BOOKS BY R. M. LAMMING

In the Dark   *1986*

The Notebook of Gismondo Cavalletti   *1985*

IN THE DARK

IN THE DARK

R.M. Lamming

NEW YORK ATHENEUM 1986

Author's Note

No character in this book is an actual portrait of anyone I have known, and the story is fictitious. The extract on p. 7 is from MS Lansdowne No. 762, translated by G.G. Coulton, and is from his book *Life in the Middle Ages*. It is reprinted by permission of Cambridge University Press.

Library of Congress Cataloging-in-Publication Data

Lamming, R. M.
    In the dark.

    I. Title.
PR6062.A48415   1986   823'.914   85-47642
ISBN 0-689-11629-2

Manufactured by Fairfield Graphics, Fairfield, Pennsylvania
First American Edition

For June and Greg Hall, and Barbara Lynch

What is the best thing and the worst among men?
Word is best and worst.
Of what thing be men most afraid?
Men be most afraid of death.

Questions between the Master of Oxenford
and his Scholar

IN THE DARK

One

Maybe it had been rash to say he would do this job himself.
He stared with horror at his books. They were transformed.
Crooked, precarious pillars of them rose from the carpet down
the length of the room, and a dangerous, leaning wall reared
up against the French windows, threatening to crash through
at any moment on to the lawn. Then there were more pillars
on the desk, and more in the fireplace. And the worst of it
was, if he brushed against any of them it might cause havoc.
Like Samson at Gaza ... yes, that was it ... that was the
image. One shove, the collapse of a single pillar, and the whole
lot might come down.

The idea appalled him. They had been packed shelf by shelf,
and even now, despite appearances, they were still in some
kind of order. If he hadn't known that, he would probably
have wept – or gone mad. Come to think of it, he would
certainly have gone mad. It was his theory: order shored people
up. Everyone needed a sense of control, at least over what they
loved.

That was why this removal business was terrible. Rough
hands on his books, filthy boots knocking over his portfolios
(that had actually happened), 'experts' man-handling his precious carvings ... and no one paying the least attention to
what he said. 'The other way up! Don't knock that! Don't put
anything on top of those ...!' Words, mere words, blown
away like thistledown. It had been a nightmare, the whole
thing. So many necessities of life were.

Then, besides the necessities, there were always malign refinements. For instance, he found it easy to believe that when
they had unpacked the books again, the removal men had
stacked them close together like this just to spite him. The old

bastard. 'Neat and tidy for the old bastard ...' He had heard them call him that: he wasn't as deaf as he made out.

Now he was going to have to work like an archaeologist, dismantling and re-locating walls and pillars one at a time, brick by brick, book by book ...

Slowly, he began to walk from the corner where the men had put his desk down to the French windows. They had left a narrow path between the pillars on this fireplace side of the room, so that if he simply walked and looked, without attempting to touch anything, he might get up and down all right.

But if he couldn't touch, how to begin ...?

As he moved, he wheezed – he often did when anxious – and his eyes picked out individual volumes, trying to read the lettering on their spines.

On his left – poets: ABSE to LEWIS. On his right, European philosophers, and beyond those – several lofty, unsafe-looking pillars twisting like corkscrews ... Essays, Critical Essays, books of table-talk ... He could see the port-red leather of his Chesterton, and topping the pillar next to that, the mottled back of his Quiller-Couch. But where were poets, MARVELL to YEATS?

Now he saw them ... On his left, and where they should be: down from ABSE to LEWIS.

At last, he reached the French windows. Here, the ancient authors were stacked, and whole sections of this wall, which blocked the view of the garden, consisted of books in series: Latin authors in dark blue binding, Greeks in red (dramatists and poets), or black (historians and philosophers). They were not, in fact, the genuine product, but Victorian translations – and the original cornerstone of his library. He had bought them second-hand as a job lot at the start, when he had first re-solved on an education, and of all his books, he loved these best.

The rest of the wall was made of texts, dictionaries, commentaries, and the whole impressive structure rose to chin height. Lawson could hardly see over it. The beech trees could be seen, of course, the tops of them at any rate, marking the end of the lawn, where the ground sloped down to the stream that was his boundary, but of the lawn itself, which stretched to the trees from the house, he could see nothing.

A draught came through the centre of the windows, and a belt of sunlight fell across the Greek historians. *Damp and light. That's bad.* Impossible to draw the curtains. Books anchored down the heavy folds of velvet, and in any case, the entire wall stood right up against the glass. Lawson felt a moment's panic. He forgot the risk of bringing the wall down, and jabbed out a finger to touch Thucydides along its spine. But this brought another shock. Dust. As if damp and light weren't enough ... Dust everywhere! He could smell it. In fact, now he saw the evidence – a grey smudge on his finger-tip – he realised that ever since he had entered the room there had been a sort of mustiness in his nostrils. He was inhaling the stuff, and every book was coated with it. Horrible. He rubbed his hand on his jacket. It was all the more vexing because, when the books had been packed, he had actually made a considerable extra payment to have them wiped, each one individually. He had supervised the whole, tedious operation himself. And as for the house, that was supposed to be clean, too. He had made arrangements. The previous people had undertaken to leave it spotless. He had only agreed to their price on that undertaking.

Obviously, they hadn't bothered.

'Don't put yourself out much, darling. You should have seen him. Barely still with us ...'

The man to his wife.

Tall, articulate and smiling, got up in ludicrously smart leisure clothes, velvet jacket and dark blue trousers on a Saturday afternoon:

'I'm sorry my wife's not here to meet you, Mr Lawson, but I dare say I can speak for her.' Here the smile had grown wider. 'As you hope to move *in* so very soon after we move *out* ...' stressing the prepositions, nothing could be wittier, '... we'll certainly see to it. Everything left spick-and-span.'

Liar.

Lawson began to tremble. He gazed weakly over the wall of books at the trees. They were still green – no one could have called them red or brown yet – but with branches showing black through the leaves. There had been strong winds in the past few weeks; any more like them, and it looked as though the trees might be stripped naked before anyone could say it was autumn. Well, that was a comfort.

His wrists tingled. The draught from the windows was creeping around in his cuffs with small, secretive movements like an insect's. To get rid of it, he bunched his fists and drew them into his sleeves. Not that he was really cold, but with a dash of imagination he could think he was, and so it was difficult to tell whether he was trembling because he was upset, or simply shivering. Either way, madness to stand in a draught ... Prompted by the thought, he turned round, looking across the irregular piles of books at a metal object on the corner of his desk. It was a handbell, a trimmed-down, brassy version of the type much used in primary schools. There it squatted, hideous thing. Over it towered a stack of French poets, ready to fall on the least provocation and push it jangling off the edge. Lawson stared. He discovered he felt sick and a little dizzy. If it got worse, he would have to ring that bell, which was stupid. All he needed was to calm down ...

From where he stood, he looked about for a chair, only there weren't any, not for sitting on. Either they were hopelessly buried beneath books, or stranded somewhere behind books ... all except one – he spotted it with dismay – the sole chair left to sit on, and that was at the desk, away down the narrow path. Near the bell. He started back up the room.

Back past MARVELL to YEATS and Quiller-Couch, past Chesterton and ABSE to LEWIS ... but this time his eyes were fixed: all he saw was the front of the desk. He had almost reached it when, without a sound, the door opened, and the woman came in.

She stopped just inside the doorway, holding a wooden tray with butter dish, a plate, a glass of milk and a rack of dark toast set on it, and she held these things well away from her, as if they were disgusting. This was a habit she had. Anything to do with him, she would hold it out like that, so that no one could mistake it for anything of hers, and seeing her indulge in this habit now he felt dizzier. His breath came and went in snatches. The floor began to shift. He put out his hand to steady himself on the nearest pile of books, and, mercifully, this pillar was a stable one: it held. He stared at her; she stared back.

Being a short man, he supposed she couldn't see much more of him than his head, sticking up over the books, looking ridiculous, and he detested her. He detested her cotton overall and her hard white face like a scrubbed doorstep. He detested her strong arms and the thinness of her hair with its little rolls of curls gathered round the base of her skull.

She stared. Then her gaze travelled over the books to the empty shelves behind him, and she said with triumph, 'You've taken on something here!'

Lawson pretended he hadn't heard. He fingered the gold lettering on the book beneath his hand – *Gulliver's Travels* – and she began to stride up the far side of the room.

'Your breakfast. I'll put it on the desk.'

'Be careful . . .'

He hurried. He saw her pushing the French poets out of the way, and slapping the tray down. He saw an elegant, gilt-edged volume topple off its pillar and land on the plate . . . Verlaine, he was sure it was Verlaine . . . and a wave of snowy milk rose over the side of the glass. He saw it fan out as it fell.

'Now look what you've done!' he cried, coming up and flapping his hand at the mess. His eyes suddenly filled with tears. Cloudy patches had appeared on the book's violet cover. And to his intense annoyance, he saw that some of the toast was saturated.

'Ruined!' he croaked. 'Ruined!'

The desk swam in front of him. He clutched at its edge. The brass bell began to float.

'You'd better sit down,' she said briskly, and her hand fastened on his arm, squeezing the jacket sleeve hard to get a grip on what was inside. All his jackets had sleeves that were out of shape. There was nothing he could do about it.

He let her guide him round the desk, and push him down firmly into the chair. When she released him, his arm ached. It was always the same. A sensation close to the one he had after a blood-pressure reading, when the tight band was taken off.

'Now calm down!'

From a pocket in her overall she plucked a duster; and then she lifted the book. A substantial half-moon and several other shapeless blots darkened its cloth. She dabbed at them savagely.

'There. It'll hardly show. You mustn't get so worked up . . .'

13

Next, she began to shuffle the loads on his desk, trying to level out the piles, but when books started sliding to the floor, she gave that up, left the fallen books where they were, and seizing hold of the bell, set that on the floor, too. Then she swiftly mopped up the milk which had seeped out beneath the tray's rim. Finally, she raised both the plate and the glass to wipe their undersides and the tray itself. And that was that. She set the moist, cold things down in front of him again.

Lawson suffered this activity meekly. He saw it all through a strange mist. He sat with his hands in his lap, struggling to steady his breath and shift the blur from his eyes; and in the end, just as his vision was clearing, she stood back, stuffing the duster away.

'It was an accident,' she said, her jaw stiff.

He nodded – nothing to be gained by shouting, it only gave her ammunition – and her face relaxed.

'I'll come in when I've had my lunch, and dust those shelves for you. Then I'll help, if you want ...'

Again he nodded, although it would be terrible. He dreaded these intrusions. She had a chilling knack of picking up a book and banging it down without so much as a glance at the title, as if books were just objects. And that was only part of it. In many ways she was like the removal men. Her handling of books implied that some people valued their time and had better things to do than squander it on print. Worse, she implied that there might, after all, be a few books somewhere which were worth reading, but that his books were not the ones. His were commonplace.

'Thank you,' he said carefully. 'After your lunch ... What time is it now?'

He could, of course, have looked at his own watch, but he owed this much to Verlaine: it was a hint, a reminder that despite this woman he lived his own life, her time was not his time, and no point in her day matched any point in his.

She studied the top of his head. That showed she understood. He knew it, he knew exactly what she was doing, but even so his fingers fluttered, and he longed to stroke his toupee, check that it was on straight. Any second, he'd give in – and how pleased that would make her! Lawson gripped the arms of his chair.

Abruptly she said, 'Same time you always have breakfast. Quarter past twelve, just gone. I've got some potatoes boiling.'

'Go and eat then,' he pleaded. 'Don't let me keep you.'

'I'll come back later.'

And with a last hard look at his head, she went.

Left alone, he blew air out through his mouth, and closed his eyes in relief. Then he concentrated on soothing away the sickness. It was all just a matter of nerves. He was sure of that because it rarely affected his appetite. He often felt hungry and sick at the same time, which couldn't be anything else but nerves. On the other hand, to bolt down breakfast on a queasy stomach was hardly civilised, and possibly it was dangerous. Soothe away the sickness first, that was it ... He'd had plenty of practice. Step number one: avoid upsetting sights – he focused on his plate, so he couldn't see the Verlaine, or the nodding pillars. Step number two: control your thoughts – Shakespeare worked well, so did Tennyson. Noble, blank verse Tennyson.

> ... I am a part of all that I have met;
> Yet all experience is an arch wherethro'
> Gleams that untravelled world, whose margin fades
> For ever and for ever as I ... when I ...

In his head, he hummed through a number of syllables and waited until he could pick up the poem again. He was never distressed by these gaps, because he knew he hadn't really forgotten: on another occasion, the words which had escaped him today would be present, each one effortlessly in its place, and probably some others that had given him no trouble today would be missing. It wasn't anything to worry about. It was as normal, he thought, as changes in the weather.

Tum ... tum ...

Flecks of light on the water, the splash of oars, white harbour steps ... and grey-haired old men, escaping from their women.

Marvellous, how this sort of thing calmed him.

Soon, he could raise his eyes, blink at the piles of books and empty shelves, even at his Verlaine, and still feel the regularity of his breathing. In his stomach there was silence, as though some excitable animal that lived in there had curled up and gone to sleep.

The early afternoon sun brought out a gratifying warmth in the shelves' mahogany, a red glow, and the stacked books waiting to be housed seemed full of a touching trustfulness, an obedience. Then the outlook, with those fine beech trees – it was far superior to any he'd had at the other house; and all at once he felt happy. It was going to be the most beautiful of his libraries. He began to sip his milk.

When the housekeeper came back, armed with rags and a tin of polish, he set to work in earnest. He had made up his mind to begin by clearing his desk and arranging the French poets either side of the fireplace, A to L on the left, M to the end on the right. With surprising thoughtfulness, the removal men had left an opening between his desk and the fireplace, so it seemed as good a plan as any to start there.

And he liked to keep some poetry near the hearth, handy for pulling a volume out and leaning against the mantelpiece while he read a soulful passage; and French, in particular, was a soulful language. Besides, it gave him pleasure to try out the accent which he had so painfully acquired from his course of gramophone records – years back, when his hearing had been better; and he liked to imagine an audience, one or two appreciative friends sitting in his armchairs, listening, mute with admiration.

Unfortunately, before he could move his poets, he had to communicate with the woman.

She stood at his side, the rags in her fist.

'Where do you want me to start, then?'

'Over there.'

He waved towards the fireplace, and in anticipation crinkled his nose. The polish she used smelled as sweet as ether, and there was something else he found an irritant: she always rolled up her sleeves to do the polishing, right above her elbows, which were raw-looking, scarlet, although he couldn't think why. It wasn't as though she worked hard. Really, she did very little. But in her cotton overall, with those elbows, she achieved the look of a perfect drudge – and an energetic one at that, the sort who glories in her slavery. Ancient Rome was probably full of them: offer them freedom, and they would purse up their lips at the insult.

While she polished, he busied himself examining the books she had pushed off his desk when she had set his breakfast down. He stroked them, opened them, looked at their spines ... No harm done, so he couldn't say anything. After that, he pretended to check Ex Libris labels: one had been glued into every book, and occasionally an edge would lift. But in fact, he spent most of the time watching her elbows.

Back and forth they went. Sharp red points.

Twenty minutes or more of that, then she straightened up, one hand crabbed round the tin of polish, the other clutching the dusters, and she made off round the pillars of books to the door.

'What are you doing?'

She stopped.

'I thought I'd work round the rest from the –'

'No, no! I want the whole of this side first. This side ... if you would,' he added, as she began to scowl.

She excelled at that, scowling. Her face would crack into downward lines from her mouth, with little crevices spreading from her nose, while her eyes remained utterly expressionless. Thanks to those eyes, when she scowled, he sometimes had the feeling that she either didn't know her face had changed, or wanted him to think she didn't know. In either case, he couldn't afford to underestimate the warning, and the last of his good humour evaporated. Snatching up a few anthologies, he hurried for the shelves. She stood and watched. He set the books on the polished wood, and they promptly slid sideways.

'You really think you can do all this by yourself?'

'I won't have people interfering with my books!'

'You'll give yourself a stroke.'

An hour later, she was helping him.

He stood on the library step-ladder, calling, 'More! Next!' while she strode to and fro, her mouth set in a tight line, and she held the books just as she had held the tray, well clear of her chest ... Oh, she was strong all right – she would have made an excellent wrestler – and there was satisfaction in her every movement. She had always known he couldn't do this by himself.

Still . . .

Up and down the steps he climbed, grabbing books, housing them; and seeing each treasure find its niche again gave him such delight that he hardly cared what *she* thought. Not for the moment, anyhow. Of course, it had upset him, having to let her help like this, but he could hate her for it afterwards. The important thing for now was that the more he filled the shelves, the more the empty shelves and all the books that were still on the floor urged him to speed up, get the job done, the whole thing perfect. He ached at his labour. His heart pumped heroically. He wheezed great sing-song sobs of breath, and wobbled on the steps, but the truth was, he couldn't work any faster: he was already working flat out.

'You should slow down,' she said.

'I'm perfectly all right!'

Something slipped through his fingers. He imagined the sickening splat as its pages crushed on the floor – there was no carpet along this edge of the room – and peering down, he knew at once that the book had come loose from its binding.

'There you are!' she said, picking up the casualty and thrusting it at him. 'See what I mean? You should slow down!' And to show that the damage meant nothing to her, she turned her back on him.

Lawson was sobered. The book lay heavy in his hands, and seemed to accuse him. All its middle section was crumpled, and, just as he had thought, the stitched back had been wrenched from its skin. Bewildering. Frightening. Dropping books had never been a fault of his. He hoped it wasn't going to be another of those things that happened more and more often. She probably kept a list of them. She was probably laughing at him now . . .

But when he looked round, he discovered instead that she was almost out of the room.

'Where are you going?'

'Telephone.'

Telephone. He hadn't heard it, but that, at least, was nothing new. He very rarely did. The Devil's invention. Stuffing the book away, he clambered down and followed her jealously out into the hall, squeezing between two tea chests to the small table and this most monstrous of intrusions, the telephone. Why everyone accepted it with such complaisance had always been a mystery to him. There should really be a device of some kind that told you who was phoning before you lifted the receiver: any fool could see that. And for him, it was exceptionally pernicious because he couldn't hear, and people wouldn't speak up.

Now he stood helplessly, while the housekeeper did the honours.

'Who?' she was saying, and then: 'I see. Well, what exactly did you want? . . . No, I'm sure he won't be interested.'

'Who is it?' he hissed.

She paid no attention to him.

'Just a very short one, then. But I wouldn't think any details . . .'

Lawson made an ineffectual grab for the receiver. She began to spell his name out.

'L – A – W, that's right. Arnold Lawson . . . Oh, I'm sure he wouldn't! He never speaks on the phone.'

'Who is it?' This time, he shouted, so that she had to clamp a hand over the mouthpiece, and she turned to him and shook her head. Then she said down the phone, 'Just a minute . . .

'It's the local paper.' She smiled. 'They want to write about you.'

'The *what*?'

Lawson felt himself reddening. He lit up inside with disgust, anger, and then with indignation: it occurred to him that she thought he was flattered.

'Out of the question! Tell them I'm out! I'm ill . . .' He waved his hands. 'Leave me alone! Just because . . .'

Just because he was rich. It was filthy. These people hunted out money like scavenger gulls swooping down on herring scraps. Lawson's face blazed, and he began to swear. He was sick, sick of them. If they came round, they'd find the door locked. He hadn't time to waste on scandal-mongers, muck-rakers . . .

She let him rant. When he finally ran out of breath, she said, 'It's not you. It's because of the house.'

'What?'

'It's very old and well known. Some important families have lived here. She wants to know what you're going to do with it. Alterations, that sort of thing. For the women's page.'

And the housekeeper's smile sent the little cracks spreading out from her nose.

'The *house*?' Lawson blinked. Then he spat his words out. 'What ridiculous nonsense!'

Bad enough to be hounded because he was rich, but intolerable, preposterous, to be peeked at not for anything to do with himself, but because of the house, bricks and mortar . . .

'Let me speak to her!'

He grabbed the phone and shouted, 'Hello! Hello, young lady?' They were always young, these gossip writers; it was a measure of his contempt for them.

Patchily a voice came back. He caught his own name, and the word 'trouble'.

'Trouble?' he repeated fiercely. 'There won't be any, I can tell you! Leave me in peace! Do you understand?'

He drew a long breath, and the telephone voice started again. Predictably, he couldn't hear: she wouldn't speak up. Only one word came through, and that was 'visit'. Unbelievable. The little bitch was persevering!

'Get off this line!' he shouted. 'You're trespassing!'

Then he slammed the phone down.

Bloody silly . . . He stood panting with his hand on the receiver, ready to snatch it up if it rang again. It didn't. An uncomfortable silence stretched across the tea chests. Lawson rubbed distractedly at a greasy mark on the table. He could feel the housekeeper's smirk, he didn't have to look, and she would be thinking, *You should have left that to me.*

'Four o'clock,' she said. 'I'll bring you your orange juice, shall I?'

'Yes.'

He nodded, glancing at her just in time to see her face changing: she must have been putting the smirk away. Well, he didn't want to know. He hadn't the energy.

To sit down with his orange juice. That would be nice.

'I'll bring it to the library.'

'No, don't . . .'

That didn't appeal at all. The unfinished job would reproach

him ... and the annoying thing about it was that he might
have gone on for hours yet, if only the telephone hadn't rung.
That newspaper girl had fairly winded him, and now he was
off the step-ladder, he noticed a pain in the back of his knees,
and a stiffness in his arms. It was inevitable: the books would
have to wait. Everything would have to wait. There was too
much to be done. He gazed at the tea chests.

'What are these? The ivories?'

'Some of them, yes. The rest are in the lounge. What about
them?'

'Nothing.'

From shoulders downwards her body moved, almost a
twitch.

'Where do you want it, then? The lounge has got dust covers
everywhere.'

'What?'

'Your orange juice.'

'I think ... I'll go up to my room ...'

'You all right?'

'Yes, yes!'

At least up there he'd be out of her way, and the mess.

'I'll just ... get a book ...' he muttered.

'All right.'

She marched off to the kitchen.

It had begun to rain, a light grey shower speckling the French
windows. Lawson stood undecided. When they were all over
the place like this, he simply couldn't choose a book. It was
impossible to single one out. So he watched the trees rising
over the ancient authors, and noticed that as the afternoon
closed in, even the greenest leaves appeared to be blackening;
also that, with the coming of the rain, the trees had begun to
sway. Watch them for long enough, and it would be easy to
believe that there was some relationship between swaying and
blackening, as if the trees themselves were conjuring up the
darkness.

Suddenly he made up his mind. Hurrying from the room, he
crossed the hall again, and poked his head into the passage
that led to the kitchen.

'Hello? You there?'

'What is it now?' She came out with the jug of orange in her hand, and the usual glass. 'What's the matter?'

'Nothing.' He paused, so the word would sink in. It was no crime to have second thoughts. 'It's just that I'll have it in the library,' he said. 'That's all.'

Two

Five days later, he made his first sortie into *her* realm. It had been the maids' parlour, and was next door to the kitchen. Now she had turned it into her own snug, nauseous little sitting-room, with all her knick-knacks set in places that corresponded to their old places in the other house. There on the mantelshelf were the simpering porcelain lady and the metallic lighthouse that was really a barometer, and, keeping them company, the plastic swan that someone had brought back for her from a holiday – a label round its neck read 'Caernarvon': otherwise, it was as white and shiny as a boiled egg. On the walls hung her loathsome calendars – bowls of purplish roses, or baskets of spaniel puppies putting their tongues out. From the curtain rail hung yards of scarlet linen convolvulus on yellow trellis work; and in the corner, just as in the other house, stood that abomination: her television. It pumped out its bluish light across the room, nothing like, yet oddly like the blue of a vein seen through the skin.

She hadn't heard him come in. Or else, because this was her realm, she deliberately ignored him. She sat with her back to the door, facing the television, and went on knitting – he could see her elbows going – but apart from that, she sat rigid. Her head rested on her shoulders with all the solidity of a small rock. She always sat like that. On the few occasions when Lawson saw her in a chair, he felt tempted to sneak up behind and give that head a good prod, just to see if it would roll off.

Over the mantelpiece, a cuckoo-clock. Best to consult that, he thought, before saying anything . . .

He had to look at it hard, because, apart from the television, the room was lit only by a table lamp in an orange shade. He had to screw up his eyes at the tiny fingers. Nine . . . fifty-five . . .

23

That couldn't be right. He fumbled for his watch. Her clock or his watch ... one of them had to be wrong, six minutes out ... and if it was his watch, he had no case against her, it was obliterated – at least the major part of it. But the other part might hold. He decided to open with that.

'I rang the bell.'

'Did you?' Her head came round. Her face showed no surprise to find him standing there. 'I didn't hear it.'

'But you *must* hear it! I have to be able to depend on your hearing it!'

Exasperation made him whine. After all, it was perfectly reasonable. She was paid to hear bells; but from the way she stood up, wrapping the wool round and round her needles, he knew that she was offended.

'I was watching a programme.'

'What? What did you say?' Damn her blasted television.

'I said I was watching something.'

'But if you didn't hear the bell,' he persisted, 'if I'd really needed you ...'

'Why don't you leave the library door open? Anyway,' she said, 'it'll be all right after Monday. That's when they're coming to ...'

He lost the rest. Gunshots and a siren sounded. There she stood, clutching those long needles in the path of the glow from the television, which made her look darker and taller, the blue light fuzzing round her edges. It was a most uncomfortable way of seeing her. A troll, thought Lawson, or a ghoul ... The idea fascinated him, and, for a moment, he forgot what he had come about.

'What did you want, anyway?'

He tried to peer past her. The voices from the corner were completely unintelligible, a chattering of primates with American accents ...

'What are you watching?'

'Oh, it won't mean anything to you,' she said. 'It's called "Ironside".'

'What's that? A ship?'

A detective. He knew. He read the reviews of these pulp things, but to let on that he knew would be to contaminate himself. She would not, of course, understand his reference

to ships. In the corner, another shot rang out, there was a
shout, and tender violin music rose behind the chatter. The
housekeeper flinched. She glanced back at the screen, and said,
'That's it. It's over. It was just finishing. Now, what did you
want?'

'I came ...' Lawson hesitated; he saw the unfortunate trend
of this conversation, but how to get out of it? '... because you
didn't hear the bell, and it was time for my bath.'

'It was *not* time.' She moved to stow away her knitting, and
her voice was bitter. ' "Ironside" finishes at ten. I was coming
straight after it.'

Then she looked up at the clock, which had not yet covered
the fatal six minutes. Lawson flourished his watch.

'By my watch ...'

'Oh, never mind.'

She snapped off the television, and the sudden extinction of
its blue light made him jump. Naturally, she noticed that. As
she came towards him, her hand was already stretching out to
seize his arm, but he dodged ahead of her into the passage and
even managed to keep his lead all the way to the stairs, though
she followed hard at his heels. He could feel her sense of injury
like a chill wind blowing down his neck. If only he'd waited
five more minutes. She had a way of making these episodes
seem so infantile. She could trivialise the most legitimate griev-
ance.

As he began to climb the stairs, Lawson hunted for a for-
mula, something cryptic and dignified that would hint at deeper values behind these pantomimes, values she missed when
she passed off his complaints as the random or spiteful obses-
sions of old age.

'Time, the subtle thief ...' he muttered. 'Wingèd chariot ...'

About half-way up, she started a harangue.

'I don't see why you make such a fuss! If your bath's a few
minutes late, what does it matter, for heaven's sake? You've
got all the time in the world!'

She had drawn close and was hovering at his side, her fingers
almost brushing his sleeve. Lawson shrank even closer to the
banister, and he twisted round to see if she meant those last
words to be irony, but, as usual, her stony face gave away
nothing. Stupid, thoughtless words – or malice?

25

'All the time in the world!'

He laughed, and immediately her scowl lines appeared.

'Well, it's not as though you've anything else to do . . .'

Now that was a typical insult. There were depths of conviction behind that remark. Lawson stopped laughing and stared at her. He watched her narrow her lips, and a look of something like doubt flickered across her eyes. Maybe he hadn't heard right. He leaned towards her. 'What did you say?'

'Oh, come on . . . I meant, now that the library's finished . . .'

'Nothing to do? And how would you know what I do? You haven't the faintest idea . . .'

'Oh, I dare say!'

She tugged at his sleeve. He leaned hard against the banister and refused to budge. Gloss it over, would she?

'You seem to forget,' he panted, 'time *matters*. You think I'm just fussing. Routine means nothing to you. Mens sana in corpore sano . . . Do you think at my age that just *happens*?'

'No, I don't think that . . .'

You don't think anything, that's your trouble. Oh, what's the point!

He shook off her hand – at least, he shook his arm, and she let go – and they went on together up the stairs. What had he done, he wondered, to deserve this pea-brained termagant? Swindled one client too many? 'Lawson's hard,' people had said, and his enemies had said, 'Lawson will bleed you dry. Watch him!' Now was he being paid back? Bread upon the waters? Just deserts?

Oh, very comical! And what *are* one's just deserts? The thought of this woman at his side as reward or punishment for any part of his life set Lawson wheezing, and when they reached the landing he had to pause, to catch his breath. She waited. As soon as he could, he snapped, 'Fetch my cardigan! The red one!'

He wanted her out of the way. It was terrible to have her marching him into the bathroom. Quite often, like tonight, he avoided it by issuing an order. Fetch a jacket or his hairbrush. And she was so used to the trick that it hardly ever occurred to her to make anything of it.

Away she stomped, down the passage to his room at the far

end – but it had been better in the other house. There, the passage had been longer, his room even further from the stairs, while the bathroom had been the first door one came to, and by the time she came back with whatever he had sent her for, he had always been safely inside with the door shut. But here, he would have to scuttle half the length of the passage after her. It made things a little desperate.

A game, he tried to think of it as a game.

The passage was lit by three bulbs hanging on long flexes, each surrounded by an airy cream shade, and as the house-keeper passed beneath them, these bulbs swung gently, so that the shades' fringes made patterns on the walls. Lawson didn't like that. He hadn't noticed it before, this shifting light. Stronger bulbs and shorter flexes, shades without fringes . . . He made a mental note as he set off for the bathroom.

A wooden chair stood by the door. He ignored it. He had to, because in his five years of acquaintance with this chair, he had never been able to train himself not to see it. Turning the knob, he pushed, then slipped his hand inside, fingers splaying for the light cord. His heart pounded. Any moment she might re-appear . . . He looked back along the passage. In the bath-room, something brushed against his knuckles. He grabbed, pulled, and white, aseptic light sprang forth obediently. With a squawk of relief he hurried in and closed the door behind him.

It was a soothing bathroom. No draughts: solid Victorian shutters sealed off the windows. And no shadows: clean strip-lighting reflected off the mushroom-coloured tiles and the grey marble. There were reassuring brass rails along the sides of the bath, and although there was a full-length mirror, it was fixed to the wall over by the shutters, so that it didn't have to be met with if he wasn't on a good day. Altogether, an obliging bathroom, with no nonsense like carpet to worry about ruin-ing. Instead, good rubber mats on the non-slip cork tiles. Purely but handsomely functional. That was what soothed him.

He reached down for the bath plug. And there she was, thumping on the door.

'Are you all right?'

He frowned at the doorknob.

'Of course I'm all right. Sit down.'

'You don't want your cardigan?'

'Why would I want my cardigan in the bath?'

He'd had to straighten up for that, and now he began again, reaching for the bath plug. He imagined the wooden chair creaking as she parked her behind, plumping herself down, and folding her arms. She never – he hadn't watched, but he knew – tucked in her skirt beneath her when she sat: the difference between a woman and a lady.

Ah, ladies ... Despite everything, this was a good day, and while the water crashed into the bath, he examined his person in the mirror.

Old, yes, but not repulsive. Roguish, you might say ... Smiling anxiously, he peered at his rouged cheeks, his hair-piece. No one, he was sure, knew about the rouge until he told them. He used so little. With the hair-piece it was different. The rich, whisky colour was obviously not his own. A distinct line showed where it met with the white sides and back. Fools thought he meant to deceive them, but no, the hair-piece was a flag, a deliberate act of flamboyance. 'So?' it said. 'This skull's not so young – what of it? Life's still sweet!'

Style. Lawson turned sideways and ran a hand across his stomach. Style, the last thing any man should lose. He patted his small, soft paunch. That was the biscuits. But never mind, it suited him. Because he was short, leanness would have made him look – shrivelled.

Then he brightened his smile, and really, from a smile like that no one could have guessed his age. He himself would have guessed somewhere in his seventies. Seventy-six, perhaps ...

She was thumping on the door again. He had to turn off the taps to hear what she said.

'What?'

'... so much water?'

'I'm just getting in!' he called back, tugging off his jacket. 'Stop fussing, woman!'

Once his clothes were off, he kept well clear of the mirror.

He was very, very white. Seated in the bath, he gazed with distaste at his legs: they seemed rather too small under the water. Busily he soaped himself. The important thing when having a bath was not to look too closely.

'Grand old eccentric,' he murmured. 'All the time in the world . . .'

He eyed the door.

Her ear would be cocked, listening for splashes, and if he didn't oblige she would call out. Sometimes, even if he did splash, she called out. On bad days, the whole business struck him as a humiliating farce, but on good days he baited her; he kept as quiet as a drowned man, just to see how long she'd leave it.

And so, as he soaped, he took great pains not to stir the water. He simply dunked the bar of Lifebuoy like a biscuit before rubbing it on his neck, then on his arms, then on the baby-flesh of his chest . . .

She left it longer than usual. He had reached his legs before she spoke.

'All right in there?'

'Of course I am!'

Silence.

Lawson raised his left leg and let it fall back into the water with a heavy slopping sound. He waited. Usually, she went on to say something else.

'I saw those boys again today!'

The boys.

He stared dully at his knees. The boys. He had a suspicion he owed these boys to 'Ironside': she had timed the news perfectly. It's unpleasant to feel angry when you're stark naked.

'Why didn't you tell me before?'

'What?'

'Why didn't you tell me?' he shouted.

'I am telling you. They were in the stream again.'

'*I* didn't see them!'

'It was this morning. You were asleep.'

He began to splash loudly, lost the soap, and flung water up at his chest.

'Were they on *my* side?'

'Oh yes.'

She sounded very sure about that.

The rest of his bath was joyless. Youth, the terrible young. A pain grew across his middle or in his head, he wasn't sure

29

where it was, but it was there. He washed quickly and methodically, his mind empty.

As soon as he decently could, he pulled out the plug, clambered over the side of the bath, and towelled himself.

'Are you out?'

'Can't you *hear* I am?'

Thrusting his legs into his pants.

When he opened the door, he found her already on her feet, facing him. She glared. It *had* been because of 'Ironside'.

'I'll settle them,' he said. 'I'll put up a notice!'

'Oh, that won't stop them!'

'Mine will.' He smiled. 'I'll put – Private Property. Patrolled by Dogs.'

But she wasn't impressed.

'They'll like that,' she said. 'That'll be a challenge.'

'Rubbish.'

He pushed his jacket at her, snatched the cardigan and bundled into it.

'Dogs'll make it more attractive,' said the housekeeper darkly. 'More exciting. Still, it's your garden ... What do you want for supper?'

The final proof that he wasn't forgiven. He loathed any bother about his diet, and well she knew it. That was why she used this trick of implying, when she wanted, that he only lived for his food.

Lawson looked disgusted and flapped his hand.

'For God's sake use your head, can't you? I've got more important things ... I've got a letter to write!'

'About the boys?'

'No!'

Stupid. Shouldn't have mentioned that. He hurried for the stairs. What he had in mind wasn't thought through properly yet. He had been waiting to be rid of her, for the hours when she'd be in bed, safely snoring. (Not that he could remember ever having heard her, but he felt sure that she did snore.) He had been waiting for night, when he could think best and he had the house to himself – a postponement that was no real hardship: in fact, he had woken up that day without any feelings at all on the matter, which was astonishing, considering.

Sleep could work these treacherous changes.

The day before, his rage had been epic. Despite the diabol-
ical nature of telephones, he had jotted down the number of
the *Herald* and pictured himself phoning up, irate, articulate,
but in the end it hadn't come to that, although it had come
close, close ... Instead, he had sat at his desk throughout the
night, composing cunningly abusive letters to the editor; and he
had presumed that after a sleep he'd know which one to send.

Who would have thought he might wake up indifferent?
Today, the afternoon had been whittled away reading Boswell's *Life of Johnson*, and to tell the truth, until a few
moments ago, the article had been in the very cellar of
his mind. Yes. If he didn't lie to himself, even now he would
much prefer to go on with his Boswell, or maybe re-read
Rasselas ...

Lawson hurried downstairs, anxious to avoid scrutiny in
case she detected any lack of purpose. Her voice came sharp
at his back.

'Well! If it isn't the boys, I can guess! Why go drawing
attention to yourself? You say what you want is privacy, so
why write a letter? That's what I don't understand!'

'Nobody asked you to.'

They reached the hall, where she was suddenly beside him,
the hard, central light making her face look whiter, stonier.
She shrugged.

'I don't think you've any idea *what* you want.'

She would make these comments. If he hadn't known how
stupid she was, some of her probes would have unnerved him.
As it was, sometimes when he looked at her, she fitted exactly
his idea of the hag that had mouthed the Delphic Oracle. It
was certainly vital to remember she was stupid. But then, the
Sibyl had probably been stupid too.

'It's nothing to do with you,' he said.

She shrugged again, and took herself off to the kitchen.

Lawson 'locked up'. By this, he meant checking the locks on
the front door and creeping down past her realm to check the
back door. He allowed himself the euphemism 'locking up'
because 'checking the locks' had a Dickensian, Scrooge-like
sound to it, which was unjust. It was only common sense to
keep a house like this one locked. His carvings alone were
worth thousands, before one started on the books ...

At the front, there was a sizeable key hanging on a hook by the door, and every night Lawson fitted it into the keyhole, then tried to turn it towards the door-frame until he had satisfied himself that it couldn't be turned any further. But at the back, there was a Yale lock, so there he had to content himself with pressing down its snig, hard. Then as well as the locks, both doors sported bolts, and although the mechanism of bolts is visible at a glance, staring at them was never quite enough for Lawson. Actually, he worried more about these bolts than he did about the locks. Of the five senses, sight, he thought, was the least reliable – you could fool yourself into seeing anything – and so he always touched the knob of each bolt-shaft to feel that it was pressed as far forward as it would go. Only then could he turn away.

After this chore, back to the library. It was a joy to enter. Everything had its place. Ancient authors, biographies, poetry and novels, first editions, rare finds and signed copies: leather-bound and cloth-bound, his entire collection stood quietly attentive between layers of warm mahogany, and it seemed to him that all these books communicated with one another. To and fro across the room they spun their silent conversations out of the finest thoughts of man, and Lawson loved them. Each book was capable of giving him intense pleasure by the quality of its pages, the feel of its spine on his hand; and this was true whether it smelt musty and was blotched with signs of neglect by some previous owner, or was a brand new, glossy acquisition. And each book was capable of giving him excitement – though not all with the same intensity – by what its black print had to say, even if he disagreed with it. To disagree, after all, was something, was to be alive. When he read a book, even a trifling one, he could feel the stirring of his mind, and knew he was alive. He loved his books for that. Besides, he loved them because they were his. There was not one of which he couldn't have said how he had come by it. He thought he felt a special affection for those found only after a long search in antiquarian bookshops, or for those which had been reserved for some other customer and he had snaffled them up at twice the price. But he also thought he loved best the first editions, bought as soon as published – demonstrations of his foresight and the broadness

32

of his taste – and on the other hand, those Greek and Latin classics ...

He loved all his books. He loved all of them best, and for many reasons. This was sanity. This was the civilised world that kept back the tides of darkness.

The strong, velvet curtains overlapped across the windows. Night was shut out. In each corner of the room stood a standard lamp, shedding a glow over the armchairs, shelves and carpet. Another lamp stood on his desk. He preferred this arrangement to central lights. In the small hours of the night, it was the corners that might have troubled him, if they hadn't been lit. Anything that happened honestly, out in the centre of the room, he felt he could face. What this 'anything' might be, he had of course no idea. That is, he had every idea and yet none. Also, why he should have a greater dread of death coming from any particular direction, he couldn't even try to rationalise. It was simply one of those points on which he gave in to the old fool in his skull, although while he did so, he scoffed.

All these lights cost money. Yes. And, 'Men fear death as children fear to go in the dark.' That's it! My second childhood! A thought which would make him shake his head as if one of them had to get out of it – either the fool or the scoffer – but neither left.

Now, crossing to his desk, he pushed aside the Boswell, and tugged at an edge of newspaper that was jutting out of a dictionary. (When writing abusive letters, he was always careful to check the precise meaning of words.) The paper was folded on an inside page, and down one side, two columns of print had been framed in red ink. A small headline read: 'GRAND OLD ECCENTRIC COMES TO WOODBOURN'.

They had made him sound like a circus. For a moment, the anger came back. He read selected lines, the ones that had most infuriated him.

'... we cannot hope to see much of Mr Lawson. In his private world he is content. He delights in his own company ...'

Couldn't a man want peace and quiet without being Narcissus?

'... rumoured that he has fabulous treasures, exotic collections of Chinese paintings and ivories, besides a valuable library'.

Splendid. Every thief in the district would have the house on his map ... though where they'd got that notion about Chinese paintings ... but then, where had they got any of this, most of it true? He screwed up his face, panting slightly as he imagined the reporter-bitch batting her eyelashes at the local estate agent, wheedling out of him Mr Arnold Lawson's previous address. He imagined her hunting through the countryside in her Mini or wretched little Fiat, and sniffing about in the town he'd come from. Which grocery had he patronised? And butcher? Ah, he didn't have a butcher! What about getting around, could he still drive? Good heavens, so he hired them, cars and chauffeurs? How old was he, then? And all this money he had, did anyone know ...? A mindless pilfering of his life to throw it at the feet of the public. Not so mindless, either. Behind the breezy chatter of the article, he thought he sensed a calculated hostility, and it puzzled him. He could think of no reason for it. Surely not because he'd been rude on the phone? It was one thing for top professionals – or downright amateurs – to go off the deep end, but from a local, work-a-day level, it was nonsense. Retribution out of all proportion. Hard little snoopers should expect insults. They had no right to take offence –

Lawson sat down. He made an effort to calm himself. He was still clutching the newspaper, and it trembled a little. There was worse to come.

'... reputation for ascetic living and literary learning, is a confirmed vegetarian. In fact, his life-style is probably unique ...'

This was the bit. This was the bit that had really shaken him yesterday.

'He prefers to work on his books and letters at night. Mr Lawson says that he doesn't need much sleep, and when most men are sleeping, those who are still awake have the best chance of snatching a good idea ...'

When had he said that? Had he ever said that? There was no denying that it had a sort of ring, the quality of something he might have said, but he would have made such a remark only to a friend, and it must have been years ago. Now he never said such things: people would think he was senile. So who had this bitch-reporter dug out? Someone who knew him well? There weren't many left.

Yes, he was still angry. He held the paper up to his eyes and squinted at it. If he ventured into the town, people would point at him and say, 'That's the old codger who's bought Wood-bourn. The one who sits up all night . . .'

His life and his business. His secret time. Why should they know these things? Did *he* want to know when other people cleaned their teeth or had their bowel movements? Surely when he chose to sleep was just as private.

'So you are. You're going to write to them!'

She was back already with the supper tray. He hadn't heard her, and now there she was, grimacing at him over the top of the *Herald*. Lawson crushed the paper into folds and shoved it under the dictionary. All this creeping about.

'Couldn't you have knocked?'

'What good would that have done?' she said evenly. 'You never hear when you're reading. You know you don't.'

True. No answer to that. He leaned far back in his chair as she set the tray down.

'Oranges and jelly. Fruit cake and a piece of cheese. All right?'

'A bit rich, isn't it?'

'I'll take the cake back then, and bring you a digestive.'

At once her hand came down and he watched the dark, delicious fruit cake rise on its plate.

'No. Leave it, leave it!'

'Sure?'

'Yes.'

'Well, good-night.'

He didn't bother to answer. He examined the tray, then pushed it from him and took out his watch. 11.20 . . . He wouldn't eat until one o'clock. Sometimes, tempted not so much by the sight of it as by the faint sweet scents of his supper, he ate earlier, but he always regretted doing so. It left too long with nothing. One o'clock. By that time he should have chosen a suitable letter. Afterwards, he might re-read *Rasselas*, which would take him through to six o'clock and bed. A constructive programme. He slipped the watch back into his pocket, and stared at the curtains. What was it, he

35

wondered, besides the boys and the letter, that worried him? Suddenly he remembered. Grabbing hold of the brass bell, he brandished it up and down until his wrist ached. The thing clanged with malicious sluggishness. It seemed to gain a hundredweight every time he raised it. He had already given up and was setting it down with a thump when her head appeared, coming half-way round the door, a half-face, glowering.

'All right, all right! It takes time to get here, you know!'

'Were you upstairs?'

'I was on my way up.'

She waited. He put his question.

'I was wondering,' he said, 'if you couldn't hear this in the kitchen, do you think it would wake you?'

She didn't know, she didn't care. The look on the half-face said he could faint, fall off the library steps, choke on fruit cake, it meant nothing to her. But then some other thought must have interceded and her expression changed: she was all false helpfulness.

'I'll leave my door ajar. Anyway, it's not long now. The electricians are coming on Monday.'

'About time.'

'Was there anything else?'

'No. Good-night and – leave the door.'

He unfolded the *Herald* again, spreading it over the plates, the jelly dish.

Where was he? Angry, yes. 'GRAND OLD ECCENTRIC ...'

Carefully he lifted the paper to make sure that the jelly wasn't sticking to it.

'GRAND OLD ECCENTRIC ... fabulous treasures ... probably unique ...'

He read these appalling phrases several times before he understood that he wasn't angry: he had lost the moment. Now, if anything – ludicrous though it seemed – the phrases pleased him.

Three

Still, nothing altered the principle. He had to make his protest.

The next day, after breakfast he went out to post the letter. He always posted his own, partly because he didn't trust the housekeeper – she might have steamed them open in the kitchen – and partly because it gave his walk some shape. Not that this second reason was important. He wasn't a moron. He could enjoy a walk for its own sake. In fact, where walking was concerned he believed in spontaneity, and provided he covered his seven miles each week, he usually left it to instinct and the weather to tell him when to walk.

Nevertheless, if he did have something to post, he enjoyed posting it. Today was Sunday, there would be no collection, but he set out with the letter all the same.

He dressed well for the occasion: a medium-weight grey coat with a yellow handkerchief in the breast pocket, a trilby, gloves, his cane. One had to keep up appearances. People were always watching the old for signs, for custard on their ties or for undone fly buttons, but they would find none of these signs on him.

There was a mirror in the hall, just outside the cloakroom, and as he stood in front of it pulling on his gloves, the woman came past on her way to clear the breakfast tray.

'Going out then?'

'Yes.'

'Going to post your letter?'

'Good afternoon,' said Lawson, turning from her and hurrying off down the passage. Questions, questions . . .

Going out by the back door had been his habit in the other place, and he saw no reason not to continue it. The business of unbolting and rebolting at the front would have made him feel that his home was derelict, and that he himself was like a tramp hiding in one corner of it. He knew this, or remembered it, and so he kept to his habit. But for another thing, he liked the secrecy. He found pleasure in sneaking round on his house and catching it unawares, before it could snap to attention – a whimsical piece of foolishness, but one that served a purpose, so it could be tolerated. Emerging from a side-path and looking up at his property from a delivery boy's angle, he had often spotted defects – missing slates and peeling paint – which could only be discovered by such an oblique scrutiny. It was justification enough.

Only, sometimes – like today – he forgot to look for defects.

Lawson breathed in deeply. The air was aromatic, a blend of bonfire smoke, ploughed fields and damp wood. And coming out on to the gravel drive at the front, he saw that the sun smiled on his house. The black porch columns shone. He stopped to survey the neatly curved edge of the lawn, and its symmetry pleased him. The tall French windows of the library pleased him, and the two grey steps that led down from the windows to the grass. There were not many flower-beds, he was glad of that: one part-time gardener should be able to manage, if he knew his job; and there would be less of that tiresome succession of plants coming and going, uprootings and plantings, than at the other place.

All in all, a good house. He smiled his congratulations, and set off for the gate.

On either side, dark rhododendron bushes. And rising behind them, tall trees that concealed the house from the road: their branches spanned the drive, and the tunnel they made, thought Lawson, was a particularly impressive, worthwhile feature, even if he didn't altogether like this shadowy walk down it . . .

Then he made his mistake. He glanced up. He stopped and gaped. Overhead the leaves were yellow. Bright, celandine yellow. Immediately his mood changed. The day before, looking out from the library windows at the trees that backed the lawn, he had told himself they were still green. But here was the truth. The sun was still warm, it was only just October, but once the leaves had turned, there was nothing to do but face it.

Autumn.

When he'd been younger, he had loved this season. Now he hated it, and the longer it lasted the more he hated it. He grew impatient with its mild days and gentle beauty. Deceit, that was what it was. As if a shrivelling and withering of things could ever be really beautiful. As if it were anything more than a pun to speak of 'cycles' when next year's seed cost this year's ruin. No, he wasn't fooled, and every year the best he could hope for was a short autumn. As October advanced he'd grow restless. 'Let's get on with it!' he'd mutter. Winter at least was honest. Winter, the testing time, when all that was weak or unprepared went under.

It never came quickly enough. First, there always had to be this slow, seductive ritual of lies. Yellow leaves.

Sunlight flickered through the branches, mottling the gravel; this made the ground look unstable, so Lawson was obliged to set one foot in front of the other very deliberately, and he was glad when he reached the gate. He stood for a time gazing out at the bungalows in the distance. They were white and neat like cheap dentures. The edge of town. Nearly all his retirement he had lived in places like this, on the edge of somewhere, and it seemed to him now that unfailingly on the horizon, year after year, there had been bungalows.

Still, he supposed the view was picturesque.

Across the lane, there was a meadow, and through it ran a river so shallow and pebbly that it gleamed like tin. Gorse bushes hunched along the banks, and there were cows. Black and white cows.

Then down the lane – a very few yards – there was a road, narrow, quiet, the meadow on one side, and fields on the other. The fields had just been ploughed. From his position by the gate, Lawson glared at them. That smell which had seemed so pleasant – now he knew it. The stench of autumn.

Stooped a fraction, and wheezing, he set off for the post-box.

Once on the road it was uphill, but hardly a challenge. The steep part only began in earnest on the far side of the box which he could see, a plate of metal painted red and set into the stone wall, just a modest exertion ahead of him. Jerkily, this patch of colour grew larger, and the white bungalows grew. He felt in his pocket for the envelope.

'*Drawing attention to yourself . . .*'

Drat the woman. It was a good letter. It said nothing that everyone didn't know about gossip writers, how they trespassed, exaggerated, and it wasn't hysterical. It was sound. He had gone through draft after draft . . .

And yet, the closer he came to the letter-box, the more his confidence dwindled. Was he over-reacting? An old man. With nothing better to do.

His head rang with disembodied voices.

'*Look at this!*' cried one, and there were squeals of girlish laughter. '*Words from that Arnold Lawson!*'

'*Who?*'

'*That recluse! The batty old man at Woodbourn!*'

'*Oh. What's he got to say for himself?*'

'*Complaints! Wouldn't you know it? And after all those nice things I wrote!*'

Lawson hesitated. He took out the envelope and turned it over to lie face up on his glove, its bright stamp eyeing him. Then he forgot where he was. The profile on the stamp was of just such a girl. Surely it was time they decently aged her? Distasteful, this youthful silhouette for a woman who was – how old? Forty? Forty-five? To portray the Queen as a sort of nymph – it was crass. He stood examining the stamp closely, and a car came down the hill –

He heard it, looked up. A virulent blue MG: it roared, it blared its horn, it was coming straight at him. For a moment he froze in amazement, and still it came. He looked round wildly and scuttled for the side of the road, barely reached it, pressed back against the wall . . . He saw sunlight strike off the headlamps. The car swerved. He felt a rush of air on his trousers. The driver had fair hair. A girl in the passenger seat raised her hands to her cheeks, and she was laughing. Then they were past, and fumes poured back across Lawson's mouth. For the hell of it, the driver gave one more blast on the horn.

Hooligans!

He leaned against the wall, gulping for air, and watched the car shrink to the size of a blue-bottle. His knees trembled, more from anger than from shock, he told himself, but that was no less troublesome. A fine thing, if he collapsed out here ... One, two ... he noted each breath, and thought with regret of his inhaler nestling in the pocket of his cardigan, in the cloakroom.

Delinquents!

He didn't dare move. Somehow, he had to steady himself. It was not much further. There was the box, almost right in front of him on the other side of the road. Lawson focused on it, and gradually he conjured up a determined calm, temporary and tenuous but, at least, effective, until in the end he felt strong enough to cross and read the white plaque that showed the collection times.

Just as he'd thought; there were none on Sundays. The first collection was at 8.30 in the morning. Still, the box's gaping little mouth seemed to beg for titbits. He raised the envelope, and let it brush the lip. He swayed, a reed in the breeze.

Come on ... he urged himself ... *you nearly got killed for this!*

Blue MGs. Blond drivers. And girls, laughing.

Suddenly he drew the envelope back, tucked it away in his coat's inside pocket, and turned for home.

He hurried. These little outings, having once turned sour, had a knack of getting worse. The sooner he was back in the house, the better. It was a lesson he knew too well, so that even after passing the Woodbourn gate, he felt only marginally safer. And sure enough, as he came to the top of the drive, there was a new shock.

Movement. At the back of the lawn – in the spinney. A trick of the light, perhaps? He stood still and watched. There ... no mistaking that! A cheerful green anorak, romping through the undergrowth.

A boy. Beating about with a stick.

At the sight, all Lawson's pent-up misery broke out. He raised his cane. He advanced. What he meant to do he had no idea, but he knew he must do something.

'You there!' he croaked. 'You!'

The boy stopped and looked round. Then he took to his heels, prancing down to the stream. There was a shout. 'Quick! Quick!'

'Wait!' cried Lawson, but the trespasser had vanished, and on reaching the slope at the edge of the spinney, Lawson came to a shaky halt. Quite obviously, he couldn't give chase down that: it was steep and slippery, and overgrown with roots, brambles. He could only stand there, making noises.

'Come back!' he croaked. 'You hear me?'

Two boys grinned up at him from the stream. They were standing in the middle of it – both wore wellington boots – and while he ranted they watched, as one might watch a strange animal.

'This is private property. Understand? Private!'

They whispered together, stared and laughed. Lawson's chin trembled. Maybe that flurry across the lawn had upset his toupee? But then gratefully he remembered his hat. And besides, the sun was behind him: he could see into the spinney far better than they could see out of it. The thought encouraged him, and he waved his cane. 'Clear off! Get off my land!'

The boys just stood there. Water swirled round their boots, and their broad faces looked up at him in silence. Lawson felt a second twinge of nervousness. *Now what?* he wondered. *I really should keep a dog ...*

He had tried that once. He had bought a large Alsatian, but the brute had shown such a predilection for baring its teeth at him, and then, the expense of the stewing steak, the biscuits and vitamins, and the bills from the vet for injections and worming ...

'Why can't we play here, mister?'

'What?'

He peered down. The faces below were pale, stubborn.

'What's wrong with us playing here, mister? The other people let us.'

'What's *wrong* ... ?' he gasped, lowering the cane.

Amazing. No rude names and raspberries. Instead, negotiations, arguments. Natives versus the settler.

'We've always played here!'

Lawson's flesh seemed to shrink inside his skin.

'Go away! I don't want you!' he flicked his hand, a movement to scare a fly, and he saw their faces harden. They altered not by the eyes nor by the mouth, but altogether, in some inexplicable way that had nothing to do with their features.

42

'I want peace and quiet!' he cried, and he could sense how shrill his voice had gone. 'You've got all the meadow to play in!'

'But it's not the same!'

No. Not dark and secret, not private property. It was a place where they would be harassing no one, and so, of course ...

Lawson rallied. His anger was legitimate. His cane came up for another menacing gesture.

'Next time, I'll call the police!' he shouted. 'I'm warning you!'

At that, the boys exchanged glances, and one of them muttered something. To his immense relief, they began to plod across the stream, and when they had reached the far bank, they started walking, scuffling the leaves as they went. To show defiance, they kept their faces turned towards him for as long as they could, but in the end they had to give that up, to keep from slipping in the mud.

One to him. He watched them go. But perhaps he should have scared them more. Seemed madder and more terrible. What if they came back? The same threat rarely worked twice. And the police could never be bothered. He considered his 'dogs' notice. Maybe he would have to try it.

Why should they play there? Why should the young have everything?

'Nice walk?'

She was coming downstairs as he reached the hall. Slowly he drew off his gloves.

'Yes, it's a nice walk.'

She stopped to observe him, so that he had to remove his hat with extra care.

'I meant, did you enjoy it?'

'Oh, most enjoyable.'

The car, the boys. He ducked into the cloakroom, hung up his hat, then came back to the mirror. He blew on it, and stared through the mist he'd made. His eyes looked more fiercely red-rimmed than usual, and on his cheeks the spots of rouge shone like labels.

'There's nothing wrong with that mirror. I dusted it this morning.'

'Did I say there was anything wrong with it?'

As he hadn't said anything, there could be no quarrel. The housekeeper pulled a face – she must have forgotten that in the mirror he would see it – and he watched, fascinated, as her reflection buckled; but it was only for a moment, before she straightened it again.

He plucked at his coat buttons.

'Did you post that letter?' she asked.

No peace. He scowled at her.

'Can't you stop pestering me, woman? Can't you see I'm tired?'

'You'd best get sitting down, then.'

'Yes. Yes.'

His chest squealed. At some time since he'd entered the house, his coat had become a layer of lead, pressing him down, and he longed to get out of it; but while she stood there, he couldn't possibly. There was the hideous chance that as he moved his arms and struggled to extricate himself, the letter would fall from the inside pocket. Such things happened.

If only she'd go ... She showed no signs of wanting to.

'By the way ...' she began, 'I'll be going out just now. Church. Unless you'd rather I didn't, being as this is the first week ...'

'And why not?' His voice rose. 'Don't you go every Sunday? Off to the charnel house? When have I ever tried to stop you? Just because we've moved ... Why not? I expect it! I look forward to it!'

He shuffled his feet. He glared.

'Let me help ...'

'No. I don't need help.'

'You shouldn't call it that,' she said. 'You've no respect.'

'The charnel house? That's what it is, isn't it? ... Don't you tell the vicar to come calling. Not on me. You hear? I'll tell him what I think ...'

'I wouldn't dream of it.'

'Ha!'

To be fair, it was years since she had committed such a folly, but Lawson still remembered a smiling, complacent gentleman who had called on him once, at tea-time. He had finally got rid of him by turning their talk to Eastern religions

44

and reading a passage from the *Kama Sutra* out loud, over the
cake. Presumably she had heard all about it, and there had
been no more vicars. All the same, in a new place he felt it
wise to repeat the veto.

'As if I would!' she said, and her lean shoulders squared
with contempt.

Shortly after five, she went. With his usual relief and appre-
hension he checked the back door after her, making certain it
was locked – although he stopped short of bolting her out.

These hours when there was no one to answer his bell, no
one to come interrupting his thoughts, were a kind of pleasant
island that was also a minefield. He moved through them very
cautiously.

For a start, before she left he always made the library as
snug as possible, full of light, the standard lamps shining benevolently, and the curtains drawn. No hint of the evening
closing in. And he always kept his orange juice to drink while
she was out.

Everything to a plan – strategies, refined through any number of her Lord's Day observances.

Settled in an armchair, he sipped the juice, rationing himself,
and at the same time, he made a critical study of the fireplace.
The house was centrally heated, so there was no need for coal
and crumpled papers, shovelling of ashes and all that, which
was just as well. It would have given her an excellent excuse
to come in whenever she felt like it, 'Just to see how the fire
was ...' But in another way, it was a pity. An empty fireplace
looks lonely, and this one in particular seemed emphatically
designed for social gatherings, celebrations. It was rich and
grandiose. The black marble surround was carved with vines
and grapes, and in the centre there were tiles in sumptuous
black and gold that would have glistened if he'd had a fire in
the grate. But there was only the grate, a dark socket. After a
while, its blind stare irritated him, so he got up and went to
his desk.

Time to put away the letter. Taking it out of his jacket, he
laid it flat on the blotter, smoothed it and viewed it with
satisfaction. He was very glad he hadn't posted it. So glad, in
fact, that he felt a stir of pity for the Arnold Lawson who

might have been sitting there, horrified by his rashness, wishing this letter out of the box and back in his hand.

I was right to trust my instincts, he thought.

Of course, his mind could go on changing. Either tomorrow or the next day, he might well experience all his anger over again and think of posting the letter. The problem was, should he act on that mood if it came, or ignore it? He would have to think. Meanwhile, it seemed best to lock this piece of worry away, in his desk drawer, and try to forget about it.

Now I can relax, he promised, as he slipped the key into his pocket.

Then he noticed his hands. They felt powdery. Quickly he wiped them on his trousers, as if he had touched a subtle poison that might work its way into his bloodstream. Dust again! It showed up grey on his knees ... But the whole desk stank of polish, so where had it come from? The drawer? A small deposit left to dirty his papers?

The slut. Never does anything properly!

He'd left everything unlocked for this precise reason. 'Wipe every surface,' he'd told her. 'Thoroughly!'

Unlocking the drawer again, he tugged it towards him and rubbed a finger along the inner edge. Sure enough! Yes! And the good white envelope ... He picked it up and turned it over. Smudged. Smirched. There was an unmistakable thumb print on the back. It couldn't be sent like that, as if he'd mauled it, fumbled with it and dithered over it. Now he'd have to change the envelope, but if he did, obviously he might be tempted to re-read the letter, then to draft another, and another ...

It was all monstrous. Slut. She probably hadn't even touched the other room ...

Lawson thrust the letter back and hurried out. As he crossed the hall, he started rehearsing reprimands.

Then I'll say to her, 'By the way,' I'll say, 'I know it can't be dust. I know how well you dust, but there's a disgusting substance in the sitting-room ...'

The sitting-room was his showcase. If he stuck to his habits, he would never actually 'sit' in it, but that wasn't the point. Here stood his great oak cabinets with glass-panelled doors – sturdy Victorian pieces of furniture full of precious jades and ivories, and here stood his highly polished grand piano, and on antique tables his valuable vases. She had unpacked these carvings and vases on Thursday under his supervision, and the dust from the boxes had got everywhere. She had promised to have 'the whole room sparkling by the weekend'. He knew her kind of 'weekend'. Not Saturday, but Sunday. It had seemed best to wait.

Well, now he'd see ... Now for the truth ...

With angry aplomb he threw open the door – and came to a sudden halt on the threshold.

The room was filled with pinkish light. It coloured the sides of the vases, sparkled off the cabinets, and a pool of it lay across the closed back of the piano. But it was everywhere, even in the spaces between things. It had come into the house without his knowledge, and the presence of it sickened him. He held out a hand, and that, too, looked faintly pink, contaminated.

Of course, he knew the explanation. Lawson groped his way forward. One of the side windows faced west, and through it the sun, as red as the flesh of a blood-orange, glared in from behind the trees. When he saw it, he drew in a quick breath. To be caught unawares like this ...

I'm having a bad day, he thought weakly. *That's all* ... He gripped the window-sill. *I should have put the light on.*

Too late. The sun held him. He couldn't move. His brain numbed. His temperature dropped: his fingers on the window-sill turned ice-cold. It was as if this blood-thing in the sky had reached in through the branches, into his body, and was drawing all his strength and every trace of will-power out of him, gathering them into its centre, to sink with it.

He was being emptied.

A long time passed.

Rescue. He needed rescue. Vaguely he knew it, in the way a man falling headlong into a pit might sense that the pit's sides are out there somewhere, untouchable.

Nevertheless, rescue came. It took the form of a white car nosing up the drive. While Lawson stood staring at the sun, he became aware of this intruder on the very edge of his field of vision, and it was so astonishing that it broke the spell: his eyes could move. He looked at it fully. A white Austin Morris,

47

a smug little town car, already pulling up in front of the porch. Where the sun caught at it, its roof pinkened.

Now what?

He didn't feel relief, although he was conscious of the fact that he had just escaped from something; but there came a rush of curiosity, and he strained to see in through the windscreen. He made out a faint blur. Did that mean *they* could see him? He took a couple of panicky steps backwards. An old man, spying on his visitors ... From the shadows, he watched the car door open, and a small woman in an over-large, cream-coloured coat got out. As she closed the door again, she glanced up at the house. Then she moved out of sight, up the porch steps. The front doorbell rang.

Now what? Now what?

Lawson hurried back to the hall, and stood there waiting, breathless, as if by some fantastic trick she might break in.

If he kept quiet, would she go away? He remembered the lamps blazing in the library. At this time of day, could their light be seen through the curtains? He should have made a point of finding out. Had he left a chink in the curtains? Not that it mattered ... If he refused to answer, whoever it was would give up in the end. They would have to ...

Jolting his nerves, the bell rang out again, very loud, and held for longer than was quite polite. It was as though she knew he was there, facing her, taking full advantage of the door between them. A small, dark woman. Certainly not the reporter; from what he'd seen, she looked too old for that – and too impractical, weighed down by her fashionable coat and an enormous handbag. No. This was someone paying a social call – a friend of the previous people, but not a close friend. They had moved house without enlightening her.

A cast-off acquaintance. What else could she be?

For a third time, the bell rang – and in the silence afterwards, it came to Lawson that he had no good reason not to find out. Why all this cowering and puzzling? One middle-aged woman didn't amount to a gang of thieves, and he had nothing better to do. Nothing, that is, in particular. In fact, his resentment of strangers was largely habit. A kind of mental rheumatism. Old age ...

To his own surprise, he reached up and drew the bolt

48

back. Then, instead of changing his mind, he took the key from its hook, and seconds later, he was peering round the door.

'Mr Lawson?'

'What about him?'

The woman's face was more lined than he'd expected. She looked about sixty. And she knew his name. Taken aback, he jerked his head as though avoiding a noose.

'What if I am?' he rasped.

She smiled, and when he saw that he smiled, too. He couldn't help it. He found she was attractive. There was a warmth and intelligence in her eyes – brown eyes, topped with masculine eyebrows. Her face was pale, delicate, but she wore a bright lipstick.

'What if I am Mr Lawson?' he said again.

'May I come in?' She was holding up her smile like a flag, some kind of signal in no man's land. 'I was just passing,' she said. 'And I thought I'd drop in ...' Her tone implied that nothing could be more reasonable.

Lawson's own smile slipped. He made all haste to correct it, but at the same time, his hand tightened on the door-knob.

'Why?' he asked softly.

'Why?'

The woman seemed at a loss to know what to do with the question, as if, by asking it, he had broken the rules, and now it was her smile that wavered, then disappeared altogether. As it went, her face became smaller, almost mouse-like thought Lawson. He waited. She stood before him nervously silent, her feet apart, holding her handbag low in front of her with both hands on the straps, and he noticed, with a pang of forgiveness, that she was even shorter than he was.

At last she said, 'Well, I read about you in the *Herald*, and I just thought ...' she laughed, 'I'd like to meet you.'

So that was it. A woman who filled her life with newspaper gossip. Annoyed, for some ridiculous reason Lawson went on smiling.

'My dear lady, if everyone who reads that nonsense comes driving up to the door, what shall I do? Sell tickets? And didn't it say I'm a *recluse*?'

'Oh, that!' She wrinkled her nose. Apparently she had nothing more to say, and as he had nothing either, she looked away from him, towards the trees.

'Isn't it a gorgeous sunset?'

'Madam ...'

Without exactly meaning to, he went out to stand beside her on the step. The evening was still warm. She smelt faintly of some perfume he had once known the name of, and it was true, he was a good two inches taller.

'Madam ...' He was elaborate. Oddly enough, he felt no desire to give offence. 'You must understand,' he said, 'I'm not one of your gregarious town-dwellers. I don't go in for entertaining.' Then he was struck by a mitigating thought. 'Do you live near here? Are you a neighbour?'

'Not really. I live in a part I don't suppose you know yet ...' Then she said a name, but standing there with her back to him like that, how could she expect him to catch it?

'You'll have to speak up! I'm deaf! Do you represent a *cause* or something?'

The woman turned with a stare, and it crossed his mind that she thought he was senile.

'A charity,' he explained. 'I get so many requests ...'

To his tremendous relief, she laughed.

'Of course not! Honestly, it's just that it said in the paper you've a marvellous library. I love books ...' and she looked past him into the house, so frankly inquisitive that Lawson's jaw sagged.

She hadn't justified herself at all. Not for a moment did he believe that she loved books. He didn't know what to believe, except that she read the *Herald*. Nervous she might be, but she was also brazen, inexcusable. And yet he didn't tell her to go.

A new silence crystallised between them. Helplessly he let it grow, and in the end she broke it for him.

'Well?'

He continued to smile, playing for time. He could go inside and slam the door. What could she do? Start ringing the bell again? Go away, feeling a fool? Serve her right. The strange thing was that he didn't feel more hostile. He wrapped his arms round his middle and rubbed his elbows – not that he was cold. Finally he said, 'Well, you'd better come in, if you're coming. I can't stand out here freezing!'

'I suppose you've got a name?'
'Moira Gelling.'
'Married?'
He pushed home the bolt.
'My husband's David Gelling, the lawyer.'
'Never heard of him. Is that what you are – a housewife?'
Now that she was in, it didn't feel good to have this woman in the house, and the question just slipped out. Women who filched prestige from their husbands were irritating. Still, he hadn't intended to be rude, and he felt it was a ludicrous question to put to a woman of her age. In confusion Lawson hurried her along.
'Here's the library. The "marvellous library" ...'
That sounded rude, too. To make amends, he waved her through, and she walked past him smiling. She seemed not to notice his insults.
'I've never been what you'd call a *domesticated* housewife ... Oh!'
She stood still, a diminutive figure smothered by a winter coat, encountering the magnificance of his books in the warm glow of the lamps. He kept his eyes on her. He prided himself on knowing a fraud when he saw one, the kind of person who enthused indiscriminately, and he thought, with a little faint hope: *Please. Don't say anything stupid!*
'Thousands of them!'
Now that was stupid. They might have been wooden blocks in covers for all she knew. He grunted with disappointment.
'Take a seat ... take a seat ...'
But she wandered over to the fireplace, and gazed at the French poets.
'Rimbaud ... Villon ... You read these, in French?'
'Tolerably well. Won't you sit down?'
No. She was away again, craning her neck at the highest shelves by the door.
'Latin and Greek too?'
'Why not?'
To stop them trembling, he curled his fingers into the palms

51

of his hands. She was behaving idiotically. Her pretence of interest dismayed him, and so did his own rudeness.

And there on the desk, making everything worse, stood his childish jug of orange juice.

'May I take one out?'

'If you must.'

Let her get on with it. He lowered himself into an armchair and watched her take out first one book, then another, skimming through them and putting them back. A fraud. She knew nothing, nothing . . . He saw her take down a yellow and green biography.

'What's that?' he asked, knowing very well.

'Pasteur.'

'Do you know anything about him?'

'A little.' She looked up. 'I qualified as a doctor.'

'Oh.'

'I just never used it.'

Flick, flick through the biography. Back it went.

Well, she might be a doctor, but she still knew nothing about books. Even the way she held them was wrong, awkward and timid, as though a bird might fly out of the pages, straight at her. It became insufferable, and all at once he blurted out, 'You don't know the first thing, do you?'

Then he sank back into the chair, recoiling.

Now there'll be a scene, he thought. *She comes here uninvited, and now she's going to argue . . .*

But to his joy, the woman agreed.

'I suppose I don't. I read a lot, but I've no taste. I don't really know a good book from a bad one.'

Lawson softened. Perhaps, after all, she was not a fraud.

'What *have* you read?' He hauled himself to his feet. 'Novels? The nineteenth century? Dickens? Eliot? And what about the twentieth? Lawrence? Conrad?'

'Some of them . . .'

As he came towards her, she moved away from the shelves, not far, but the action pleased him. He saw it as an acknowledgment that everything belonged to him.

'What do you think of this?' Before he could stop himself, he took a fat book from one of the lower shelves and pushed it into her hands. '*Vanity Fair*. Have you read it?'

52

'I can't remember ...' She turned the book over diffidently. 'This is very old, isn't it?'

'Ha! It's a first edition!' He snatched it back, and as he did so, her expression became wistful. Also, suddenly she looked tired. For some reason, this embarrassed him and he began to pontificate.

'If you haven't read them, read the giants first. Go back to the start. Richardson, Fielding, Thackeray ... You should really begin with Richardson, but I don't suppose you'd cope with that ... And never mind Jane Austen! I know you women all read *her*! No. Begin with Thackeray ...' Replacing the first edition, he clawed out a modern copy that stood next to it. 'Here! A cornerstone of English literature! Though I don't know that I'd say "taste" ... If it's "taste" you want, it should be Eliot ... But get your grounding first ... Take it! Take it! You may borrow it!'

'Really?'

Ah, generosity. And he had hinted at his range – a considerable range – in a field where she was plainly ignorant. He was enjoying himself. Definitely not a fraud, he decided. He detected in her a craving for guidance. Tentatively she opened the book at the back and began to read an advertisement on the flap of the cover – a list of companion volumes. Even that, he felt willing to pardon.

'I shall be most interested', he said, 'to hear how you get on with it.'

'It's very kind of you.'

'Only don't go telling everyone. I'm not a public lending library!'

Her smile returned.

'Are you really a recluse?'

Lawson sniffed. He shuffled away to his chair again, and this time she followed.

'Recluse ... eccentric ... words ... labels ...' He gestured loftily. Then, in a fit of happiness he giggled, and settling himself in the chair, he winked at her. For this one fraction of the hideous day, he felt festive. The woman stood, staring and trying hard not to stare at the top of his head. He patted it.

'Do you ... Sit down, sit down ... Do you approve of toupees, ma'am?'

53

'... It's rather *bold* ...'

'An honest woman. Her price is far above rubies! And how old do you think I am?'

She sat down carefully, taking her time about replying.

'Eighty-ish. Eighty-one, or two ...'

'Oh, you flatter me!' He was vexed, but he laughed. Of course, she was a doctor. He should have known that she would come near the mark.

'I'm eighty-seven,' he said. 'What do you think of that?'

Well, what was she supposed to think? Why did he make these appeals? By adding three years to his age, what was he trying to excuse in himself?

But she only smiled and shook her head. She couldn't have known he lied.

'I've had quite a life!' went on Lawson. 'The women in my life have been nobody's business!'

'Oh, I believe you!'

To his delight, her words were richly insinuating. And in the next moment, she rubbed her legs against each other, a slight, coquettish movement. So it was still there – his charm! And the woman was a flirt! These simple facts opened his heart. He understood. He knew her species of loneliness, and he felt a surge of anxiety for this visitor who knew nothing about books.

'Why don't you take your coat off?'

'Oh, I can't stay.'

'What? Are you cold?'

She certainly looked cold. She sat huddled up, as if fending off an icy blast.

'No, but my husband's supper ...'

'Ah.' Lawson grimaced. 'The duties of the hearth. And I thought you said you weren't domesticated.'

Then he got flustered. He drummed on the arms of his chair with his fingers. All this talk of leaving, confound it ...

'When you've finished the Thackeray,' he waved at the room, the shelves, 'I've plenty more to show you.'

It was merely an observation. He took care to stop short of a promise, but all the same she brightened. Her eyes followed the sweep of his hand, and she said, 'How I envy you all this!'

'Yes. It's quite a collection.' He nodded complacently.

54

'But how do you put a thing like this together? Did you buy up whole libraries, or ...'

'Scratching and saving. Hard graft!' His voice shrilled. 'None of this was given to me. I sweated for it!'

'Really, it's another world.'

She looked almost religious. Gazing round at the shelves, she evidently realised what they meant – the love and labour in the place. Her face was awestruck. She couldn't have been more different from the woman who'd entered the library.

Lawson had forgotten such sincerity, and now rediscovering it put him in mind of his role as host, the attentions due to appreciative guests. He became conscious that it was the sherry hour – and that he had no sherry.

'Would you ...' He half rose. 'My housekeeper's out ... Would you like some orange juice?'

'Yes! I would!'

It wasn't said out of courtesy; he could tell she meant it, and he hurried to fetch a glass.

Here I am, entertaining, he marvelled, smiling to himself. But somewhere along the passage to the kitchen, he stopped, overwhelmed by his folly. A stranger. What did he know about her? And he had left her alone with his books! He had a split-second vision of her scooping something into that cavernous handbag ... He turned back. Stupid! Incredibly stupid of him! He doubled his pace ... and arrived at the library door only to see the woman still in her chair, leafing through the Thackeray.

'I couldn't find one!' he gasped. 'I ... don't know where she keeps them!'

'It doesn't matter. I ought to be going anyway.'

As if this setback were a prompt, she got up, straightening her coat, while Lawson worked at controlling himself. Hurtling down the passage like a mad cat was not to be recommended, and he had to put a hand to his chest to help regulate the heaving.

She came across to him with the book and her handbag. For such a small woman, a bag that size was an absurdity, and he wanted to tell her, but he hadn't the breath. It was easier just to shamble out ahead, to the front door.

'I'm so glad I came,' she said. 'When I've read the book ... perhaps you'd come to tea? I could drop you a note.'

55

'No no!' He hated tea. Favoured event of predatory vicars. A superfluous, decadent business that made for obesity. 'I rarely go out!'

'Well ... I'll drop a note. Or else ...' She looked towards the telephone, but he pretended not to see. He busied himself with the key, the bolt, wheezing softly, and when he turned round again, her eyes were sharp with professional appraisal.

'Asthma!' he panted defensively. 'Nothing to do with *age* ...'

'A nuisance, isn't it?' She held out her hand. 'Goodbye, and I'll look after this!' flourishing the book. Her hand, the first he had actually held in his own for months, felt like soap – smooth and cool. Lawson let go of it quickly.

'Just don't go telling every Tom, Dick and Harry ... I don't want hordes of callers!'

She laughed. He opened the door. And now that the visit was over, she became girlish, flushed with her own audacity.

'I won't tell a soul!' she promised. 'You have my word!'

Her voice warned him not to believe her. She would talk all over town.

Again, as she passed him, he smelt her perfume. Her short, pale legs negotiated the steps. A small woman, leaving. He called after her. 'Would your husband be at this tea?'

'I shouldn't think so. Why?'

'Just you? Well, read the book. Read the book!'

'I will.' Looking back at him, she staggered in the gravel.

'Your shoes are ridiculous!'

He meant all women's shoes, but it came out wrong.

'Goodbye!'

He watched her toss his Thackeray into the back of the car, and he stood, hand raised, blinking, as she switched on the headlights.

The sunset had dulled. Now, a dark slate-purple lay over the trees. From his position on the steps, it looked as though the drive tunnelled through a solid mass, scarcely less black than itself; but as the woman drove away, beams of yellow light picked out tree-trunks and branches, breaking the illusion.

Then the car turned out into the lane, and the tunnel walls were solid again.

Four

A bored, spoilt woman, escaping from Sunday. She had called on a whim, and on a whim he had received her. There wasn't much more to it than that, and there would be nothing more, once he'd got his book back.

Yet he was re-vitalised. After Moira Gelling had gone, he turned the key on his letter to the *Herald*, and it seemed a matter of complete indifference to him whether he ever saw it again. Then, when his housekeeper came in, still got up in her church-going best, looking pious and carrying a tray of soup and crackers, he lashed out with a witty attack on charnel houses – something he'd not had the fight to do for a long time. He succeeded in turning her white with hatred, which was always enjoyable on a Sunday. He liked to prove her a hypocrite.

That night, he read Byron – *Don Juan* – looking up between cantos to smile at his books.

'Thousands of them!'

Oh, the small brains of women! He felt effortlessly, benevolently superior. It was happiness, he recognised, based on nothing, but still permissible: life was largely made up of nothing. And before he went to bed, to demonstrate how truly alive he was, he left a note on the hall table.

Today, kindly dust the sitting-room.

He slept badly. There was still that peculiar interlude with the sun – that pink light – on the edge of his mind, where it required constant suppression. Not that it mattered. He rose at noon quietly convinced that his new day would be a pleasant one, and not even the two clumsy electricians, fiddling and banging in every nook of the house, could undermine him. Nothing that happened, and nothing he undertook could mar things. He felt lapped in contentment. He forgot all about the letter. By a more or less subconscious act of will-power, he kept the boys out of his grounds. In the Yellow Pages, he scrutinised ranks of solicitors and found: *Gelling, D.* Then he looked up Gelling, D. in the main directory. When the electricians had gone, he took his first edition *Vanity Fair* from the shelf, and began to re-read it.

But on the Tuesday he felt ill at ease. By then, the old fool in his skull had worked himself into a state, waiting for contact, invitations ... And that was nonsense. Really, he couldn't care less. On the other hand, he thought, it would be interesting to know just how long it took a woman like Moira Gelling to read a book. A real book.

What if she couldn't stomach it? Would she simply let things drift?

No, no. Sooner or later, *Vanity Fair* would have to be returned, and a bored woman wasn't likely to post it ...

On the Wednesday, he took to prowling round the library, fingering various novels, and talking out loud to the armchairs.

'So you've never read Scott? You should! It's fashionable to run him down of course, but even so ... And Stevenson. I think you might like Stevenson. *Jekyll and Hyde.* Now that you *must* read!'

The week slid into rain, a grey blanket wrapped round the house. He crept about inside its folds, sensing the dampness in his bones. In the middle of Thursday afternoon, he pulled a travelling rug out of the cupboard on the landing, and draped it round his shoulders. By the evening, all his optimism had turned to mildew.

The housekeeper noticed this change, as she noticed everything, and her tone was hard with barely concealed eagerness.

'Are you ill or something?'

It was seven o'clock. She had just set down his lunch tray: cheese sandwiches and egg custard.

'What's that supposed to mean?' Raising his eyes from his book, Lawson saw exactly what she wanted: she was alert, poised to take over. 'You'd like that, wouldn't you,' he whined. 'Can't I have a bad day without you thinking I'm ill?'

58

She shrugged.

'You've been in such good form all week ...'

'*Good form?*' He pushed his head clear of the rug. 'What do you think I am? A racehorse? A greyhound? Oh ... go away ...'

'You sound terrible. Maybe I should call a doctor.'

'What for? Anyway, I haven't one! I haven't registered yet, have I? ... If you want to be helpful, turn the heating up. And bring me some milk ... *hot* milk.'

'It's stupid for a man of your age to be without a doctor.'

'Just fetch the milk, woman.'

She did something exasperated with her hands, and he thought – not for the first time – that hands like those could easily strangle him. He presumed she longed to let them. If only she could have been sure ... Twenty years of narrow, calculated service. Doubtless she felt there ought to be a harvest at the end of it, but as she wasn't sure there would be, she kept those hands under control.

Away she went, the righteous slave, to boil up milk that both of them knew he wouldn't bother to drink.

All Friday, the rain continued. After school, boys in brightly coloured anoraks scampered like savages through the trees. He growled at them from the library windows. He sent the housekeeper out to shoo them, and had the satisfaction of seeing her headscarf turn limp and black, clinging to her head as she stomped back through the downpour.

Then the weather mended, and his mood lifted into a strange calm.

One week, or even two or three, he reflected, was not so long to take on a novel. Not for a woman. Besides, he saw he had fallen into a trap – one of the many set by age. He had over-excited himself about a sort of bubble – what else could he call it? – a sudden froth, and this had led to a disproportionate despair. But now he was sane. He folded away the travelling rug. He spent several hours with *Pickwick Papers*; and in his chest, a pain which he had hardly known he felt, eased. He determined to have his Saturday bath as usual. The blessings of normality.

'What's the matter now? Why aren't you running the water?'

'Nothing. Just ... getting undressed ...'

He disliked spiders. This one was the size of a small tin lid – a Germolene tin – and it was not black but dark brown, which was somehow worse. He had stood for about a minute watching it. He saw it thrust out a leg, stretching it up the smooth side of the bath, find no grip, retract, then thrust out another leg, pushing it out like a thread almost to snapping point, and find no grip ...

He was faintly shocked by this activity.

Get rid of it!

Yes, but how? He should have drowned it. Turned on the hot-water tap, and cooked it. But the size of the thing had made him hesitate: it was big enough to be animal – and having failed to play the executioner in the first few seconds, now he found he couldn't.

He was worried for this spider.

There was nowhere for it to go – not unless it could squeeze back down the plughole, and either it had already tried that and given up, or it couldn't try, because it had no idea where the plughole was, miles away down the bath. Or maybe they were places to escape from, plugholes. A hopeless situation, anyway. Lawson peered closely. As he watched, it crept for a couple of inches along the base of the bath, then began again, stretching up the curved wall of its prison. Was it panicking? Maybe even spiders had their moments of insight. Would it start running round in circles? Or was this other urge impossible to overcome – this slow, painstaking search for a grip?

She began to thump on the door.

'Do you need help?'

'Certainly not ... Don't come in. I'm having trouble with my bowels.'

'Why didn't you say?'

He looked round for an apparatus. In the rack above the washbasin, there was a plastic mug. Lawson seized it, and hurried back to the bath. Carefully he lowered it; his hand trembled, the inverted mug trembled ... Would it be wide enough? What if the brute didn't all fit in? He imagined with shivery distaste the feel of the thing, scuttling over his fingers.

So far, so good ... As he reached towards it, the spider shrank, buckling its legs ... Coiled for a spring? What if it could jump? One second, docile there beneath him, the next – half-way up his arm ...

But the spider crouched, seemingly paralysed, as the heavens closed over it. The rim of the plastic mug made contact with the bath. Lawson panted. He had it, but not entirely. It had managed to scale a slight, but impressive distance up into the bath's curve, and so the mug wasn't sitting straight. Round the rim, there were gaps. At any moment, a leg might poke out ... He steeled himself for some such sickening detail, but nothing happened. It was keeping still, waiting. On to the next stage. With his free hand, he fished in his trouser pockets. Paper ... Usually he carried jottings – lists, dates, quotations – round with him, though when he wanted them ... To his relief, his fingers curled on something that felt like a folded page from one of his notebooks. He pulled it out and very slowly pushed it under the mug. Would such a flimsy barrier hold? Well, now for the bad part: the scooping up. He couldn't put it off. Bending nearly double like this was agony. His chest felt tight, and reddish blotches swam before his eyes.

In one move, he flipped the mug upright, securing the paper across the top with his thumbs. Then he stared at the bath.

Nothing. He had it. The spider was between his hands. Dizzily Lawson straightened up and staggered back, the blood rushing from his head.

'What are you doing in there? I can hear you moving about!'

From her tone, he could tell that her patience was exhausted, but he hadn't the breath to answer. He stood looking at the heavy bathroom shutters, with their stiff catch. To open those, he would have to set the mug down, and risk ... what? That the spider would somehow scrabble up inside and push the paper off, heaving it off with its back, like a chick hatching out? He didn't know. He would have to look into the strength of spiders. They might be like ants – every one of them a Hercules.

'I'm coming in!'

'No!'

But she came anyway, her face armed for a crisis, her sleeves rolled up, and he swayed at the sight of her.

'You – shouldn't!' he panted. 'I didn't tell you to!'

'What's that?' Seeing him on his feet and fully dressed, for a moment she looked crestfallen, but then her eyes had lit on his hands. 'What have you got there?'

Lawson backed. She came on with quick steps, her mouth set, and seeing it was no use, he cried, 'Take it! Get rid of it!'

He held out the mug. She clasped it, and lifted the paper. Then she muttered something, and her eyes betrayed a small, mean enjoyment. She moved towards the toilet.

'No, no!' he gasped. 'Outside! Don't kill it!'

Her tongue clicked, but she drew her arm back. Striding across to the shutters, with one hand she pulled them open and pushed up the window. Then she flung it out.

A few days afterwards, he had her order a car, and as part of his exercise in sanity he ventured into town. She disapproved of that, as she disapproved of all his independent outings. She clearly resented his rare displays of wealth: hired cars, chauffeurs. She never failed to make it plain that old men should stop at home.

When he was dressed and ready to leave, she insisted on brushing his overcoat, and she thumped him hard between his shoulder blades.

'You'll be able to register today. Get a doctor.'

'Possibly.'

'You should.' She stood back, examining her handiwork. 'And you'd better take your scarf. That chill of yours could come back worse,' she promised. 'There's a cold wind.'

Down the passage to the back door ... He laboured to get out of reach, but she followed at his heels, and when he stopped at the sight of the Mercedes, she almost walked into him.

'Anything wrong?'

'No ...'

Sparkling black. She was supposed to have asked for any colour but that – the uniform of cabs and hearses. Still, he wouldn't fuss ... He hurried out, climbed in, and finally, once the car door was shut she left him in peace. He relaxed into the plush seat. Woodbourn drifted away from him. All was well. A warm, smooth car, and the driver – a ruddy-cheeked man of about fifty – was gratifyingly silent.

It was good to be on the move. Lawson gave a full minute

to praising himself for his enterprise, and to picturing the housekeeper. Stony-faced, she would have gone back to her tawdry little sitting-room, and there she would perch, knitting, knitting, watching the clock. How many scarves and socks and tea-cosies made up twenty years? And what did she do with them all? Church bazaars, jumble sales ... Her needles jabbing against each other ... But, of course, at some stage in the afternoon she would lay the needles down and go prowling through the house – prying – which was why he had spent the greater part of the day before locking things away. Not that the woman thieved. She was deadly honest in that respect. She would hate to give him such a good cause for sacking her.

He touched the letter in his pocket. Over the week he had realised that this piece of bluster to the *Herald* was never going to be posted – so why have it cluttering the place? It had occurred to him to tear it up, and so he would. This afternoon. Dispose of it in a public convenience. To have done it in the house was out of the question. The stiff, good quality paper might have blocked the pipe, and then she would have guessed.

'So you didn't send it after all? I knew you wouldn't. But why didn't you put it in the wastepaper basket? What have you got to be ashamed of?'

Nothing could induce him to give her so much satisfaction.

His mind was made up. He gazed out at the scenery.

In the meadow, the cows looked oddly humped. On the hill, the washing outside the bungalows flapped. She was right about that. There *was* a wind. Well, he'd forget her. As they came close, he peered at the bungalows contemptuously, and pronounced judgment: *Rabbit hutches!* Then, by association: *And they breed like rabbits!* He pulled a face, remembering his own marriage.

At the top of the hill, there was a halt sign, and here the chauffeur said something.

'Eh?' *Devil take the man!* Lawson had to lean forward. 'What was that?'

The Mercedes changed gear.

'I said, where's it to be, sir? The High Street? Or the new shopping precinct?'

'How should I know? Drive around. Let me see both!'

'Right you are, sir. No cars allowed in the precinct, but I'll drive as close as I can. If you want to get out, there's a handy car-park ...'

'Barbarians!'

Lawson settled back to be entertained. Plump-thighed girls in mini-skirts; a cyclist struggling against the wind; frowsy women with carrier bags ... Sealed inside the Mercedes, he could observe the people of the town as phenomena. At the sight of an elderly woman out walking her Yorkshire terrier, he smiled scornfully, because she was stout: another one who'd let her waistline go! A tray of frozen chickens being carried into a supermarket gave him a moment's agitation:

That's right! Wrap them up in polythene. Oven ready. Force-fed and mass slaughtered ... but we needn't think of that!

'Do *you* eat meat?'

He snapped the query at his chauffeur's back, and watched the blue jacket straighten slightly before the answer came.

'Me, sir?' Wary eyes showed in the driver's mirror. 'Meat? I like a nice chop ... or a piece of gammon ...'

'Tch!'

Lawson expressed his displeasure without vouchsafing any more words on the subject, and they drove on in silence.

The town itself was a challenge. It looked alarmingly like the other town, the one he had just left. There were the same grey and brown pebble-dashed houses with small, unloved gardens; the same red-brick schools, and the same depressing corner-shops ... but it couldn't be just like the other place. The similarity had the feel of a code that hid some vital message. The towns were seventy miles apart, and it had cost him not much under a thousand pounds to move from one to the other, besides all the pains of buying the house. So it had to be different.

Then he thought of Moira Gelling, and reaching forward, he poked the chauffeur lightly on his collar.

'Whereabouts is Williston?'

All he could remember of the address in the telephone directory.

'Up the back of town, sir.'

The man at the wheel sounded glad to be sure of his answer this time, and he kept his eyes on the road.

'Pleasant area, is it?'

'I suppose it is, sir. Big houses and that.'

'We'll drive back through it.'

'As you say, sir, but if you were wanting to see it in daylight, it'll take us half an hour to ...'

'We'll go when I say so!'

Lawson frowned at the man's head with its dead straight hair-line showing below the rim of the cap. This was *his* afternoon, and he meant to be in charge of it.

He made his purchases in the High Street. New gloves of soft leather, some hard lead pencils, and a golden box of Swiss chocolates, monarchs of their kind – but these were not for his own consumption. For himself, he bought boiled sweets. He also bought a bag of peppermint creams for the chauffeur, who was suitably overcome and his ruddy face turned purple.

'That's very kind of you, sir, I must say ...'

'Never mind that. Just you drive around and show me everything. I want to *know* this town ...'

They drove out past the gasworks and back past the hospital. They saw the borough cemetery with its wrought-iron gates, and they skirted the deplorable concrete shopping precinct with its prams and bright green rubbish boxes. Lawson made comments, and the driver laughed politely.

It was a short afternoon. By half past four the sky was darkening, and the first rain bubbled on the car windows. Lights burned orange in the shops.

'Is there anything else I should see?'

Slumped in his seat, paper bags scattered round him, Lawson began to lose the spirit of the occasion. He felt tired, and peculiarly bloated.

'There are some fine old churches ...'

'Well, I don't want those! Isn't there a playhouse? Aren't there any monuments?'

The chauffeur considered carefully, and at last he offered, 'There's a war memorial down by the labour exchange ... We did have a theatre, but it's the cinema now.'

'Philistines!' said Lawson.

'Did you want to see it, sir?'

'What?'

'The cinema ... did you want to see it?'

'No. Here ...' He stretched, waving a piece of paper. 'Take me to this address. I have to register.'

In the mirror, the chauffeur saw. Twisting his shoulders slightly, he reached back, but Lawson wasn't in the mood to wait. He let go; the paper fluttered on to the man's lapel; then he sat back with a grunt, leaving the fellow to squint at his writing.

'But this is very near where you live, sir. Shall we go to Williston first?'

'No.'

Why explain? In fact, he had his reasons. Now that it came to it, he felt an urgent need to be in and out before the thick of the evening surgery, when the whole place would be a germ-farm, people coughing, temperatures blazing away. And quite apart from all that, he could do without the audience. The last time – eight years before – he had blundered into an audience, and it had done nothing to beautify the unpleasant little ritual: How old was he? Did he have diabetes? Could he take penicillin? Impersonal, methodical probes, watched by a row of calculating faces from the chairs ranged round the wall. *A new doctor at* his *age. Hardly seems worth it, does it?* Oh, he knew what people thought.

Glumly, Lawson unwrapped a sweet and popped it into his mouth. He had selected a doctor late one night by reading the list in the Yellow Pages, and writing down the first name with a local number. That would do. What was the good of inquiries? He had little faith in the medical profession. Any fool could prescribe inhalers for his asthma, and as for other things, well, he'd rather they didn't.

He sucked his sweet, pulled out his wallet, and inspected his medical card.

The chauffeur's hint was justified. It made a long detour to drive home by way of Williston, especially coming from the surgery which turned out to be on the bungalow estate, almost back at Woodbourn. But Lawson was paying for compliance, and he got it. The Mercedes crawled down avenues and into crescents, out again into drives. There were few 'roads' in Williston, and no 'streets'. There were not many street lights either, but those there were stood taller than their downtown

66

counterparts, and instead of common-or-garden yellow light, they gave out a fur-soft, violet shine.

Lawson stared at it all morosely. He had been ruffled by the doctor's receptionist. She had asked: Did he want to make an appointment? – and had seemed surprised, even disapproving, when he'd said no, he didn't.

Implying, of course, that if something was found too late, he need only blame himself....There was a touch of the vulture about these girls who worked for doctors, and about all medical females.

Moira Gelling is a doctor. He had forgotten that.

He studied the houses. Mock Tudor, mock colonial, mock Regency ... Soon, he was trying to remember the full line in the telephone directory: Gelling D. ...? Hopeless. He had no idea. He struggled to make out some of the names on the gates. 'High Poplars.' 'The White Posts.'

Tea and cakes in one of these? Why not? If she repeated her invitation.

The Mercedes purred through the drizzle. By now, the roads were so wet that whenever a car came from the other direction, which wasn't often, its headlights sent twin blurs of luminescence skimming over the tarmac. Then the car would pass with a whooshing sound, which he just heard. Wrapped in his coat, Lawson became more and more uncomfortable. The coat sleeves cut into his armpits. The boiled sweets seemed to have pumped him full of air.

Why was it, he wondered, that every house in Williston had the look of a fortress? He knew he lived in something of the sort himself, but that was different: an old man, to all intents and purposes living alone. Whereas these were family houses. Did they have to look so defensive? A great many were set back behind stone walls, and most had a garrison of trees. Only in one or two of the smaller roads did walls and trees give way to privet hedges and feathery little gates, with short walks to the front doors. But even there, the actual houses had a closed-up look, as if they were under siege, and it seemed to Lawson that the lamps which shone out through the curtains were far from welcoming. They were jealous, watchful, and warned people off.

Irritably he rubbed his nose. He took a sweet out of the bag,

67

then dropped it in again. This wasn't at all what he wanted. He wanted to be back at Woodbourn, in his library.

Hard on the dawn of this realisation, the chauffeur said: 'Any particular house you want me to slow down near, sir ... just give the word.'

He stared in horror at the black cap.

'Why should I want that? I've no particular interest!'

'Right you are, sir.'

'Take me home!'

They headed out of the district.

Lawson smarted. What unmitigated lunacy. He wished he'd never heard of Williston. Now his day was ruined ... By the time they passed the bungalows, everything was wrong. He had pains in his bowels. His back ached. There was a draught from somewhere. He regretted the cost of the car hire. An expensive afternoon. The whole trip was supposed to cheer him up: now here he was, depressed. And while he sank, the chauffeur rose, jollier and jollier.

'Lovely bit of country, this, sir! Living out here, near the town, in the country. It's the best of both worlds, isn't it?'

Silence.

'My brother used to work that farm behind your house. There's a water wheel up the back there. You should take a look at it, sir. It's very old.'

The weather was worsening. In the drive, the trees shook: the tunnel they made seemed on the point of collapsing.

Round the side of the house in silence. With a discreetly rebellious lurch, the Mercedes stopped. The rain came down in slanted darts.

'Here we are, sir. Home in time for tea!'

Promptly jumping out, the chauffeur ran and opened the passenger door, stooping forward as he did so, apparently ready to dash back into the car himself, as soon as he had the old man out of it.

An insult. Lawson stiffened. There were still a couple of wet, windy yards to the house, and suddenly he shrieked, 'Get me an umbrella, you fool! Ring the bell and get me an umbrella!'

He sat tight. The ruddy-cheeked man gaped, then he scampered away, rain bouncing off his cap, his trouser-legs catching splashes from the puddles. Lawson watched, and was soothed. His money's worth. He watched the wretch ring the doorbell, and draw his neck into his jacket.

There followed an unacceptable interval. The housekeeper took her time.

Bitch! thought Lawson, discovering all at once that he had expected this. *She thinks it's me out there! Give him a bit of a soaking. Do him good. That's what she's thinking!*

Again the chauffeur pressed on the bell; and then at last the door opened, revealing her flat, overalled figure and her long face in the dim light of the passage.

The chauffeur spoke: she listened, glaring towards the car, and after a moment, Lawson saw her lips move. 'Wind ...' she was saying, something to do with 'the wind ...' An anxiety seized him. *'So he wants an umbrella, does he? He'll be lucky, in this wind!'* Something of the kind ...

A risk, yes. If it turned inside-out – farcical: the joke on him. He could only hope for the best ... Slowly, he straightened up; he let his chin jut out. She saw, of course, and first she shook her head, then she vanished inside while the chauffeur hovered in the doorway. Seconds later she re-appeared, bearing her own, mustard-yellow gamp. This she thrust at Ruddy-cheeks, who came scuttling back, wrenching it open ...

Fortunately, the thing held.

'Someone called while you were out.'

'Oh?'

Thinking he might be cold – so she said – she had heated up his orange juice, and he grimaced as he sipped it. He loathed it hot.

'A woman.'

'Who?'

He looked up quickly, too quickly. The housekeeper smirked.

'She wouldn't say. She didn't come in. When I said you were out, she left this.'

From the depths of her overall came a pale blue envelope, and her hand, while not exactly doing anything out of the ordinary, gave a fine pretence of crushing it.

Hastily Lawson dropped his eyes. There were flecks of pulp

in his orange juice: he studied those. His heart had started to pound.

'You should have left it on the desk ... Not that it matters,' he said. 'Just put it down. I'll read it later.'

He took a sip to keep from staring.

'I told her that you don't like visitors.'

'Thank you.'

Carefully he curled his left hand round the glass, to join up with his right hand. She was watching every movement. He could feel her jealousy raking the air between them.

'I thought you said you didn't know anyone round here. You told me that was why you wanted to live here.'

'Did I?' he said politely, glancing up, and there was her face, packed with stingy rectitude, like ... he groped for an image ... like the plaster copy of some minor saint – one of those tight, scoured souls never asked to intercede about anything. His patience snapped. 'What if I did?' he snarled. 'Circumstances change, don't they? Do I have to tell you everything?'

'I think you should.'

'Oh, you do, do you?' His cheeks were burning. At the very edge of his eye, lurked a ghost of the blue envelope. She had set it down miles across the desk, closer to her than to him.

'It's only common sense,' she said.

'Hah!'

He was speechless. He settled back and puffed out his belly at her, behaviour that brought a slight, downward turn to her mouth.

'What if you were ill?' she said.

'What?'

'If I don't know who your friends are, how would I know who to let in? To see you?'

'You mean – if I were dying!' The glass fused to his hands. His voice rose in a brittle arc. 'You think about that a lot, don't you?'

'Oh, for heaven's sake ...'

'You ... you succubus! Get out! Witch! Harridan!'

Orange slopped on his sleeve; balls of spittle flew across the desk, but she stood her ground. She watched him from behind two deepening lines of scorn, one either side of her nose, and

70

she clucked, very softly so that he couldn't hear, but he knew, he saw –

'Always reading things in!' she said.

'Get out!'

She turned with dignity, and left the room.

After that, he couldn't read the letter at once. First, he had to use his inhaler; then he sank back in the chair and tried to sort out a tangle of emotions. He was glad, glad that the bitch was so completely mystified. It filled him with a peculiar warmth to think that Moira Gelling had given away nothing, not even her name, although she must have been pressed for it. In her silence towards the housekeeper, wasn't there a sign of sympathy? A small alliance? It felt like it. He hoped so.

He contemplated the shade on his desk-lamp.

So he hoped, did he? And what on earth was he hoping for, exactly? Who was this Moira Gelling? A woman he didn't know, whose life had no natural meeting point with his, who had wheedled her way in ... And yet, he hoped! He felt the victim of an absurd exposure, as if someone had pulled his socks off.

For a long time he stared at the desk-lamp. He had an idea there was something wrong with it, something his eyes kept skimming over ... and suddenly he noticed, low down on the join of the shade, the beginnings of a pucker, a sly break with symmetry. The glue was drying out, and the elaborate stitching, which he had always presumed held the thing together, was only ornamental after all. A crack was forming; not there yet, but promising itself.

Quickly Lawson looked away, and from that disturbing object, his eyes fell on the envelope.

Of course, it would be an apology. The woman had come to her senses. She quite understood his desire for seclusion. She hadn't finished the book yet, but when she had, she would send it back by post. She wouldn't bother him again ... All this she had hoped to explain, and to say goodbye, but since he wasn't in ... A swift correction of errors, sealed up in an envelope.

Lawson reached out and grabbed it. Then he weighed it nervously on his hand.

Whatever she said, it was short. A single piece of paper.

He imagined her. Bunched up in her coat, waiting on the porch step, preparing her smile – to be confronted by the housekeeper! And when? When had she called? He couldn't ask the bitch. While he was playing the spy in Williston? The thought that, if he had come straight back from the surgery, he might have been in time to see her was so exasperating that, for once, he couldn't be bothered with his paper-knife: he ripped the envelope open, gutting it like a fish.

Dear Mr Lawson,

I'm scribbling this, just in case you're out when I call this afternoon. I must tell you how very much I'm enjoying *Vanity Fair*, and I've come up with a better idea than tea. (You sounded rather against that.)

Why don't you come to the Poetry Society? It was started only a couple of years ago by a group of people like myself who want to learn a little, and we're still a very modest gathering, although I hasten to add that not every member is as ignorant as me! Our next meeting is at 8.30 on the 17th, at the Hydro. It'll be a talk on Coleridge. I would be so pleased if you'd come along and tell me what you think of us! You will come, won't you?

Looking forward to seeing you there,

Moira Gelling

Confound women! The lines shifted, they danced together and broke apart again. As if to make up for the pale, discreet envelope, her handwriting was decidedly showy, with flourishes on the loops and capitals. Confound women! If tea was bad, 'societies' were the end. Perhaps there was some way out of it? Lawson read the letter again. Was the tea invitation still open, or had she withdrawn it? 'Looking forward to seeing you there . . .' That sounded final.

Ghastly. A 'society' was worse than anything . . . And without doubt, they'd be after him for a subscription. Maybe that was the only reason . . . No. It wouldn't do to think so . . . But could he write back and say he preferred tea? What had he said that day in the hall, as he let her out? He had better be consistent. What had he said about tea? Something disparaging ...

And in his despair, he seemed to hear Moira Gelling comment, *'These old boys! They never know what they want!'*

Trapped. A cantankerous old fool. He wrapped the letter round his fingers. If he hadn't been out, they could have talked, everything would have been different. He saw it now. What he'd said about 'tea' had flustered her: she didn't know what was suitable, and this 'society' business was an attempt not to seem frivolous. He had brought it on himself. Yes, yes. His own fault.

His stomach rumbled. Confound women, always making a mess, worrying too much ... He thought of the chocolates – a gift, to take to her tea – and sighed.

Unrolling the letter, he smoothed it out again, the flat of his hand across her signature, the gigantic M, the whale's jaw of a G.

What to do?

He puzzled, until an unwelcome, alien decision lodged in his brain. It was like a bone in the windpipe, impossible to ignore; and a minute later, he was heading for the kitchen.

'Ahem!'

The housekeeper's arm moved with deadly precision, chopping fruit. Bonk ... bonk ... Her knife flashed as it rose and came down swift and hard on the wooden board. Under the bright strip-light, she looked colourless – even her scarlet forearms had become blanched – while in her movements, there was apparently neither thought nor feeling.

'Ahem!' he said again, and this time she glanced up.

'Why didn't you ring the bell?' she said.

'I believe I was rude to you.'

She held the knife in a butcher's grip, and was silent.

'I apologise.'

'That's all right.'

Bonk ... bonk ... She went on slicing bananas.

73

Five

From its Gothic exterior, the Hydro promised to be hideous, and so like other hotels he had known that, long before he reached the top of the steps, he could guess where he'd find the receptionist's desk, and what kind of covers graced the chairs in the lounge.

Debating Societies, Luncheon Clubs, Literary Evenings ... These hotels, which hired their catering staff by the hour and concealed long corridors of shut-down bedrooms behind fresh flower arrangements – oh, he knew them! It was the fate of the retired to haunt such places in pursuit of 'leisure interests', company and so forth – and he had done his share of haunting, but that was long ago. He hadn't been near a place like this for years. Eight or nine of them.

Now ... here he was ...

The device in his right ear buzzed, like a tired bee. An imbecilic thing. He was only wearing it out of an inconvenient fear of letting Moira Gelling down. He knew what could happen at these functions. Since he wasn't a member, he might be obliged to sit at the back, and the accoustics were bound to be terrible. It wouldn't do, if anyone accosted him, to make some stupid remark that showed he hadn't heard a word; and these amateur speakers always mumbled. But it was, truly, a loathsome, fatuous device, this hearing aid, its pink plastic rosy against his yellowed skin.

Reaching the top of the steps, Lawson turned ill-humouredly to a shadow that flittered with some impatience at his elbow.

'That's enough. You can go ... but don't forget, from half past nine, I want you waiting in the foyer ...'

'Right, sir!'

The driver shot away. Not Ruddy-cheeks, this time. In fact

there was cause for complaint. They had sent him a youngster
who had taken the corners at fifty, a dandy who wore his
trousers tight – there he went, turning out his knees as he
skipped down the steps, brushing without apology past two
ladies who were just beginning to climb. A lout. Money, reflected Lawson greyly, secured very little these days.

He postponed going inside. He stood beside the revolving
doors and looked across a razor-slit of lawn at the car-park,
and the car roofs shining in the moonlight. It was most appropriate weather; the sky was like a clear bowl that somehow
held the moon and stars in equilibrium, to each its own share
of brilliance ... He could even see a faint smoke-like trace of
the Milky Way ... and suddenly, it seemed a fitting moment
to prime his Coleridge. Straightening his shoulders, he began
to chant.

> 'The moving moon went up the sky
> And nowhere did abide;
> Softly she was going up
> And a star or two beside.
>
> Her beams bemocked the sultry main,
> Like April hoar-frost spread ...'

To his satisfaction, the words came out in a rich bass. He
paced them with great deliberateness.

As they came up the steps, the two ladies slowed to listen.
Lawson was perfectly aware of them. They had the full faces
and big eyes of pampered cats. Both wore unavoidable per-
fumes. He chanted on:

> 'But where the ship's huge shadow lay
> The charmèd water burnt alway
> A still and awful red ...'

He stopped. There was an exchange of feline glances, then
the ladies came hurrying up the last steps with nods and the
lively smiles of sane folk humouring an eccentric.

'Good evening!' they shrilled.

'Good evening!' Lawson smiled comfortably. They were exactly as he had anticipated, and more in acknowledgment of

75

his own foresight than of the gentle sex, he touched his hat. Heartened, one of them, breathing across a fox-fur collar, ventured, 'Are you coming to Coleridge?'

And what else would he be doing, declaiming *The Ancient Mariner* on the steps of the Hydro?

He strove to suppress his sarcasm. 'Madam, I believe I am.'

The ladies tittered. They kept at a small distance, as if to imply that they knew he might be dangerous.

'We'll show you where it is,' said she of the fox-fur. 'You've not been before, have you?'

'How very kind.'

He allowed them to herd him between the blades of glass and round a semi-circle into a reception area of the usual staggering unoriginality: red, patterned carpet, pseudo-mahogany fittings. The receptionist's alcove was on the left, with the staircase rising behind it, and beyond that were delicate signs in primrose yellow to the Ladies and Gentlemen. On the right, the dining-room doors, firmly closed; and then there was a passage with yet more signs: To the Lounges, To the Bar. Tall palm trees of a synthetic variety stood about in tubs, while straight ahead shone a wall of mirrors, in which Lawson caught a glimpse of his short, beswathed body emerging from the entrance, one stout woman in front of it, and another stout woman behind.

The fox-fur lady said:

'We have our meeting in the smaller lounge – that's straight through the main one – but if you want to leave your coat in the gentlemen's cloakroom ... Or would you rather keep it on?'

'Why?' he demanded. 'Don't they have any heating?'

'Oh yes. In fact, it gets quite warm ...'

'Then why should I keep it on?'

Breaking free, he followed the sign for Gentlemen.

ZZZZZZZZZ ...

A man coming out as he went in held open the door for him, smiling and saying something or other, but it might have been anything. The bee had stirred. ZZZZzzzz ... Lawson tapped fiercely at his hearing aid.

Then he realised he was alone. The door through to the lavatories was shut, and in this outer room there was no at-

76

tendant, no one – only a row of coats on a metal gibbet, and one ornate chair, perhaps borrowed from the ladies' room, backed up rather oddly against it. Immediately he sat down, carefully stretching his legs out to keep the trouser creases sharp. Respite. He sat very still, trying to gather his resources – and discovered he had made a mistake.

A bad one. Stopping at a half-way point like this did nothing to help his nerves. He caught himself wishing he hadn't come. He felt less and less sure he was up to it; and as his confidence ebbed, it left behind a jagged edge of bitterness. Coming out, being sociable ... it took such courage, and no one understood. Oh, they thought they did. They read all the basic signs – his rouge, the toupee, the tremor in his voice – a hundred things that set him apart, and from these they reached the fullest possible realisation that he could never be one of them. Too old. But they couldn't guess the rest: what it was like, to be 'out of it', sensing everything they thought of him, carrying their exclusion round with him in every cell of his body. No ... they couldn't begin to understand what an ordeal it was just to be among them. He supposed they thought it was a treat.

Well, I can't stay here ...

He got up miserably, arranged his coat on a hanger, and left his hat on one of the wall pegs. Then he blew on the cloak-room mirror. A mist formed. Through it he straightened his tie, wiped his mouth with his handkerchief, and rubbed his cheeks beneath the spots of rouge to soften the contrast. Finally, he checked the zip on his trousers, and then he sallied forth.

The smaller lounge ... He hurried. Down the passage, through the larger lounge in which the management had thoughtfully doused the lights, in case anyone had the temerity to sit in there, and from the shadows, someone fell in at his side. A male voice asked: 'Are we going right for the poetry meeting?'

'I think so.'

The question was reassuring. Lawson turned to nod at this fellow newcomer – a grey-haired individual with a strong beard and the look of a schoolmaster – but in the next second, his heart quailed. He found the man was staring with academic intensity at the top of his head. Even in the semi-darkness, was his toupee so conspicuous?

'What's the matter?' he gasped.

'Pardon? ... Ah! This must be it!'

Together they burst into the Hydro's inner sanctum, with its cosy lights and flock wall-paper.

Lawson's first impression was of familiarity; it could have been one of a dozen society functions that he remembered: the more or less reasonable, well-intentioned faces, the little table set by the windows, with a glass of water and hard-backed chairs for the speaker and chairman, the other, comfortable chairs drawn up informally as if for a home-made picture show. Yes, he recognised the set-up. So far as the 'Coleridge' was concerned, he knew what was coming: the unaccustomed speaker, the foolish questions. But some things disconcerted him. He had expected maybe two dozen members, but here were forty or fifty; and what was more, there were almost as many men as women. This, in his painful experience of literary evenings, was most unusual. Even more astonishing was the age span. Mingling with the grey heads were men still in their middle age, and women still in their thirties, also, to Lawson's discomfort, a contingent of teenagers, dressed like plumbers in smudged jeans.

'*A modest gathering.*'

Moira Gelling, he thought, with all the indignation of panic, *is a liar*!

The Society was robust. It was a crowd.

Frozen by the door, he searched for her. At this stage of proceedings, all the poetry took a liquid form. Members milled about in the space behind the chairs, holding whisky or sherry glasses. His eyes blurred with the effort to single her out. After a minute or so he groped for his watch. 8.25 ... Surely she must be here? If he stood at the door for much longer, he would look ridiculous! He fumbled with the watch chain. Would it be best if he just sat down? But when he looked up again, the way was blocked.

A plain, somewhat puffy-faced creature in wide spectacles stood before him, her mouth puckered into the artificial smile that young people take for tact, her hands gripping a sherry glass.

78

'Excuse me ...' She advanced, and he scowled. She had a namby-pambiness he could nose like rotten meat, and in her voice there was that sugar-sweet coercion: *I'm using all the right words, so you see, you can't be rude!*

'Excuse me ... but would you be Mr Lawson?'

She very scrupulously avoided staring at his head. Obliged to notice her, Lawson felt no obligation to be nice. Condescension from the young was insufferable and besides, plain women depressed him.

'Are you *looking* for Mr Lawson?' he asked sourly.

'Well, yes, I am.'

She smiled all the harder. Revolted, he thrust out his neck at her.

'And what would your Mr Lawson be like?' he demanded. 'You see me. I'm old. I'm short. I have a paunch. I wear a dark brown toupee. I paint my cheeks ... Does that fit your description? Your Mr Lawson was described, I suppose?'

The girl laughed, like air escaping from a balloon, and her round cheeks pinkened.

'I'll just tell mother ...'

She vanished, pushing through the crowd.

In Lawson's ear, the bee hummed, and he presumed he hadn't heard correctly. Well, good riddance. He had scared her off, that was the main thing. Anxious to avoid any more encounters, he surveyed the chairs. No one was sitting down yet. If he moved smartly, he might have a seat at the front after all, where he could hear. But it would be a risk. These societies had their petty traditions. He might park himself in a place reserved for some particular member, and that could cause an awkward scene at the last moment. He imagined it, struggling to rise, apologies and protestations, then, just when everyone else was seated, trotting down the room, looking for an empty chair at the back.

I'd do better to sit in the middle from the start ... His hands prickled with sweat. A thousand curses on Moira Gelling! Where was she?

I could just turn, he thought, *and leave.* A beautiful idea, flawless like a poisonous berry, and so tempting that he couldn't bear to stand by the door for another second.

'Please ... excuse me ... thank you ... thank you ...'

He began to nudge his way towards a chair.

'If you'd just ... thank you ...'

'Mr Lawson, wait!'

Moira Gelling, dressed in a yellow frock that was much too young for her, with frills round the neck and sleeves, came pushing, smiling, holding out a sherry glass. She was dazzling. She wore geranium-red lipstick, her hair was freshly rinsed a magnificent silver-purple, and she rubbed through the crowd like an excited débutante to stop at his side, a little breathless, laughing. Behind her towered the plain creature of the tact and spectacles.

'I'm so glad Rowena spotted you! I was trying to keep near the door, but somehow I got carried away!'

Moira Gelling's laugh was astonishingly loud and vulgar.

'Not bodily, I hope.'

He felt stiff, he sounded stiff. He blinked at this immature woman, and wondered if he had it in him to smile. Then he discovered he was already smiling.

'Here!' She pushed the glass at him. 'Have a sherry. I haven't touched it. Ro, would you get me another? ... You do drink sherry?'

'Madam ...' Coleridge ... books ... sanity ... Helplessly he waved her offer aside, and shook his head.

'Oh, there's time!' she cried. 'We're always late starting. Go on, Ro, bring me another. And you take this one!'

'Well ...'

Bewildered, he obeyed. When had he last drunk a sherry? He didn't want it, but he could see that he pleased her by taking it. She laid her hand on his arm. Out of habit, he flinched; but her touch was light, and he found he couldn't resent it.

'I'm so glad you've come!' she said. 'When I didn't hear anything ...'

'Should I have written?' He was pained, thrilled.

The woman smiled. 'Come up front. Ro can catch up with us!'

How nimble and happy she is! he thought. *She's enjoying all this. She enjoys people ...*

Together they worked their way down a line of chairs. Although it was true that she barely touched him, she guided him along, acting like a partner in some strange dance, and Lawson caught a whiff of her perfume. It was the one she had worn that Sunday evening. He wanted to ask its name and felt he mustn't; but still, he had to say something, if only to distract her from his clumsiness – he kept bumping the chairs with his knees –

'Who *is* that Rowena girl?'

'Ro's my daughter.'

'Impossible!' The love and pride in her voice had shocked him. He faltered, and her touch became a fraction more perceptible.

'Oh? Why?'

'She's ... too big ...' he spluttered.

Moira Gelling laughed. He heard her with dismay, and then, something in the sound – something that agreed with him despite the love, and told him he was forgiven – set him laughing with her. She brought her face close to his.

'Ro takes after her father. He's big, too. She's very clever. Especially at Latin and literature.'

She would be.

They reached the side of the room and edged towards the windows.

'Is your husband here?'

'Oh, he never comes. Shall we sit? Is this all right?'

She had led him to the centre of the front row, and he was flattered – a fact that vexed him. *Another sop for the old fool!* He grimaced at his appointed place.

'All right?'

'Yes, yes ...'

Sinking down into it – a soft, welcoming chair, with cushions – he sighed deeply, and gulped the sherry.

Then he held court. She had obviously thought it out in advance. She brought a chosen few to shake hands and murmur civilities – women mostly, quickly slithering into the chair by his side, so that he wouldn't have to rise – and to each of them she allowed a quota of four or five sentences, before whisking them into the crowd again. All of this continued to be flattering. Jealously and expertly, Moira Gelling seemed to be establishing proprietorship, and after his first wave of disgust, which soon got lost in the sherry and the

81

friendly smiles, Lawson felt happy to humour her. In defiance of his gloom in the cloakroom and of any lurking scruples, he told himself that he might as well accept these attentions with good grace: his ego needed some polishing; and only the last of the chosen – a thin, dramatic woman with teeth like white piano keys – came close to upsetting him.

This person, who was introduced as the 'lady chairman', spoke in the strenuous way of females who pretend to find everything complicated.

'So you've bought that lovely old house at Woodbourn? ... What a challenge!' she cried.

'How do you mean? A challenge?'

'Oh, because it's enormous, isn't it? Really hyoo-ooge!' – making a pipe of her lips, she managed to imply that through the word flowed countless evils, if one knew how to look for them.

'It's big. What of it?' Lawson fidgeted. Deciding she was stupid, he was rude. 'I'm rich. I can afford a big house. I don't have to scrub the floors myself, you know!'

'Oh ...' At this reference to his wealth, the woman paled. Her hands fluttered: nothing could have been further from her mind. Her smile stretched all the way back from her teeth.

'No! What I meant was – such a responsibility! A house like that ... All those empty rooms! I know it's silly, but *I'd* be frightened ...'

'Frightened of what?' Now he hated her. She was talking of ghosts and ghouls, or some such drivel, and he detested things of that kind. Anything for effect. Always ready to relish a shiver. Well, he wouldn't go along with it! He waited, charged with venom, but the woman checked herself. She fingered her necklace.

'Frightened of what?' he repeated.

Her skin formed bags beneath her eyes, and, as he leaned towards her, these actually seemed to bulge, while by secretive jerks she moved her head away from his. Suddenly, he could sense her fear. So far as he could tell, she had lapsed into some indecent terror of old men, something best kept private, and loathing her, he rejoiced at it. The devil take her spook-mongering!

Then at last, she laughed.

'Mice!' she cried. 'It sounds ridiculous, I know, but I'm terrified of mice! I was brought up in a vicarage, and these big old houses, unless you live in every room ...'

'That isn't what you were going to say!'

'Pardon?'

'No!' he insisted, his voice rising.

But the woman stood up, turning away with a sharp appeal. 'Excuse me ... Moira, shouldn't we make a start?'

And so to Coleridge.

It was the bearded schoolmaster – a commercial artist, as it turned out – who gave the talk. Dull stuff, cribbed from one or two critics. Lawson didn't have to listen, he knew it all: he had spent the afternoon reading one of those critics. So he concentrated only on the poetry.

> ' 'Tis midnight, but small thought have I of sleep;
> Full seldom may my friend such vigils keep!
> Visit her, gentle sleep, with wings of healing ...'

Coleridge. Generous, tragic – a crippled giant. Even here, in this cosseted gathering, Lawson was able to feel for him. In fact, to his surprise, the poetry seemed to affect him more than ever. A spirit who had known all there was to know about the horrors of darkness, the miseries of insomnia ... Yes, he had a lot in common with Coleridge. No one sitting in the rows behind him could have a more intimate understanding. All these other people: what notion could they have of those hideous hours before dawn? But Coleridge had known, and, for a few rare minutes, Lawson felt himself to be vindicated. It was a privilege, no less, to share his horrors with such a poet.

He prayeth best who loveth best ...

The line was not one quoted by the speaker, but apparently fell of its own accord into Lawson's head, and he knew exactly what it meant. Against the darkness there was one defence and only one: a simple trust in the universe, which minds like his – barbed and analytical – could never hope to possess. And so they were damned, both he and Coleridge. But what glorious damnation!

Emotions swelled. Sorrow surged through him, and a curious

tenderness towards his fellow beings. He felt close to suffocating. 'May all the stars hang bright above her dwelling!' brayed the commercial artist, and Lawson glanced sideways at Moira.

She sat with her skirt rucked up, so that her legs were exposed above her knees. She had propped her chin on her hand, and her face in repose looked old, menaced. He could see the folds on her neck. He wheezed softly. The room was hot. It was possible he would faint – and what if he didn't? The more emotional he became, the more it was torment to sit still. Suppose he touched her? He wanted to. Frightened by these thoughts, he tried to focus on the speaker.

On and on ploughed the talk through interpretations of imagery. The spiritual qualities of moonlight. A passage was read, describing the night when Coleridge carried his infant son into the garden:

'And he beheld the moon, and hushed at once
Suspends his sobs and laughs most silently
While his fair eyes that swam with undropped tears . . .'

A beautiful passage. Father, son, the silence and the yellow moon beams . . . it had never failed to move him. A glimpse of that simple trust . . .

On the arms of his chair, his hands trembled. Something horrible was happening. The soulful words had begun to hiss like serpents, and behind the serpents, the bee had stirred. Ssssss . . . zzzzzz. The moon shattered. The infant squawked. Sickened, Lawson slapped the device in his ear. The din got louder. He began to fiddle at tiny adjustments. With the skill of the desperate, he managed the serpents . . . Then, a thin, penetrating screech, as hard and bright as a needle, shot across the room. He started. He half rose. He clawed at his ear-lobe. He saw the speaker, mouth wide open, staring at him, the old man in the front row. He saw Moira Gelling turn her head, her expression one of shock or derision, and he shrank back into his chair. More adjustments . . . Another screech: it rose to a banshee pitch, then fell away into crackles. To Lawson, even those seemed thunderous, an electric storm inside his skull, but Moira turned to the speaker, who lifted his voice and carried on, addressing the back of the room.

84

Lawson burned. Inside the respectable suit and freshly laundered underclothes, his body twisted, melting like a candle. Coleridge had gone for ever. All that mattered now was dignity, and how to preserve it. He ached to pluck at Moira's wrist and whisper, 'Can you still hear it?' And more than that, he ached to get away, out into the purchased dignity of the Mercedes that waited in the car park. Just thinking of it made him dizzy. To escape ...

He gave himself up to the crackles, and the meaningless drone of the artist.

'Why didn't you turn it off?' asked Moira. 'It gave me the fright of my life.'

After the clapping, a short break had been declared. Coffee, before the questions. And Moira Gelling had rested her hand lightly on his sleeve again. Lawson was speechless. The woman laughed, very gently squeezing his arm, as if they could share the joke.

'I can't see why you put it on!' she said. 'You weren't wearing one that Sunday!'

'I put it on for you!' Distressed and relieved, he blurted the truth out. 'I wanted to be sure I heard. For you.'

'For me?'

She smiled, and for the first time he saw a hint of cruelty, the slight, capricious kind that he had often seen in flirtatious women, especially those who are easily moved. She leaned towards him.

'I can hear it now,' she confided. 'Why don't you turn it off, before the questions?'

'You can still?' Lawson straightened up and looked round wildly. 'Then I think I'd better go ... I see other people are leaving!'

'Oh no, you mustn't. It isn't late. I'll get you a coffee.'

'No, I ...'

'Please!'

He couldn't fight her. She hurried away, and he slumped deeper into his armchair. *She's trying to put it right!* he thought. *She's trying to prove that a spine-chilling screech in the middle of a talk is nothing so terrible. Brazen it out.*

Instinct told him she was right.

While she was gone, with great reverence he touched the thing in his ear, and this time it obeyed him. When he switched it off, it went off. At once the babble of voices receded. He was wrapped in a pleasant blur, and gratefully he closed his eyes to enjoy the privacy of an ostrich. A short-lived indulgence. He was being watched; he felt it – an irritating sensation like an insect on his face – and opening his eyes, he found Rowena Gelling, her stocky figure bending towards him, her spectacles glinting.

'Hello . . .'

She asked a question which he didn't hear, but from her tone it was easy to guess: 'Did you enjoy the talk, Mr Lawson?' He grunted, trying to shrug her off with her awkward smile and the faint smell of deodorant that rose from her shoulders. How old was she? Eighteen? Nineteen? The child of Moira Gelling's last fertile years. He decided to look past her at the wallpaper.

Stoically, Rowena offered another topic.

'Mother's been telling me about your library, Mr Lawson. It does sound marvellous . . .'

And here mother was, handing him a coffee.

Lawson saw the cup and heard the word 'library' at the same moment. *His* library. *His* books and treasures – gossip for the Hydro! Before he quite knew what he was doing, he had snatched the cup and hissed furiously at the mother's face: 'How dare you? I said I don't want every Tom, Dick and Harry . . . every over-grown schoolgirl . . .'

Moira Gelling stood stricken. A mingling of fear and guilt narrowed her cheeks and softened her eyes. She resembled a trapped, frightened animal, and seeing it, a delightful quiver ran through Lawson's body. She had betrayed him, but she cared. Her lips moved. He turned back swiftly to the daughter, who looked pasty and offended.

'Get your mother to bring you down,' he growled. 'If you want to see it. If that's what you want.'

Then they were rescued. The lady chairman called for order, and questions.

Six

At eight o'clock the following morning, he was still awake.

As soon as he had recovered from the disasters of the poetry meeting, he had gone into the sitting-room, raised the lid of an Indian chest that stood in there, and taken out a cardboard box full of photographs. He had carried it back to the library, and spread the faces on the desk, like patience cards.

Ghostly people, nearly all of them dead. And even if they were alive, they wouldn't have known him now, while the man they might have recognised as Arnold Lawson, he himself had trouble believing in: middle-aged, belligerent, always dressed in smart suits, a womaniser who drank whisky – but was never lavish. Tight with the brass. Hard in business. He knew he had been this man, but not exactly from his memories. In his present guise as old, deaf and asthmatic, he knew it as one knows a legend, and parts of it – especially the sexual part – felt suspect. He tried not to think about it much. But when he did start thinking, he often blundered into areas where the legend grew complicated, threatening to vanish. The truth was, none of these women staring out of the photographs had liked him. Least of all his wife.

Elizabeth Violet ... A studio portrait of her, sweet with Edwardian innocence, smiled anonymously up at him. She might have been anyone. Her round face showed no particular traits of character. She might have been a distant cousin – but she had been his wife: a whining, sponging, bird-witted companion for fifteen years. He could remember that. He had blanked out specific incidents, but the flavour remained: a blend of revulsion and bitterness on his mental palate. Now, as late as this, what did it matter? She had married twice since then. Twice, that he knew of. Was she dead? A petted creature like her might last for ever. Lawson turned the photograph over, and read the address of the studio stamped on the back. He didn't care.

As for the others – portraits mounted on thick card, informal snap-shots curled at the edges, face after face – they had all, he supposed, been after his money, and he supposed he had known it at the time.

Often, when he and a woman were pictured together, the woman rose at his side like a sick giraffe, and her eyes, staring madly into the camera, seemed to cry, 'Don't think I belong to this clown! This little buffoon here!'

Had he been to bed with all of them? It was a muddle. He forgot to look at the photographs, and forced his mind to turn back through a long vacuum. Only one recollection came to him promptly and sharply. A hotel in Bournemouth. A woman, laying aside her pill-box hat, sitting cross-legged on the bed and unfastening her blouse.

'Darling, just one very small thing. But it makes no difference really. I hope you don't mind.'

'What's that?'

'I'm menstruating.'

He remembered what the man had done, how he had grabbed the first thing to hand – a metal ashtray – and thrown it at her, shouting, 'You filthy bitch!'

It had caught her above an eyelid. They had gone on for more than a year after that, and Lawson, if he ever thought of her, could still see the scar – but that was all. Her name was lost to him.

Faces ... He cleared the desk, and laid out more. Business colleagues, rivals, even the odd friend. 'You should watch out for Lawson, or he'll bleed you dry!' Resenting his success. To daunt him, they had limbered up their public schoolboy accents. Men who had faced the cameras with such jolly smiles and an arm around his shoulder, as much as to say, 'You see how small he really is!'

And now he was nothing.

The desk-lamp shone on his photographs and made no secret of how faded they were, faded and brittle like discarded plastering. Who was it who had said, 'Live too long and you'll be dead in your own lifetime'?

He must look it up. Keep alert.

Nervously, he selected a picture of several people in dinner jackets and fingered it, then another, until, by degrees, what he remembered became remembering. Separate occasions, ancient wrangles and ironies came creeping back; there was a taste of whisky on his tongue. Old angers flared in him, and went out. He smiled at old triumphs. His sense of the alien in his younger self began to fall away, and Moira Gelling ... uninvited, she returned to his thoughts. This time, he could recognise her. Here was the woman he had always wanted, who had never wanted him. Or if she had, he had never found her.

But now, surely – Lawson rubbed his face in agitation – there did exist a relationship? True, he had only met her twice, but what did that have to do with it? The difference between an acquaintance and a relationship was nothing to do with time: good God, he ought to know; he'd had thousands of acquaintances of every type, people clambering about in his life every day for years, and time had never made them closer. What was needed was sensitivity, and Moira Gelling, he thought, had that. She was treacherous – all women were treacherous – but she was ... she was ...

He groped for words. Genuine? Sympathetic? Yes, yes, and other things. Spontaneous ... Blinking across the room, he ransacked his vocabulary, and as he did so, the library seemed to draw in round him, warming him with its rich, good presence, so that after a minute, his head was flooded with happiness. He gaped at the crowded bookshelves and indulged in a wave of gratitude that swept out towards them, then back towards himself.

He had so many resources. Such self-respect. And life was for living.

So, at eight o'clock in the morning, he was still awake: the penalty for excitement. He had gone upstairs at six as usual, lain flat on his back in the sheets, as if blown over by a miracle, and watched the dawn. (There was always a gap in his bedroom curtains.) He had imagined he heard a twittering of birds somewhere in the eaves. He had watched the sky turn blue, the brilliant blue of deceptive October, and when at last he had closed his eyes, a bright shape made by the gap in the curtains had throbbed behind his eyelids. Then he had amused himself by turning to the wall and opening his eyes again, so that this shape stood out in front of him, a momentary phantom. Games of the old fool.

He tossed. He looked at the clock on his bedside table. Just gone eight. And still awake.

I've got to make an effort! he thought.

Around nine, he did sleep. He dreamed of a mountainous place in the moonlight where he was digging a hole with his hands: he had something to bury, he worked in a panic, and the earth was full of heavy stones. He woke up with a jolt. His pulse raced. Ten to eleven. Pulling on his dressing gown, he shuffled to the chair by the window, and sat there, staring back at the crumpled bed. Another failure. There were so many. It was to safeguard against sleep losing its place in his life altogether that he had a rule: he never gave in before noon. So he dozed grimly in the chair for an hour.

'Sherry?'

She brought out the word coldly, quickly, and he thought of a stone cracking open. That was it. He was Moses. He had struck the rock in the wilderness.

'Dry Sack and Bristol Cream,' he explained mildly, enjoying himself. 'And a bottle of Gordon's Gin...and you'd better get some tonics.'

He tapped the dome of his boiled egg. She stood in front of him and watched. Sitting with his neck cricked in the bedroom chair had given him a headache, but he didn't mind. He was happy.

The housekeeper wasn't.

'I don't know what's come over you,' she probed fiercely. 'Why do you want to start drinking again? I thought you were all for discipline and healthy diets . . .'

He smiled, easing off the dome like a lid and slipping the spoon into the soft yolk.

'Doesn't it occur to you I might want to entertain?'

'*You?* Excuse me if I'm wrong, but don't you hate visitors? It's been ten years . . .'

'So?' He took a bite of toast and munched it. He felt fully

in charge of the situation. 'I'm not a machine,' he said gently.

She peered down the length of her nose. She wiped her hands on her overall, not that they were wet. 'It's that woman, isn't it? The one who came here?'

'It is.' Oh, the glory of it! Lawson beamed up at her. 'I don't see that it's any business of yours, but – yes, I expect that lady to call from time to time ...'

'You're mad. You know what she wants, of course ...'

'I do? What, pray?'

'Well, if you don't, you should. She's after your money.'

'And you aren't, I suppose?'

It came out like an observation on the weather – he couldn't stop it – and the housekeeper gasped. He could see the fury curdling in her face, so that from plain stone her features turned to marble, full of strange mottlings, but he refused to let that worry him.

'This is a very tasty egg!' he told her. 'And a bottle of whisky. Dimple Haig. Put in the order today.'

'I certainly will not!'

'What?'

'I won't do it.'

Lawson's happiness froze like a nervous rabbit. Her hands cradled each other, knuckles prominent. She was testing him ... hoping for hysterics. Carefully, he laid his spoon beside the egg-cup; he studied the plate, and only when he was sure that he wouldn't be betrayed by a fit of wheezing, did he look up again.

'It isn't good for you!' She tilted her chin. 'I'd be being irresponsible.'

'Oh, you'll do it!' he said. 'You'll do it because I pay you to do it!' – and his voice was strong, there was not a tremor in it. Lawson heard himself with amazement. They were both amazed. The housekeeper's head came down. Her eyes flickered. She apparently meant to say something, but changed her mind. Abruptly she turned and flounced away.

'Well, don't blame me if you have a stroke!'

'I wouldn't dream of it!'

The rest of his egg had no taste at all, but he ate it anyway, trying to ignore the fact that his hands were shaking; and as he ate, now and then he looked up in resolute enjoyment of the sunlight that poured in through the French windows. A beautiful afternoon. Autumnal, suspect, but nevertheless beautiful. He could see that the sky above the spinney was an intoxicating, blemish-free azure ... He might take a stroll. Get out of her way for a while. Safer, to explore his feelings in the open ... At the very thought – this coy reminder to himself of certain feelings – his happiness took a small bound.

Then it froze again. Someone was out there! Lawson pushed back his tray, and squinted. A thin figure was bending over a flower-bed at the far end of the lawn. One of those smart-alec boys? Damned cheek. Stealing plants, by the look of it! And today, of all days, when to potter round the garden was the very thing –

Snug in the wall beside him was an aspirin-sized disc, and reaching from his chair, he jabbed at it. Damned boys! Well, he'd send the bitch out! At least there was some consolation in that – knowing how she hated the job. If the boys ignored her, she came back in a rage – he could tell from her face as she crossed the lawn – and if they ran at the sight of her, as they did sometimes, she seemed to resent that even more. Yes, he'd send the bitch out. He pressed hard, until his finger ached. There was no sound in the library, but it eased his heart to know that the bell was jangling through the kitchen and her sitting-room and her bedroom, all her parts of the house. Good. The louder it rang, the better. He wanted her to come running.

As for the boy – brazen little vandal – it was true! He was actually tugging up plants by their roots! Lawson gave a shout – a meaningless sound, a battle cry. Then he relaxed his pressure on the disc, so that he could start again, pushing harder ... But in the next moment, the bell was forgotten. The figure in the garden straightened up: a silver-haired man in his shirt sleeves.

A silver-haired man ... Lawson hurried to the windows. And now he could see a spade, fixed in the earth beside this stranger. Pettishly he rubbed the glass and gaped out. Then he wished he hadn't. The man outside was looking straight at the house. Did he sense he was being watched? Did he think that someone had waved? He gave no clues. He stood there, motionless, staring; and with an unpleasant twinge of guilt, as though he was the one intruding, Lawson stared back.

He wasn't aware of the housekeeper's entry.

'Can't I even have my lunch?'

She came looming up behind him, so that he started. He turned on her bitterly.

'That man out there . . .'

'Who?'

She peered over him through the glass, and feeling her breath on his cheek, he shrank into his cardigan. Outside, the man turned back to his spade.

'Oh, him!' she said. A peculiar indifference entered her voice. 'He's called Briggs. You said we needed someone, so I put a card in one of those shop windows on the estate. Six hours a week. Ten shillings an hour. That's what you paid at the other place.'

'But . . . you should have told me!'

'I meant to.' She was smug. 'All that talk about alcohol put it out of my head. He called this morning . . . we had quite a chat. He brought excellent references.'

Preposterous. He had always vetted his own staff. She knew it. This was deliberate. It was invasion. Lawson couldn't trust himself to speak. She watched him coolly. 'Even *I* can read references!' she said. 'He's worked for some very good people. There's a letter from a bank manager and . . .'

'That's not the point! You should have let me see him first!'

Faintly, the housekeeper smiled.

'All you said was, we needed someone. You said nothing about wanting to see them.'

'But you know I always see them.' He waved his hands. 'I'm the one who's got to pay! I'm the one who knows what I need . . .'

Her smile broadened. Whether or not she was entertained, she apparently meant him to think she was.

'Now don't you go upsetting yourself,' she said quietly. 'I'll put these on your desk, shall I' – and before he could answer, she strode away to slap down the gardener's references, which had been ready and waiting in her pocket.

'Good afternoon.'

Lawson approached his new employee with caution, and a

smile remarkable for its insincerity. The fact was, gardeners unnerved him. He had explained this to himself by arguing that he was an intellectual and any manual worker was beyond his understanding, but it was a sham explanation. He could pass the time of day with road-diggers, builders and dustmen, and feel perfectly at ease; he saw them as sensible types in useful occupations, whereas gardeners he found irritating, threatening ... They reminded him of priests. Like priests, they had their calendar of mysteries – seed-times, cycles and seasons – only, unlike priests, they never forced their doctrines down his throat, and maybe it was that, their self-sufficiency, which he found sinister.

'Afternoon.'

The silver-haired man lifted his foot from the spade, turning to his visitor with narrowed eyes. He smelt of earth and sweat. There was no servility in his manner; he wasn't bothered by meeting the boss, and after he had scrutinised Lawson's face for a couple of seconds, he nodded at the drive.

'Plenty of work down there, I'd say. All that ivy. It'll have to come off.'

'Oh?' said Lawson, glaring. 'Are you saying you can't manage? Six hours a week seems ample time to me. It's not a particularly big garden.'

Longer hours, more pay ... If the fellow tried it on, he was ready for a fight. But the issue sank into the earth. Briggs, or Biggs, or whatever his name was, seemed not to see the implications. He drew an arm across his mouth, then applied himself to his spade. To Lawson's surprise, he drove it into the curve of the lawn.

'Oh, I can manage all right.'

A slice of grass fell away, leaving a clean new edge to the flower-bed, and when he saw that, Lawson was pleased. Order, the definition of boundaries, the reduction of chaos – with things like that, he could sympathise. If only gardeners kept to them! He watched the spade take a second slice, then a third, and he dawdled by the man's shoulder, advancing down the flower-bed with him. Beneath his shoes the grass felt spongy, and now that he really looked at it, he discovered that it wasn't the bland, inevitable green he associated with grass. It was a startling emerald.

The gardener voiced a few thoughts.

'Space for annuals here ... Give a splash of colour ... About plants and that, do I come to you or the missus?'

The skin on Lawson's neck crawled.

'Are you referring to my *housekeeper*?'

'Aye, that would be it.' Briggs, or Biggs, went on digging. 'Do I go to her?'

'No. Never!' *Her* choice, taking root and flourishing all over the place! 'You come to me! Choose the stuff yourself ... whatever you want ... I'll give you cash in advance ... Always to *me*. Remember that!'

The gardener, if he made any reply, only grunted. Slice after slice, the sods flopped forwards into the flower-bed. Lawson fell silent. Soon, the flower-bed ended and he was standing on the gravel. There was a final thrust of the spade; then both men looked back along the way they had come. The curve of the lawn was sharp and pure. Mathematics and pegged-out guide-lines couldn't have bettered it – an extraordinary feat, thought Lawson, and there it was, that touch of the sinister: a skill like that, it wasn't normal.

'Right,' said the gardener. 'Now it's back to the start and tidy up. You haven't got a wheelbarrow, have you?'

'No ... but you can have one. I'll give you the money for it.'

The man only nodded. Lawson felt he was in the way and retreated a pace. Then he stopped again. Damn it all, he was the boss. Why should he go before he wanted to?

How old was this character? Seventy? Sixty-eight? He longed to ask, and knew he wouldn't. A bad idea, to appear too interested. He noted how crumpled the gardener's face was, and in his voice, there was a sense of years, the passage of years ... On the other hand, Lawson knew from experience when someone was bellowing at him, making one of those special efforts because he was deaf, and Briggs – or Biggs – was innocent of that, yet everything he said could be heard. His voice was naturally strong. Then, another thing, the man was fit. Despite the digging, his chest moved in and out with an enviable regularity.

Young for his age. And anyway, he's not so old.

He would have given a lot to be seventy again.

'Well ...' said the gardener, shifting his hold on the spade. He eyed his boss, and seconds passed. Then he simply turned his back, and headed up the lawn.

Typical of gardeners.

Lawson didn't stop him. How could he?

I should call him back, he thought. *I should make it clear that I'm the one to say when we've finished talking* ... But he knew it was impossible, a pettiness: the blue sky and immaculate curve of the lawn – they made it one. He began to stroll away. It was all most unsatisfactory. He'd had it in mind to give instructions about the boys. He wanted this fellow to scare them off whenever he saw them ...

Still, the day and the man – both felt wrong for that, in any case.

Seven

By the end of the month, there were no more golden days. Bitter mists set in. Dawn and twilight, they prowled round the garden, and the hours in between were overcast, ice-cold. The colour died out of things. The housekeeper brought down his winter vests and aired them in the kitchen, their bleak shapes stretched on racks from the ceiling. Behind the pantry door stood the whisky, sherry and gin bottles, and half a dozen tonics. As the days passed, her face wore darker and darker lines, like heavy-service granite.

Lawson made no comment. After their scene about the alcohol, he didn't dare. His behaviour was exemplary, until the day of the visit – a day on which the housekeeper was looking worse than ever. Then he hardened against her, and when she brought the bottles into the library, he said, 'Tonight, I want you out of the way ... You could go to the cinema.'

'Oh, thanks very much. And what if I don't fancy struggling out in this weather?'

'I'll pay for a taxi.'

'No you won't,' she said. 'You're not *bribing* me to hide myself! I'll sit in my room and watch television ... Oh, don't you worry. I won't come running out to tell her things about you!'

'I don't know what you mean. She wouldn't listen, anyway. It's just that I want the place to myself ... Haven't we got a tray to put these bottles on? That silver one ... where is it?'

'I was going to polish it.'

'Well, hurry up. And bring some sherry glasses ...'

He had written to Moira, confirming his invitation, suggesting a date, and a note had come back: 'Rowena and I will be

97

delighted ...' Hang Rowena! But perhaps she wouldn't have come alone? There were proprieties – small-town proprieties ... An evening visit differed from one at twilight. Drinks after eight had connotations.

Oh, rubbish. He was thinking in terms of fifty years ago. But still, he believed it. Without the daughter, she wouldn't have agreed to come, not in the evening.

Fastidiously he checked details. The soap in the downstairs toilet: it was new, just out of its wrapping, so he held it under a running tap for a while. Bone-dry soap implied things – either a host who tried too hard, or a dirty host who never washed his hands. Next, the corks in the sherry bottles. He pulled them out and pushed them half-way in again. Embarrassing, to have to struggle with corks in front of people. And after that: the golden box of Swiss chocolates. It stood unwrapped beside the whisky glasses; he opened it, and allowed himself just one delicious soft centre – a coffee cream – so that the rest of the box looked more inviting – luxuries to be eaten, nothing for show. As for the house, it stank: the sweet, penetrating smell of polish was everywhere, but he had to reconcile himself to that. It was the price he had to pay, apparently, and he felt ready to put up with anything so long as Moira Gelling didn't find he lived in dust and cobwebs. That was one of his greatest fears, and oddly enough, the thought of her previous visit did nothing to reassure him. Somehow he discounted that. His only reassurance lay in the gleaming shelves of the library and the shining glass of the cabinets in the sitting-room. He looked at those, and forced himself to forget about the smell. Fresh flowers in the hall ... and all the carpets had been hoovered – the red staircarpet looked particularly magnificent. The whole house was a going concern. It seemed packed to the roof with life, vibrant and waiting, longing for its visitors; and despite the fact that Moira Gelling wasn't due until eight, from six o'clock all the ground-floor lights blazed for her.

Dressing for the occasion took a long time. He agonised. What he wanted was to look casual but not cosy, none of the carpet-slipper image ... In the end, he matched up a blue, corduroy smoking jacket with a pair of brown and yellow check trousers that he hadn't worn for years. Miraculously, they still fitted. Then, instead of a tie, he chose a mustard-coloured scarf in pure silk, tucking it into his shirt collar – a rather expensive, pale blue shirt. The general effect came out all right. At least, he thought so. Finally, he decided that he wouldn't use the rouge – he looked flushed enough already – but he put on his newest toupee, which was a brighter, jollier specimen than either of the two he kept for everyday wear.

Then he went downstairs to eat lunch – a cheese pudding that stuck in his throat. What if they got the time wrong, and arrived early? He imagined them walking in, the sight of the bowl on his desk, with the little spoon. Catastrophe. He sent the food away, barely touched.

Seven thirty ... Half an hour to go. He took out a copy of *Mary Barton* and sat with the book on his lap, making no attempt to read it. Now and then he ran his hand across its leather cover, but at eight o'clock he gave up doing even that.

Ten past eight ... His ears strained. They felt as though they were stretching into saucers ... Then at last they heard a swish of wheels on the gravel, a thudding of car doors. Lawson stayed where he was. Seconds later, the porch bell rang, and only then did he get to his feet.

Moira Gelling, like a schoolgirl in a pleated skirt and jumper. The daughter, bovine in a dress of plain grey that accentuated her shoulders.

After the first breathless civilities, the business of hanging up coats and much fussing about the amount of gin in the tonic and which sherry would do for the girl, he arranged things to his satisfaction. As soon as everyone was seated, he waved magnanimously at the bookshelves. 'There you are!' he cried. 'You wanted to see them. Help yourself!' and Rowena responded eagerly, rising from her chair to advance across the room, hands at the ready. Lawson watched with conflicting emotions. It made him shiver to think of this mooncalf touching his things. He was shocked by the greedy delight on her face as she stretched up for a book. But it served his purpose. It left Moira to himself, and as if she knew that this was what he thought, when he turned back to her, the mother raised her glass playfully, crossing her legs. This set him smiling like a child.

She had returned his *Vanity Fair*. What was more, she had read it. She thought Becky Sharp was a wonderful woman. Thackeray was wonderful. What a scoffer he was! She could go along with that, being something of the kind herself ... People were laughable, really ... But he had left a lot out, too ...

Muddled perceptions, she offered them to Lawson with a sort of flirtatious honesty, neither pretending to have given more thought to the book than she had, nor that the thoughts she did have were inevitably stupid. Once or twice, she asked questions – 'Oh dear, don't you agree?' 'You think I'm wrong, don't you?' – frankly appealing to his wider knowledge. And all of it felt like flirtation.

Lawson grew mellow. Settled in a chair with a goblet of whisky, he delivered opinions on Thackeray – safe opinions, well backed by research and the pile of notes in his desk; and he had the joy of seeing a mute respect overtake the fun in Moira Gelling's face, while from the corner of his eye, he saw the daughter look up from the book she held, and listen.

The hypocrisies of nineteenth-century society, fortune hunters, pernicious aspects of the class system, disastrous marriages of convenience; he wound his way down a long list of topics, speaking with wit, and, he felt sure, genuine touches of brilliance – but he never lost his thread, which was no mean achievement. Always he returned to Thackeray. He was also careful not to bore her. Whenever it seemed even remotely appropriate, he paused, in case she wanted to comment. This was not a courtesy he often bothered with, but it brought its reward, one he hadn't known how much he wanted: she suddenly turned the conversation right away from literature, to himself.

'You seem to be saying marriage hasn't changed much ... And you, Mr Lawson, didn't you ever marry?'

'Arnold!' he protested. 'You must call me Arnold! Yes, Once. When I was a young fool ...'

'For a moment, I thought that woman I saw here last time ...'

'Good God, no. Really, my dear Mrs Gelling ...'

'Moira.'

'Well then, my dear Moira ... don't you credit me with any *taste*?' They both laughed; the pasty face of the daughter glowed in the distance. 'Besides,' he cried, 'having been through it once, never again, I said, and I mean to stick to it!'

'But why?' said Moira, smiling. 'There must have been plenty of women, plenty of opportunities.'

'Shackles on the mind! I don't care much about the *body* ...' he spat the word out, 'but to have your thoughts tied to some other, piffling little brain ...'

'Oh, now come. Not every marriage is like that.'

'No?' He felt a flash of annoyance. 'Obviously, you would say that! You belong to societies that your husband takes no interest in. You go visiting people, people who don't even know you ... You think you're married and free as well. But it's not that simple!'

'How do you mean?'

'Well ...' he flourished his hands. 'Are you *happy*?'

At this question, the gauche presence of Rowena Gelling seemed to billow across the room – and he saw the mother flinch, which pleased him, although he couldn't have said why exactly. He answered the question for her. 'Of course you're not happy! To be free, if you're married, means living with a stranger, keeping your mind to yourself. Anything more than that, and you're a slave. Slaves aren't happy. But being married to a stranger means deceptions, doesn't it? After all, you've got to *behave* as if you know each other. You've got to go about together as if you want the same things from life. It's all wrong. Deceptions can't make people happy either. I'd far rather settle for less. With a hired *non-person* in the house, there's no pretending, and believe me, it isn't any lonelier!'

He took a sip of Scotch. On a theme like this, he knew he could sound fanatical. Already, there was a tremor in his words. His audience waited. He counted to five before going on more slowly. 'Now that creature I employ, the one you saw. She cleans, cooks and shops for me. Nothing else. And do you know how long I've had her? Twenty years! And in all that time, we've never had a single conversation. Not a real one. She hasn't the brain, of course. But the main thing is, I've always kept her at a distance. Quite good-looking, too, when she came. Thought she'd snaffle me up.' He laughed, the crowing laugh of an old man. He heard it, found it deplorable, and hurried on. 'For all I know, she still goes to bed dreaming of lace and wedding bells. Status and money ... that's all a marriage means to her. She has no idea of *minds*.'

Moira Gelling listened, on her face a sharp, inquisitive expression.

'Even if you didn't want to marry again,' she said, 'what about love?'

'Oho. What about it?'

His lack of charity hadn't shocked her. She had spared not a thought for the housekeeper. Lawson's heart sang. What she wanted was titillation, comparing romantic sentiments, and, flattered, he raised his glass; his cheeks grew hot; he pontificated. *I'm showing off*, he thought, but by then his voice was soaring over the carpet, and there was nothing he could do about it. 'Love! ... "Let me not to the marriage of true minds ..." I'll tell you what I think. Love exists only in the free, and so it's self-defeating, because to be free – as I've said – a mind has to keep its barriers up. It's no use giving in to someone else. When the freedom goes, the love goes. And do you know the worst of it? We're all of us half mad. Join our minds together, and then we're totally mad. The sanity in both of us is cancelled out.'

She was watching closely.

'You seem sane enough to me.'

'That', he leered, 'is because I've never lost my freedom! And you're free too. That's how you're sane enough to know that I am. You say you're married, but I can tell that your mind isn't ... You may not be happy, but you haven't been trapped ... You and I, we're the same sort. We can enjoy the paradox. Because we've kept the barriers up, there's still a bit of love in us ...'

At his words, Moira pinkened; and Rowena Gelling's face rose swiftly out of its book like a pale grub, so that he felt compelled to turn to her and demonstrate that the conversation was adult, all perfectly well in hand.

'What have you got there?'

Unintentionally he snapped the question. The very sight of the girl was a kill-joy. She was sitting on one of the library's modest ladders, solidly on the top of it, and she held the book in both hands, like a Bible.

'Livy,' she said.

'Oh . . .'

The girl's voice conveyed a challenge. She meant him to understand that she knew her Livy inside out. She had probably studied him for A Level.

'She has a passion for Latin,' said Moira softly.

From behind her spectacles, the daughter regarded Lawson with the utmost politeness, yet he knew she loathed him. Her shoulders had risen. She looked even broader and whiter than when she had arrived, and her mouth had become a small, disgusted O.

A dirty old man, he concluded, prickling. *That's what she sees. She understands nothing.*

'Livy . . . Titus Livius,' he moved his tongue across his lips. 'Born . . . some time around the time of Christ . . . Did you know he was born in Padua?'

'Yes. They called it Patavium.' The girl clapped shut the book and put it back on the shelf with a little push on its spine, just as if she owned it.

Lawson's voice rose.

'You know about Roman history, do you? Read it all? Cicero? Tacitus?'

'No. Not all of it.' Rowena Gelling was primly contemptuous. Her tone implied that it was absurd to ask the question of someone her age, but give her time . . . 'Of what I've read, I like Livy best.'

'Pah. A fabricator.' Lawson banged down his whisky glass on the arm of his chair. 'A downright liar. All his politicians talk like heroes, and all his heroes talk like politicians . . . Know all the poets too, do you? Horace? Ovid? Catullus?'

Moira shifted her legs uneasily. He glanced at her. She was grey with alarm, and her eyes had darkened. Quickly he looked away again. On the ladder, Rowena sat hunched and stubborn.

'I know some Catullus . . . and Virgil.'

'Oh, you do, do you?'

The young, the unforgivable young. Jealous of their mothers, jealous of their elders, demanding time and respect and wisdom, all the good in life and all of it together, and at once.

He pushed himself forward in his chair, and words came

tumbling out of his mouth like old coins.

> ' "Nobis ... nobis cum semel occidit brevis lux
> Nox est perpetua una dormienda ..." '

'You know that, do you? You can translate that?'

The girl returned his stare.

'I *think* I can ...' – but her face had gone marvellously blank. He waited. The walls of books, the light from the standard lamps, the soothing comfort of his armchairs, he felt he had ranged them all against her. This library was his, this fragment of the civilised world which she so obviously coveted, and where she trespassed. A silence stretched between them, and it was not the girl who finally broke it, but Moira.

'Well!' she laughed. 'I lost *my* Latin years ago! I'm very impressed with both of you.'

'Never mind. Never mind.' He got up, waved his hands. The unpleasantness was over. Dismayed by the pain in Moira's laughter, he rushed to make amends.

'Much more important ...' he panted, hurrying to the drinks tray and grabbing the box of chocolates, 'have one of these! You mustn't refuse. Believe it or not, I bought them specially for you.'

'Really?'

'Yes, it's true.'

Humbly Lawson worked at smiles. He rebuked himself. He had allowed himself to forget that this woman loved her monstrous offspring. Now, here Moira was, all pinched with hurt and tension.

'Please ...' He bowed before her. Lifting the shield of paper from the chocolates, he desperately scrunched it in his fist. 'Please ...'

'How terribly wicked!'

So this, at least, he had got right: she liked expensive things. The reproach began to slip from her eyes. Moira Gelling wriggled with pleasure. Her fingers fluttered across his hand, then came down with precision, plucking out a dark smooth oval: rum and raisin.

'You must have one too,' she said. 'I'm not indulging on my own.'

'I will. I will.'

Overwhelmed by her forgiveness, he snatched a chocolate, any chocolate, and thrust it into his mouth. A huge nut whirl. When it cracked, he thought his dentures must have broken. The impact travelled painfully round his skull – but what did it matter? Moira Gelling was laughing again, and this time, in the sound all he heard was enjoyment.

'Rowena?' He turned with the box, a peace offering, and the girl came lumbering slowly down the steps. She moved towards him with her forehead crinkled, as if she had loftier things to think about than this patching up of harmony.

'I think I've got it now . . .' she said.

'I beg your pardon?' Eagerly, he proffered the box. In Rowena's spectacles, he could see two miniature reflections of himself.

'That was Catullus, wasn't it? "For us, once the brief day is done . . ." '

'Have a chocolate!'

Her hand reached out, while her voice hammered on.

' ". . . there is an everlasting night to sleep through." That's right, isn't it?' and she bit into the soft centre, chewing with unnecessary thoroughness.

He showed them his treasures. In this second half of the evening, he made a considerable effort to be nice to the girl. After all, was she to blame for those hideous lines from Catullus? *He* had chosen them. And the horror on her mother's face had been ample compensation for Rowena's Latin acumen. Another link had been forged, one more in the alliance: Moira Gelling had sided with him against the narrow pride of youth. Oh, she hadn't said anything, but she had looked at the girl in such a way that he had loved her for it. And now, for her sake, he forgave the daughter. Opening all the cabinets in the sitting-room, he brought out item after exquisite item for Rowena. He invited her to hold an amazing Chinese puzzle – intricate spheres of ivory, locked one inside the other – not only that; he allowed her to hold several of his jade figures, which were far more precious than the ivories. He talked at length about Chinese dynasties, jade and Tao, and on all these subjects the girl displayed a gratifying ignorance. She hadn't even known that jade could be white, like cloud or smoke, and admitted as much, which made her seem just a trifle less stupid.

'But ...' She peered at him through her spectacles. 'How did you collect all this, Mr Lawson? Have you done a lot of travelling?'

'No. I haven't.' He preened himself. Having exposed her scholarship and ignorance in rapid succession, Rowena had become diffident. 'All my journeys have been in my head,' he boasted. 'I've worked hard. There was never the time for gallivanting. I'm entirely *self-made*, you know,' and he laid a good deal of stress on the word that mattered, because young people never realised. The education they took for granted: in his day, it was like loaves of bread in a starving city – craved as much, and as difficult to come by.

'Yes!' He beamed at her. 'I started from scratch ... My father worked in a bottle factory. He brought home 12/6 a week.' The statements came out confident of their dignity, honourable ambassadors among the carvings and the vases. Rowena's head ducked in homage. On the palm of her hand she held a diminutive jade horse, and the foreign loveliness of this object was apparently making her more and more uncomfortable with her own lumpish body. He could almost feel her trying to shrink: head down and stomach in.

'A dainty little thing, isn't it?'

She nodded.

'Life isn't worth living without some beauty in it. That's what I say.'

Again she nodded.

'Manchester. London. Antique shops and auctions. Private dealing sometimes. All these things, I paid for every one of them with sweat and graft. You know what graft is, do you?'

'Yes,' she murmured.

'Oh, is that right? Do you now?' said Lawson quickly, and then he checked himself. Not the same quarrel over again. Silently, he lifted the figure off her hand, set it in its place and locked the cabinet door. But it was all too tempting to needle her.

'I suppose you think it's odd, an untravelled man like me, born in the slums of Manchester, collecting Chinese carvings?'

'Oh no, not at all ... I don't think where you're born ...'

'Let me tell you,' he interrupted, and now he was speaking to the ox-like dullness in her, 'if there's anything you want in life, it's no use saying, "That's not for the likes of me." You've got to make up your mind to it. "Why not me as well as another?" That's the way you've got to talk. And then you go out after it. If you don't do that, you end up with nothing . . .'

He shouted this sermon, because of the music.

Moira had preferred the piano. She had wandered off as soon as he began to explain the Chinese puzzle, which had surprised and disappointed him at first, although within a few seconds he had seen a virtue in it. If she couldn't be bothered with the carvings, well, at least she was honest. He could remember women cooing over his ivories who wouldn't have known or cared if he had shown them pieces of plastic, and other women, breathing over every separate item, as if they were trying to inhale the collection's worth in hard cash. Moira's reaction was infinitely superior.

He suspected, too, that she had wanted to give him the fullest possible chance to make peace with Rowena.

For some minutes, she had sat at the piano leafing through a pile of music, and then, raising the lid, she had begun to play, softly to start with, but after a while not so softly, until in the end she was thumping the tunes out. 'Old Man River.' 'Tiptoe through the Tulips.' She played extremely badly, banging down the keys as if she thought she could bully emotions out of them; and when something more seemed called for, she varied the rhythm, adding impetuous little spurts that had no right to be there. Such a wild, crashing din to be made by such a small woman. Lawson was reminded of her handwriting; and by the time she had the music thundering out, the badness of her playing didn't seem to matter. In fact, while he had bawled his pep-talk at Rowena, he had actually been losing interest in the carvings – not that he could have gone on shouting about them, in any case. And then, to cap it all, as he fell silent, Moira broke into song. 'I'll Take You Home Again, Kathleen . . .' A loud, cracked voice.

Rowena crimsoned.

But Lawson felt no awkwardness. Rather, he sensed his own voice lifting to the melody, and in the next second, out through his lips came an extraordinary baaaing noise, which he knew must be deadlier and more comic than any sound that Moira could make. So what?

He abandoned the cabinets. Hurrying to the piano, he stood with his hand on its polished back and sang – a horrible sound, no doubt, but the glass in the cabinet doors could crack for all that he cared. He was enjoying himself. He was glad that Moira couldn't sing either. He relished her lack of talent. If she'd had a beautiful voice, he would never have dared join in. As it was, they could wail out the old songs together ... the good old songs of the 1930s ... the war years ... Of course, he and she ... they didn't hark back to the same 1930s ... In the war, she must have been young, whereas he was already middle-aged. Still, what of it? They had heard the same music. 'Tea for Two.' 'We'll Meet Again.' They could share their nostalgia, even if there was a quarter century lying between his 1930s – or his war – and hers.

Meanwhile, Rowena had slumped palely on to the sofa; she looked dazed, and at the sight of her, Lawson couldn't help wondering just how far this singing carried. As far as the kitchen, and 'the maids' parlour'? It was good to picture the housekeeper, her face stiff with disbelief, coming out into the passage to listen. The thought doubled his happiness. He sang with all his heart.

Later, when he went to fill the glasses in the library, he stood beside his desk for a moment, and let the whole caco-phony sweep over him: Moira, singing on her own, miles out of key, backed by all those gloriously dishevelled notes from his Steinway. 'Smoke Gets in Your Eyes.' He smiled round at his books. Yes, he loved them, but they weren't everything.

The evening became a gala performance. More than an hour of piano and singing. Lawson thumped out tunes himself – 'Shenandoah', and 'Camptown Races' – bellowing the lyrics. Then Moira did what she could with 'Greensleeves', crooning away so hopelessly that he began to giggle. Soon, Moira was giggling too – from her safe place on the sofa, even Rowena smiled – and then they went on singing, until they were hoarse.

At last, a quietness settled. Enough was enough. Moira stayed sitting at the piano, she seemed reluctant to leave it, but Lawson sank back into an armchair. He smiled. He smiled at Rowena. He sighed with pleasure. Moira sipped her gin, and gazed round the room.

'This is enormous, isn't it? What are you going to do with it all?'

'Pardon?'

His head was full of music, reminiscences. He wanted to talk about music halls: he had a confession to make. As a youngster, he had disapproved of all such places and kept well away from them, except for the rare, terrible treat. He had been so set on bettering himself.

'All these rooms,' said Moira. 'I don't see how you can possibly find something to do with all of them. Not if they're all the size of this one.'

'Well, they aren't ... And anyway, I don't even try. Not with the rooms on the second floor.'

Moira's eyes widened.

'You mean, they're *empty*?'

Didn't she approve? Lawson swallowed his Scotch defensively.

'Two bedrooms are in use, of course, on the first floor. And both of the bathrooms. And a room for the luggage and so on. But what could I do with the attics?'

'Oh ... Can we see them?'

'What?'

'The attics? The empty rooms?'

'I never go up there ... Why? It must be filthy up there ... Very dusty ...'

'Oh, let's go up and look at them. It's such fun, imagining what could be done with a place!'

Lawson led the way, up the stairs. He had only been on the second floor once, and that was before he had bought the house, on the day he came to view it. He had gone up and put his head round doors, sniffing for any trace of damp. Now, as he walked into room after room, he was astonished to see the mounds of furniture left behind by the previous people, pushed out of sight up here: battered old chairs, a baby's high-chair, fold-up card tables, lamp stands and bedheads. And then there were tea chests, not to mention the cardboard boxes and large, decrepit suitcases.

And something else he hadn't expected: there was no electric light. Not a single bulb to the whole floor. There was only the light from the stairwell, so that on one side of the landing, each door opened on to a pit of darkness, in which the clutter of bric-à-brac was only just detectable, vague shapes, black against black; whilst in the rooms on the other side, the moon, shining through the dusty windows, gave the upturned chairs and boxes a kind of aura, a watchfulness.

By tacit agreement, they all ignored the darker rooms, and concentrated on the moonlit side.

'I had no idea', mumbled Lawson, 'that there was so much rubbish up here.'

The dust felt gritty on the soles of his shoes. It was cold in these attics, and he shivered.

'I'm glad there's no light,' said Moira. 'I can imagine it better.'

Their voices echoed, striking off the naked floorboards. Whenever she stood near a window, Moira's eyes looked bright with excitement – wide and bright in a chalk face.

For every room, she had different thoughts. She would leave Rowena on the threshold, and, with Lawson at her heels, squeeze between the piles of junk, until she had come as close as she could to the room's centre. Then she would make her announcement:

'This is the kind of room ... you know, where they spread the apples out ...

'Now this must be the butler's bedroom!

'I think we've found the linen room ... This is where they do the needlework!'

'Why give a room to that?' he objected. 'That's not like you, domestic trivia.'

'Oh, don't be difficult. It's important. There's got to be somewhere to mend the sheets and keep the serviettes from fraying and sew your buttons on. But you needn't worry, you've got maids to do it. They sleep in those rooms over there, across the landing.'

'They do?'

She sounded so sure, he almost believed her.

'Two. And of course a scullery maid. And don't forget you've got a butler!'

She was speaking softly because of the echo, and Lawson had trouble hearing her. How serious she was. How much she cared about this fantasy. He was delighted and bewildered. In every room, while she stood silently feeling for its heart, he waited at her elbow, shivering and panting slightly, aware of the smell of gin on her breath. Sometimes, when she turned in the shadows, her face was smooth, she didn't look old at all; then he wanted to kiss her, and there was a joy in him, as secret and extravagant as a conjurer's bouquet hidden inside his jacket.

The last room had no rubbish in it. Plain and small like a cell, it faced the moon more squarely than the others did – a moon of gelatinous silver drifting round the side of a chimney – and here he watched as Moira suddenly stretched out her hand in front of the window, her fingers turning white.

'Isn't this beautiful? We could be ghosts,' she told him. 'Visitors from some other age.'

Lawson smiled and shook his head. The idea didn't appeal to him, but he wasn't going to say so. Whatever she wanted, this woman and her fantasies. In any case, she didn't need his comments. She had turned to the door.

'Ro, why don't you come in?'

The daughter entered, clumping, and came to stand beside them. Lawson shuffled away a few paces.

'I think', said Moira, 'this room's mine.'

The claim sent a shock-wave through him.

'What? How do you mean?' he gasped. Then he tried to laugh it off. 'Anyway, you can't have this one ... it's the smallest!'

'Yes, I know, but I like the way the ceiling slopes – and that chimney ... I come here when I want to hide, or look at the sky. I *can* have it, can't I?'

To complete his confusion, there was genuine appeal in her voice, and he hastily said yes.

Eight

When they had gone, he could think of only one thing to do: down another glass of whisky. It was much more in the spirit of things than those evil banana sandwiches waiting on the kitchen table. *In the spirit* . . . Ha! Lawson spotted the pun and smiled: the old fool had an excellent brain; no one was going to catch him out, just because he'd had a few!

There aren't any flies on this one . . .

He knew that the evening had been heresy, the kind that pundits swore would knock a couple of months off his life, but what they were talking about, of course, was mere existence. Tonight had been life, and it was worth a month or two. Massive with happiness, he sat dozing in the library, until his bladder called for attention, and sent him on a strange, swaying journey across the hall and along the passage to the toilet. When he came back, he chose a different armchair, and discovered a book by sitting on it. *Vanity Fair*. He tried to read. Impossible. The moment he looked at the print, his head began to jangle with music, and in the space behind his eyes, a smiling Moira Gelling intervened, so that the words were nothing but smudges. He soon gave up, and sat with the closed book on his knees, like a pet cat.

He had meant to show her one or two other first editions, but it hadn't happened somehow. Maybe next time.

Next time . . . Lawson yawned. He consulted his watch. 2.25 . . . His eyelids drooped, his arms felt heavy . . . and now he found there was a question, jostling through whatever else he thought about.

Why not go to bed?

Because, he told himself, *it's only half past two.*

Yes, but why wait up till six?

'Routine,' he muttered.

He had planned to offer her Scott and Mrs Gaskell; now it would have to be next time. If there was one.

Standing in the porch, jittering with the cold, he had asked her:

'You'll come again, won't you? Soon?'

And she had squeezed his hand.

'Thank you. Here's to the next time!'

What was that supposed to mean? At her convenience? In the new year? He could be dead and buried by then.

'I'm drunk,' muttered Lawson.

He got to his feet and went to shelve the *Vanity Fair*, but the gap where it was supposed to fit careered away from him. It took patience and cunning to ram the book home.

Then he headed out of the room, leaving all the lights on.

Ahead of him stretched the staircase, and blinking at its scarlet carpet, Lawson suffered a revelation: what he had always taken for a carpet was, in fact, a vast tongue, levering him up into the darkness of the house; and there, with any luck, he would be swallowed into sleep.

Up, up the tongue . . .

As he climbed, he thought, *A poem, that's it. I'll write her a poem. To show exactly what I feel.*

'Who was that at the door?'

'Boys.'

'Who?'

'Boys.'

'What did they want?'

'A penny for the guy.'

'You didn't give them anything I hope? Barbaric custom! Were they those louts who come tramping through my garden?'

'I really wouldn't know.' She folded her arms, and looked down at the tray. 'I see you've hardly touched it again,' she said. 'That's two days now. That'll teach you!'

'Rubbish, woman . . . I'm just bored with your cooking. Can't you . . .' he waved at the dishes, 'liven things up a bit?'

'You won't eat this and you won't eat that, and you expect miracles.' Her arms came down round the tray, like pincers.

'I think I'd better call that doctor. You'll only get weak, if you don't eat.'

'I don't want a doctor . . . I'll sack you if you do!'

'There's gratitude for you. You'll eat what you get for supper, or tomorrow I'm calling him.'

It was true. He wasn't well. A curious sickness had come over him. The sight of food caused waves of queasiness. He had been like this from the moment he got out of bed the day after Moira's visit, and although he had done his best to conceal the fact, gulping down great lumps of the glutinous porridge or caramel custard she set before him, the housekeeper knew.

'Alcoholic poisoning! That's what it is!' she told him, with all the satisfaction of a Calvinist. She was unbearable.

Well, and possibly she was right, but he didn't think so. Hang-overs never used to last this long. It was something else, something that had him gasping for breath, his hands trembling unaccountably, and he felt so weak, that it was an effort even to read. He also felt extremely irritable, but then, why not? The chaos in his body was affecting his mind, fogging it up just when he needed it crystal clear for the Muse, and prosody.

He would write down a line:

Before I knew you, in some other life

then sit staring at it for long, blank hours. Or he would become all too aware of the anarchy in his stomach and have to get up and prowl round the library, while he belched or farted for relief.

Before I knew . . . Before I knew . . . he would scratch out the line, and start again.

If old Time kept a pawn shop, I'd redeem . . .

Redeem what? Cynical and pornographic thoughts mobbed him. No, no. Perhaps if he read a few love poems? But the words lay bleak and random on each page, like dead insects; and he had to read a verse through several times before he could make any sense of it.

You'll come again, won't you? Soon?

A nasty little cheat of a word, soon. When exactly was soon, pray? Twelve months ahead might be soon to some people. He experienced surges of bitterness. More than once, he crumpled up his poem, and dropped it into the wastepaper basket.

But if he didn't eat, things could only get worse. He admitted that. Oh yes, the bitch in the kitchen was right, as usual; and after her threat about the doctor, he made up his mind to eat whatever she put on his supper tray. And he did. A flaccid square of quiche. Pink blancmange.

That night, he tried Macaulay — *History of England*; the cheese-lined pastry repeating on him, the sweetness of the blancmange sticking to his palate. He struggled with the heavy splendour of Macaulay's prose, trying to stow-away inside it and ride out his biliousness. The palms of his hands sweated. At last he felt too sick to go on. Then he shut the book and sat clutching it for comfort: it was one of a series – solid, expensive volumes making a bid to last as long as civilisation did. Generally reassuring – but not tonight. The good brown leather, the noble gilt of the lettering on the spine – they had suddenly become inadequate. No use denying it. There was definitely a pain in his chest. It felt as though someone had picked up a hand-drill and was boring a hole between his shoulder-blades. Quite a sharp pain, if he were honest ...

Heartburn. A familiar complaint. He diagnosed it out loud to the carpet.

'I've got a touch of heartburn ...'

Gripping the arms of his chair, he sank low, stretched out his legs, and stared at his feet. It was always possible, of course, that he was wrong. Not heartburn, no, not this time, but the other thing. Heart-attack ...

He imagined the tricks of the pain, returning new and excruciating just when the worst already seemed to be over, iron talons clamping round him – and he imagined his fright.

What'll happen, he thought, *is that I'll try to get up; I'll fall forwards on to my knees. That's what people do.*

Labouring for breath. Just one more breath.

If this one isn't my last, the next one could be ...

He wheezed, tight little squeals that he heard, and he thought of his inhaler, but he couldn't move to find it – and what use was an inhaler?

Gently he stroked the Macaulay. A thumping had started between his ribs. Now it was accelerating. He could picture the whole catastrophe so vividly that he knew it was inevitable – just the blink of an eye away – and what could he do? One thing was certain: staring at his feet wasn't going to help. Slowly, he brought his head up, and what he saw was the standard lamp that stood at the far end of the room, near the curtains. It poured out its light in a wide, benevolent circle, and the whole thing's steadiness baffled him: the wooden stand so upright, the electric bulb still shining, as if life went on for ever –

I'm going to collapse!

And in the morning, *she* would come. She would find him curled up on the carpet, like a fossil. He could picture the scene, he believed in it, and yet it was incredible. He didn't believe in it. If he lived for a thousand years, he would never believe in it. The idea of his own death was no more than a flimsy transfer sticking to the surface of his mind, a borrowed idea, that couldn't have come from his own brain.

Please, no ...

He let go of the book and waited helplessly. Nothing happened. Only, after a measureless sort of void, an infinite time, the pain in his chest eased, and his heart began to thump less frantically. Maybe he was fooling himself ... but he felt he should acknowledge this improvement and, with extreme caution, as if he were dismantling a bomb, he drew his watch out. Five past four ... Only two more hours till daylight. It occurred to him that he might live, and this seemed scarcely less bizarre than the thought that he might die. Grunting softly, he moved his feet; he sat a fraction higher in the armchair and concentrated on health, life. The volume of Macaulay had slipped down by his elbow, and there it lay, forgotten. He policed himself, inspecting every turn of nausea, and he cursed the housekeeper's pastry.

'Damned indigestion ...' He patted his belly tenderly. 'Incompetent bitch.'

But at noon, when he groaned at her scrambled eggs, and she marched straight out to phone the doctor, he made no protest. Six hours flat on his back in bed, wide awake and noting every twinge of gut and muscle hadn't done much to remedy matters. The heartburn had gone, and for that he was grateful, but his hands still shook, and in his chest, a feathery sensation rose up like a bird at any slight annoyance – a flake of soap on his trousers, a spot of milk on his side plate. And he still felt sick. A doctor might, when all was said, be worth putting up with. Just to end the inconvenience.

'He'll be here around three.'

Lawson pretended he hadn't heard. She had come back smartly with the news, striding up to his desk before she delivered it, which was quite unnecessary.

'I said, he's coming at three.'

'Is he? Thank you.'

He had taken out a notebook and was writing down an address – no one's in particular. Anything would do, so long as it showed that his thoughts were elsewhere, and that whatever else he was – off-colour, out of sorts – she couldn't call him ill. He ignored her. After the address, he wrote his name. When she started to move away, he kept his eyes on the book, listening for the bang of the door. She often slammed it when she had the advantage – especially if he refused to admit she had. He waited, breathing on the page. Silence. Did that mean she was still there, watching? Or to spite him, had she sneaked off like a thief, leaving the door ajar for once? In the end, he took a risk: he glanced up, and, thank God, she had gone.

Lawson relaxed. He closed the notebook – then began to succumb to panic.

Doctor. In that one word lay whole tribes of tinkering technicians, the cold-blooded tribe and the jolly enthusiasts, the spuriously mystical and the raw bullies, all with their sharp eyes and needles, their little adjustments and pronouncements. What would this new man be?

No ... He mustn't raise his blood pressure.

He began all over again his poem to Moira Gelling.

> When roving spirits such as yours and mine
> Meet in the marketplace of this world's ...
> ... this world's ...

The housekeeper had taken away the eggs when she had gone to phone the doctor, perhaps fearing he might eat them after all, but she had left the milk, and Lawson sipped it guiltily: the Muse was dead; what mattered were the rumblings in the poet's belly. The milk was sweet and tepid, exactly how he hated it. Liquids that were neither hot nor cold revolted him: they had a teasing or deceptive quality that somehow posed the question: Are you *sure* you know what this is? Not unlike the drizzle – except that the drizzle was a killer. Through the windows he could see it, drifting grey across the lawn and muffling the spinney. Neither dry nor honestly wet, it hardly seemed to be anything, but you breathed it into your lungs and found yourself with respiratory trouble. It was as light as gossamer, but it sank through any amount of clothing and chilled you to the marrow. For much of the time until the doctor came, Lawson sat with the glass of milk held against his stomach, and looked out at the weather, censuring it. Maybe he should have moved to the Mediterranean. Drizzle wasn't the only thing that killed. So did snow, and the bitter winds . . .

He caught himself in a senile thought: *The weather wasn't as bad as this when I was young.*

The old fool in his skull, playing up again. By way of counter-attack, he refined a line of poetry:

Meet in the heart of this world's marketplace . . .

Then the door was pushed open.

'This is Dr Hewitt.'

Lawson felt suddenly cold. He hadn't heard the doorbell, and no car had come to the front. She must have given instructions on the phone: 'Please would the doctor drive round the back of the house? I'd like to have a word or two in private . . .' By the time her clock had cuckooed three, she had probably been poised, ready and waiting at the back door. Now she strode in like a farmer's wife bringing the vet to the cowshed, her sleeves rolled up to expose her forearms, and already her mouth had settled firmly into a curve that said, 'No nonsense!' Oh, the woman was jubilant. She came in with indecent gusto.

And now what? wondered Lawson. Did he have to make an

effort, and hoist himself out of his chair? But really, he argued, why should he ... less than a hundred per cent, and in his own house ...? He commenced work on a scowl. He had made up his mind about this scowl hours before. He wanted to make it perfectly plain that he abhorred this kind of intrusion – and was unafraid. He wanted his face to put the doctor right. Instead, his mouth fell open.

Dr Hewitt was a shock. Young, wretchedly young. His corn-yellow hair, undisciplined and abundant. He was pink-cheeked and handsome after a schoolboy fashion, and he advanced with a bustling lack of curiosity about his surroundings, banging down his case on the nearest chair with one hand, while with the other, he was already pulling off his quilted waterproof jacket. A young man, who valued his time.

Lawson gazed at him in horror. Meanwhile, the housekeeper took up a stand by the fireplace. She clasped her arms across her pelvis, and all at once Lawson realised that she meant to stay there.

'All right, all right!' he snapped, jerking his head round. 'We don't need *you*!' Then he saw the significant look she threw at Hewitt as she made for the door.

A disapproving pause followed. Hewitt smiled a touch too heartily, and when he did speak, his words came out with determined breeziness.

'Well now, Mr Lawson ... Your housekeeper tells me you're off your food?' He stood inclining forward, ready to pounce.

A rugby man, thought Lawson dismally. He felt decidedly reluctant to come out from behind his desk and let those eager hands get at him. Maybe he wouldn't have to. Abandoning any thought of a scowl, he tried a smile of appeasement.

'Wouldn't you be off your food,' he said, 'if your cook had a face like that?'

Hewitt responded with a snigger – a brief one, so as not to waste time.

'Indigestion,' mumbled Lawson, 'palpitations ... I feel sick ...'

'Any pain?'

'Some.' The young man's eyes were as blue and clear as a summer sky, and Lawson could feel his own eyes widening, staring back, trying to stave off the scrutiny.

'Right. I'll just examine you . . .'

'Must you?'

'Of course.' Hewitt looked surprised. His blue irises grew brighter, and at the same time, they seemed to crystallise. 'It'll only take a couple of minutes,' he said; and as if that dealt with the sole possible objection, he turned to his black case, snapping back the clasps so that the thing sprang open like a shark's jaw. Stethoscope, syringes, metal tubes for thrusting into ears, spatulas for throats and little white prescription pads: they were all in there. Hewitt wrapped the stethoscope round his neck, and advanced towards the desk. Lawson shrank. An examination might reveal anything. He knew that from the past. They came up with surprises he had never dreamed of. A stomach ulcer when he was sixty. And in his seventies, a small lump on his back which, the doctors said, was harmless, but it had brought him under the knife again, even so.

'Now, if you'll just . . . Do you need any help?'

'No! . . . thank you.' Hopeless. No way out of it. Lawson fought off his cardigan, and fiddled with his shirt buttons.

'What's your date of birth, Mr Lawson?'

Ten minutes later, Hewitt's ballpoint moved in business-like hieroglyphs over a prescription pad. Stricken with suspense, the patient could only tell the truth.

'That makes you . . . eighty-four.'

'What about it?'

Was this a hint that he should be ready to go?

'You're in excellent shape for your age.'

'Do you really mean that?'

He put no trust in Hewitt's round, juvenile smile, and when an answer didn't come at once, he felt like leaping to his feet and shouting for one. Almost every doctor did this: start to give a verdict, then break off to finish writing a prescription. A deplorable abuse of power, that was what it was. They should speak out, or shut up . . . But it wouldn't help to appear neurotic. Lawson forced himself to keep quiet. With great care, he started fastening his shirt. There was barely the strength in his fingers to push the buttons through.

'Well, your heart's pretty sound, if that's what you're worrying about. But you've been overdoing it, haven't you? Getting over-excited, eh?'

A fatuous conspirator, the doctor beamed at him.

'*Over-excited*' ... *like some damned puppy!* Lawson felt his face turn red, and not with embarrassment.

'Then you've got that asthmatic problem,' continued Hewitt serenely. 'You've got to keep an eye on that. Slow down. And you'd better keep off the alcohol.'

'Oh, she's told you about that, has she?' Apparently there wasn't going to be any drastic news about his health, and Lawson was relieved, but he didn't feel relieved: he felt anger. 'Interfering bitch!' he whined.

Hewitt put away his pen. He had sobered up considerably while making out the prescription, but he still maintained a general air of optimism, and Lawson's rage had no effect whatever.

'Why can't I have a drink from time to time? You said yourself, there's nothing wrong with my heart ...'

'There certainly isn't ... for a man of eighty-four. But wear and tear, you know, wear and tear.' The black case snapped shut; the waterproof jacket was pulled on, and the cheery smile was renewed. 'You'll be all right,' said Hewitt soothingly. 'I'll leave this prescription with your housekeeper.'

'I'll thank you to give it to me!'

He knew it was irrational: if the woman had a mind to poison him, she could do it any day of the week – she probably did – none the less, it went against the grain to deliver up his health to her. Lawson got to his feet with remarkable alacrity: shirt tails flapping, he scuttled forward, and snatched the paper that Hewitt was holding. Mercifully, it came away intact. And then, at last, a flash of annoyance crossed the young man's face.

'Now, look. You can't go out for that yourself! I want you to take it easy ... In fact, for a couple of days, you *must*.'

'Must?' repeated Lawson.

The prescription quivered in his fingers: he saw he would have to give it up again and that he ought to do it promptly, before Hewitt played his own game, whipping it out of his hand. He was going to see it borne away to the kitchen, to be explained in detail with every why and wherefore – to her.

'What are you giving me?' he demanded, squinting at the names and figures. 'I won't just swallow anything that's put in front of me . . .'

'There you are!' She had lost no time in coming to claim her victory. She squared her jaw at him: an undervalued woman, proved right. 'I told you,' she said, 'and you wouldn't listen. Now it's bread and milk, and medicine and tablets, and quiet living.' She sounded particularly pleased about the last part.

'Oh, leave me alone!'

'That's exactly what I'm going to do. I'm going to get these things before the chemist shuts.' She was already belted into her raincoat, her head wrapped in a paisley scarf. 'Anything else you want, while I'm out?' It was obvious that she hoped he would never set foot out of the house again.

'Just . . . go to hell!'

'Temper, temper.'

Off she went, tossing her head, a travesty of feminine outrage. He waited until the door had closed, and then he shouted after her, 'Don't think this is going to stop me. I'm not giving up!'

At once the door swung open. Her white, angular face shot back at him. He lowered his eyes to his book. Best not be provocative. Best not get himself 'over-excited'.

Nine

On November 5th, he received a note from Moira Gelling – belated thanks for a most enjoyable evening. He replied immediately. The poem was still just fragments of a skeleton scattered about in his desk drawer, so he chose instead a few short words, dashing them off with what he hoped was style:

The thanks are all mine. Come back soon.

Hewitt's 'couple of days' were up, so he went out to post this vital communication before he could start elaborating, and by the same post, he sent off to a firm in Manchester for his usual Christmas card. Yes, he was feeling better.

Forty-eight hours of mauve-coated pills – tranquillisers – and a medicine that looked like a poor grade of whitewash had done their trick. Now his heart had turned bourgeois, working away inoffensively; his stomach received its bread-and-butter pudding without a murmur, and his hand was steady on his pen.

He rediscovered his happiness. Having once flared up too high, this emotion, which had everything to do with Moira Gelling, was now well under control, and Lawson didn't tamper with it. He could feel it there inside him, that was all that mattered, and he shied off trying to analyse what it was, precisely.

He simply gave up worrying. Thanks to her note, he now had not the slightest doubt that she would be back.

'We must talk more,' she had written. 'We have so much in common.'

Had they? Never mind. The words were clearly meant to be words of promise, and as to the puzzle of when she might or might not come, he was through with panicking about it. In order to be hale and chivalrous when she did come, he made up his mind to be sensible, he would wait patiently.

It was equilibrium.

In fact, on the evening of the 5th, he was feeling so relaxed and amiable towards the universe, that some time shortly after eight, he pulled back the library curtains to watch the sky for rockets: showers of blue and gold, green and scarlet, arcing back to the earth: trite, he had always said, and madness – money up in smoke – but secretly, he thought them beautiful. For half an hour or more, he kept vigil, although, because the library windows faced the spinney, and beyond that lay a stretch of open farmland, there wasn't much to see, and what there was showed low down near the horizon, miles away. Nothing rose above the spinney trees, filling the sky directly over his garden, as he would have liked. Still, he watched, and he saw a group of orange stars, and a comet tail of vivid emerald – hints and glimpses among the branches – so he wasn't disappointed. On the other hand, if he had gone up-stairs, from his bedroom window, he could have looked out in the direction of the bungalow estate, where the rockets were probably spectacular, and this thought finally got the better of him: he was about to act on it when suddenly, out there in the spinney, he detected intruders. Shadows moved. A match was struck – he distinctly saw a red point of flame – and in the next moment, the erratic brilliance of a sparkler, metallic white, burst out from the undergrowth.

Children, on the far bank of the stream. Presumably on the far bank. Hastily he drew the curtains. He had no desire to work up a rage.

What good will it do? he asked himself. *This side of the stream ... that side of the stream ... arguing doesn't stop them. They are what they are, the young, and you can't talk them out of it. No one tries to tell a wasp not to sting ... It's just the way of things ...*

The mauve pills, he noticed, were admirably efficient. He found he'd had enough of fireworks anyway. He took down a volume of Robert Burns. A thin layer of dust lay on its closed pages, and he blew it off, quite calmly.

'When I was young,' he turned the cigar slowly in his fingers,

124

a substitute for a whisky glass, 'we used to build bonfires in the streets. We collected rubbish for days – old mattresses, newspapers, whatever we could lay our hands on. We built those fires so high that some of the women fussed about the houses catching. Not that they ever did ...' He chuckled. 'A close thing, once or twice, though. Sometimes, people got scared and talked about going for the fire brigade, but it never came to that. They were some fires, those were ... but we could handle them! Backstreet boys have a knack for it. And there were no cars, of course, no petrol, so it wasn't so dangerous.'

'Were you happy as a child?'

Moira Gelling, curled in her chair with a gin and tonic: somehow, she had led him into this. Lawson smiled awkwardly. Memories cluttered his brain like scenes in a camera obscura, where yesterday and for years of yesterdays in every compartment labelled 'childhood' there had been nothing but a black void.

He didn't answer Moira's question; it was meaningless; but he wanted to talk.

'We drank our tea out of jamjars. One time, we found a whole box of rusty key rings on a rubbish dump. We were for ever scouring the rubbish dumps. We took those rings home and polished them up, then went round the houses, selling them.'

'Were you *so* poor?'

'We got by. But there wasn't a book in the house, except the Bible. Not a spare shirt. And we had one pair of shoes each. My mother had one dress for Sunday, one for the week.'

His mother, with her terrified, smoky face, her jittery, parboiled hands. He shuddered. He hadn't thought of her since – since he couldn't remember when. She was unmentionable, and he had mentioned her.

Moira shook her head.

'It's amazing,' she said. 'I can't imagine you with five brothers and – how many was it?'

'Annie and May.'

'Two sisters. I can't imagine you as a boy at all.'

'Why not?' Offended, he blew out cigar smoke vigorously. 'I haven't always been old, you know. I wasn't born like this ...'

'Of course not. But it seems to suit you.'

'What? And what about yourself? You were a girl once, weren't you? How would you like it if I said I don't believe that? Have you always been middle-aged with grey hair and wrinkles ...'

'Now calm down, Arnold.'

He puffed hard on the cigar and studied the ring of saliva round it. He didn't like to look at her. He hadn't meant to be hurtful. This was what came of giving up the tranquillisers, but he had wanted to be wide awake for her, on form. At last, he glanced at Moira nervously.

She was smiling.

'You're so obsessed with age!' she said. 'As if it mattered!'

And there she had stung him again.

'Hah! It's easy to talk ... easy for you!' he cried. 'The sands of time ... they aren't running out for you yet, are they? Wait till you've had your three score years and ten! Wait and see!'

Moira sipped her gin, and shrugged.

'And when you left home ... how old were you?'

'Twelve.'

'And ... just like that? No note? Nothing?'

'No note. Nothing.'

Nothing. He was standing on the narrow stairs. He could hear his parents breathing in their sleep. The door to their room was open – they hardly ever bothered to shut it. Shapes beneath the blankets, flesh and breath and exhaustion: what was there to be private about? Clothes draped over the bed-head. He looked back at their door and listened, then he was looking down the stairs at another door, which boasted a pane of glass above it. Through that glass, light shone in from the lamp across the street, flooding up the stairs to meet him.

'Yes,' he said. 'I just walked out. I never went back, and I never wrote. I suppose you think that was heartless?'

'I don't know ... Yes.'

'*He* wouldn't care!' Lawson jerked his head as if someone was standing beside him and, for an instant, he had in his mind such a lifelike image of his father that he wasn't even surprised by it: a short and wiry figure, thin nose, tight mouth, eyes ferrety with resentment. 'He was always saying we had to look out for ourselves!'

126

'But what about your mother?'

'Oh, I suppose she went to the charnel ... to church, and prayed. God bless little Arnie, make him see the light ... She was great for the prayers, my mother!'

He laughed, and the sound embarrassed him. He banged his cigar hard in the ashtray until it was dead. It didn't seem right, talking of things like this with a cigar in his hand: it must look like bravado, and he wanted Moira to know that he was a man of feeling. He wanted to tell her about the times he had almost gone back, or looked up one of his brothers ... that he was human, every escape he had made in life had cost him ...

Instead, he asked, 'And what about your own childhood?'

'Oh, I was happy.'

'You were.' He stated it. Of course. She raised her glass again, and her gold bracelet, a heavy vulgar chain, crowded with charms, dropped back up her wrist.

'Happy,' he said.

'A tomboy. Nesting. Fishing. Messing about in boats. We lived in Devon. There was a lighthouse on the headland, about five miles away. I used to ride out to it on my bike.'

'Ah.'

He closed his eyes. A rocky coastline. Narrow lanes, hedged with fuchsia, foxgloves and convolvulus. Yolk-yellow gorse. White cottages. Sunlight on the sea. He could smell the honeysuckle. He heard young people laughing on the sand. Love of life, happiness – so this was where she got them from! Lawson sat back with his eyes shut, listening to her descriptions, and smiled gratefully. Quite simply, Moira Gelling was a happier, more generous person than he was, because she had been given more. Cause and effect, an elementary illustration of the sort he welcomed. It made sense of people. It did away with any troublesome questions to do with moral character or resilience. It absolved him.

Moira, once she began, didn't need a prompt. On and on she talked – picnics ... lobster potting ... And one day, she had tried to scale a cliff and slipped, which should have been the end of her, but her skirt had caught on a rock. A drop of sixty feet or more, and there she had dangled ... And another time, when she and a friend had gone rowing round the headland, a storm had blown up, and if they hadn't been spotted by a fishing boat ...

As she talked, her voice was warm; it was strangely deep, and all these descriptions of her childhood seemed to be not words – sounds that she could use again as often as she felt like it: Lawson had a sense that they were far more precious than that; they were something she could spend once only, and tonight she poured it out.

Not words. Life-blood.

His eyes opened wide. How tiny she looked, and deadly white. Draining herself. He had to stop her ... He struggled to his feet and hurried forwards.

'... Christmas,' she was saying, 'we used to go out to the farms and sing carols. Sometimes there'd be snow by then ...'

He snatched her glass. She stopped in the middle of her sentence and stared up at him.

'Another drink?' he wheezed. 'All this talk ... all this childhood ...' He moved away quickly to the bottles. 'What about Dylan Thomas, eh? Do you know "Fern Hill"? Remind me, and I'll read it to you. Not an honest man, in my opinion. Overrated ... but "Fern Hill" ...'

The gin bottle slithered in his hands, a glass fish. He mixed the wrong proportions, and stood with his back to her, trembling, looking at a splash of alcohol on the tray. What she had done was terrible. Too much feeling. Far too much. Veins slit open. He felt the past was everywhere. Pools of blood on the carpet.

'Arnold, what's the matter?'

Softly she came up behind him, and touched him on the arm. A maternal touch – or was it a doctor's?

'Don't *do* that!'

Forgetting he held her glass, he spun round, furious, and a streak of liquid shot out from his fist across her blouse. As the saturated cotton darkened, he gave a sheepish laugh. He couldn't think what else to do.

'Oh, God ...' She peered down at her front. 'Look at it!' She dabbed and plucked at the wet patch. 'Have you got a cloth or something?'

Ice-cold: the change in her voice was more than he could bear. Lawson went weak with misery.

'P-please,' he stuttered. 'An accident ... don't be angry, Moira!'

Desperately he reached out, and squeezed her hand.

The housekeeper's jealousy grew. Soon, it found distressing, petty outlets. For one thing, his meals deteriorated even further. There was no more fruit cake, and the portions of every other sweet, including his favourite chocolate ripple ice-cream, dwindled and dwindled. He saw that they threatened to vanish altogether. Then she took to serving new, unpalatable concoctions – cold potato soup, lumpy vegetable rice – and when he complained, she was all astonishment ...

'I thought you didn't care about your food,' she said archly. 'A thinking man has better things to do. You've told me that I don't know how many times.'

'Yes, but damn it, a man's got to eat.'

'Well, what's wrong with it?'

'Wrong with it?' He tapped the plate of congealed macaroni. 'It's disgusting. You're doing it on purpose. I know you are.'

'Of course I'm doing it on purpose. Plain living, the doctor said. Someone's got to see that you don't kill yourself!'

Even more unpleasant were her frequent, querulous remarks about the housework. Since she had always gloried in her role of martyred drudge, flaunting her silence, Lawson found these outbursts sinister. They suggested a process of change in the woman, a departure from the old, familiar strategies.

'The woman in the newsagent's ... She was saying only yesterday, she doesn't know how I manage.'

'Well, what do you want? A daily help? An odd job man? You've always managed before!'

'Just so long as you know what people think. A place like this means work, work, work. It needs constant attention. You've no idea. That's all I'm saying.'

Then, the final insult. One night, as he sat in his bath, contemplating the half-moon wrinkles beneath his stomach, she opened the door. He looked up to find her watching, and in his rage and surprise, he hurled the soap at her. No harm done. The soap bounced off the door-frame, and she closed the door again without a word.

When he came out, she explained prosaically, 'You were so quiet in there, I thought you must be dead or something.'

On nights when Moira Gelling called, she kept to her room beside the kitchen, and from there, he could feel the whole cache of her displeasure like some unstable element, radiating a dark power down the passage. It filled the air he had to breathe and with every visit it grew worse, so that he couldn't be anything else but jumpy, irritable.

And in ironic complement to all these, he had another problem. He began to find Moira herself exhausting. Too whimsical. As the weeks passed, she got on his nerves more and more, and this upset him, especially since he counted the days, even the hours, that separated him from her. Moira was the guardian of his happiness. Her visits had become like footholds on a slippery surface, and without them he could only fall. Yet he couldn't deny it, the more they saw of one another, the less they pleased each other. He found she had no logic. There were days when she refused to take the most important conversations seriously. In fact, although she now came down to see him surprisingly often – once a week, sometimes twice – and although she sat in one of his chairs and drank his gin, her mind could be somewhere else altogether. She would smile, and admire the books he showed her, answer his questions, agree or disagree, but Lawson would suddenly sense that he was talking to himself. He couldn't understand it. Was she bored? If she was, why did she come? She always claimed she was interested, and, for the most part, he believed that, but this other thing could happen so quickly. One minute, she would be sparkling, laughing and arguing; the next, although nothing had changed and she went on talking, he felt that she wasn't there.

He spent a lot of time puzzling about it. One idea he had was that her brain was so undisciplined, any real discussion tired her, and maybe she needed long, vacuous spells to recuperate. Another idea was that she drank too much; but what he really suspected was that she was preoccupied, she had something on her mind that mattered infinitely more than anything they talked about, and it kept drawing her back to it, like a magnet.

And maybe it's something she wants to tell me ... only she doesn't know how ...

130

His imagination would run riot. Moira Gelling, confessing to a growing sense of attraction, love ... Why not? Why not? But he took great care to counter-balance these fantasies with some practical consideration. Probably she wanted money after all, and couldn't bring herself to ask him for it.

A mystery. It both angered and excited him. And what could he do? Whenever he sensed one of her peculiar mental absences, he became dogmatic, shouting opinions at her, trying to break through, bring her back – and sooner or later, back she would come all right, possibly snapping at him, or with some fatuous, teasing remark that shocked him, although it set him grinning like a schoolboy. But there was no detectable pattern to it. Sometimes she came back in silence, while she just sat there listening – odd, how he could tell – or she might come back with an interruption, even though whatever she said was so frequently irrelevant, whether her mind was absent or not.

Once or twice it occurred to Lawson that she didn't really like opinions. She was far more interested in long, emotional celebrations of all they had lived through, but he could only take so much of that, and he was for ever tugging their conversations back to intellect, argument. It wasn't always what he wanted, but he did it, and it didn't help.

There was strain between them, and jarring, so that he had quickly discovered that every visit Moira made felt a little more dangerous than the last one. This fading in and out of hers, and almost everything else she did, could be so irritating that there was a real possibility of a quarrel. He saw that; and in his fear at the thought, he would make up his mind to be careful. He mustn't jeopardise these visits ...

But every time she came, his resolution failed, and the jarring continued, until one night, things went badly wrong.

It was the end of November. Moira arrived tired and somewhat breathless, carting one of her outsize handbags, a straight-edged, ugly contraption of patent leather which so obviously weighed her down, that as they entered the library, Lawson lost his patience and blurted out, 'What do you keep in that ... that suitcase?'

He tugged angrily at the handle – only as a gesture, a way

of saying, 'This bag here. This is what I'm talking about!' –
and Moira paid him back by letting go, so that the bag's full
weight lurched into his hand and his shoulder ached at the jolt.
Then she left him standing with it, pink-faced, foolish, while
she wandered away to a chair. It was the sort of trick she
played occasionally, if he was rude; she seemed to enjoy inviting his rudeness to run its course. So what now? Should he
scuttle after her, and tamely put the bag by her feet? He wanted
to, but already she was smiling, as though she knew he
wouldn't dare do anything else, and that decided him. He bore
his prize to his own chair. He sat down, and investigated the
clasp. A cheap, stiff clasp. There were two metal twigs, and
one had to be pushed back past the other ... Moira watched.
After a painful effort, he succeeded, and the bag yawned wide.
He began to rummage.

The silky lining was smeared with lipstick and powder. Her
purse was also smeared with make-up ... There were several
letters, in or out of envelopes, and on one envelope, he noticed
bright red imprints of mouths where she had pressed her lips
to remove her excess lipstick. Car keys. Nail file. Handkerchief.
Item by item, he pulled them out and piled them on his lap. A
pen. Another one. An old address book, so worn and crumpled, it looked ready to disintegrate. Powder-case. Lipstick. A
packet of Spangles ... A slim, tattered notebook.

'What's this?'

Everything smelt faintly of her perfume, telling him he trespassed.

Moira had got up again, and gone over to the drinks tray.
She had never helped herself before, but in the circumstances
he saw he couldn't comment.

'That's for notes,' she said. 'I jot down thoughts ... things
I've read or heard. Things from the Poetry Meetings.'

He sniffed at the book's creased cover, then flicked the pages
to produce a cinematic blur of writing. Secrets. Would she
tolerate his reading them? A glance at her told him nothing.
She began to pour out gin. Delicately, he opened the book and
squinted at a page. Then at a second page, and a third.

Chocolate box stuff. He felt his mouth twist. He was disappointed, but he was pleased, too, because he had known the
kind of 'thoughts' a woman like Moira would collect.

'Ha! You don't believe in any of this, do you?'

'Any of what?'

'This mawkish stuff. This "One far-off divine event To which the whole creation moves" ...'

'That's Tennyson,' said Moira stiffly.

'I know what it is!' His cheeks burned. 'I know it's Tennyson ... and this!' He pitched his voice high in derision. ' "If thou shouldst never see my face again, pray for my soul. More things are wrought by prayer than this world dreams of ..." '

'I think that's beautiful,' said Moira. 'I'd have thought you'd approve.'

'Oh, it's magnificent *theatre*!' He clutched the notebook and smiled at her lividly. 'That's what you think, is it? A hot line to heaven? Someone up there, listening?'

His heart was pounding. He had become superbly alert. So far, they had avoided this, religion. Now here it came, and he knew he shouldn't go into it, but he wanted to. He had to. The quotes had started up a scornful fury in him. It was not so much the lines themselves as finding them there, gathered in and treasured by her.

Moira came back slowly to her chair, and he saw that she wasn't smiling. In fact, either because she was tired or because of what he had said, her skin had mottled slightly, which made her look surprisingly unhealthy, even not quite clean. For some reason, this made his own smile all the broader.

'What are you angry about?' she said. 'No one's trying to convert you.'

'I should hope not! An intelligent person in the twentieth century ... You can make excuses for Tennyson, I grant you ... but it's time we learned to do without the mumbo-jumbo.'

'Well, I think it's silly to argue about these things.' There was a small table beside the chair, and she set the glass of gin down without tasting it.

'Silly?'

Lawson's temper rose by another notch, while at the same time, he felt a twinge of alarm. Her face was so haggard, so unhappy ... What was he doing, poking about in other people's notebooks? Starting in like this? He could sense the chasm that threatened to open between them. Maybe he should pull back ...

He thrust her notebook down, into the depths of her handbag. Enough. He wouldn't argue.

'Anyway,' said Moira. 'I know you say you don't believe in
God, but I'm sure that you do at some level. There's no smoke
without fire. I've heard you say, "Good God", and "Damn"
and things like that . . .'

'Never.'

'I'm sure I have.'

Then his last restraint snapped. He bundled her letters and
pens and all the rest of it into the bag like the junk they were,
and banged the bag down on the carpet. There, as he hadn't
bothered to secure the clasp, it veered over on to its side,
gaping.

'What if I do?' he scowled at her. 'God, damn . . . just words.
I can say what I like, can't I?'

'Of course, but . . .'

'Don't start telling me what I believe in. I know what I
believe in! Scio scire . . . Science and proved facts. That's what
I believe in.'

'Oh, is it?' Suddenly, she seemed to be mocking him. 'What
do you mean, you believe in it? Not you, Arnold. After all
you've said.'

'What?'

'About ageing. You can't think science has all the answers.'

'Not *now* . . . Not for you and me, as if *we* mattered . . . but
all the answers, yes, in time,' said Lawson, and he said it so
fiercely, he almost meant it. The truth was, he had no such
absolute faith in science or anything else. She had twisted his
meaning, and he had let her; he had spoken too quickly. Well,
it wouldn't happen twice. He sat bolt upright, primed by the
splendid thump of his heartbeat. If she *wanted* to argue, so be
it.

Moira smiled, and said something.

'What? Speak up.'

'It doesn't matter.'

'Of course it matters.'

'I said, you must wish you'd been born a hundred years
from now. If science is going to find all the answers.'

'Possibly.'

'I mean, of course, if there *is* a world a hundred years from

now. Think of it, Arnold. They might have done away with
old age by then. People might be living for ever.'

That winded him. He slumped back, astonished by her
cruelty.

'They might,' he said.

She had more to offer.

'But I don't suppose it would be everyone, do you? Think
of the population problem. Unless they did away with repro-
duction, and *that* isn't likely. People need to reproduce ... So
it would be immortality for the few – the great brains, and one
or two of the very rich ... I wonder if you'd be rich enough?'

He shook his head dumbly. This was new, this bitterness
from her. He felt completely at a loss, and so did she,
apparently. They stared at each other.

In the end, Moira picked up her gin.

'Oh well,' she said, 'why should anyone want to live for
ever? What would be the point, just going on and on? The
important thing is to enjoy life, that's what I say. Love and
leave it. The readiness is all. There you are, I know my *Ham-
let*,' and her tone implied that, so far as she was concerned,
there was nothing more to be said.

But Lawson rallied. He was back on familiar ground now.
He knew this kind of 'ready' talk, this facile nonsense propa-
gated by people who didn't have to wake up every day saying
to themselves, 'So, hello! We're still here ... Nothing's happened yet!' and he heard himself crying, 'Don't try to make it
sound like packing an overnight case! No one's ever ready!
There's no such thing! Ask any old down and out. Ask those
wretches they shove into homes ... Just because they sit all
day like cabbages ... Just you ask them! You say you're a
doctor – you should know. And what about priests? Not exactly impatient, are they, to get knocking at the Pearly Gates?
We ... we're limpets. We cling for as long as we can.'

'Of course,' said Moira coldly. 'You would say that. People
like you. Because you've dismissed religion.'

'Oh yes, I've dismissed it! My dismissal, as you'd call it ...
it only took me twenty years of hard study. I've gone through
every one of them, all the cults of the corpse! And Buddhism
... that's something better, I admit, but in the end it's just
another dodge – pretty it up, hush it up ...'

135

A trace of spittle seeped out from the corner of his mouth, and he wiped it off with his hand.

I'm not behaving well, he thought. *I'm making her hate me.* Yes. She sat there on the other side of the chasm they had created, and her eyes were hard. Her face was set against him. She was full of loathing for him, he decided, and fear.

But when she spoke, her words came out quite gently, like a last appeal.

'Religion must be very important to you, then. Or you wouldn't have had to fight it like that, would you?'

'All humbug. The lot of it.' He laughed, but Moira didn't. He had pushed her from him, miles and miles away. He had started this, and now that he saw the result, Moira so pale and remote, a desolation crept over him. His rage collapsed. He felt ready to weep with loneliness. If only she could understand. If only he could bring her into the emptiness of his universe. If she could share it with him, he would never be alone again.

He learned forward eagerly.

'Don't you see ...' he began, but she interrupted him.

'You're so arrogant, Arnold. Really, you don't know everything. You can't write off the whole world's spiritual experiences, just because *you* haven't had any.'

'Did I say I haven't?' He blinked with hurt at her words. 'And I ... I may be arrogant, but at least I'm not a simpleton! I don't just swallow what I'm told – the way *you* do!'

Moira was silent. She sat utterly still, watching him. Thin and imploring, his voice went reaching out to her.

'Hocus-pocus ... fabrications ... Don't you think I wish it wasn't? Take any religion ... I'm not against them for the sake of it! Take Christianity ... Cobbled together! A bit of myth from Egypt, a bit from Greece and Persia ... A few Jewish platitudes ... This and that, odds and ends ... Had a look on the scrap heap, have you? Eh?'

Then at last her face did change, first becoming soft, then grey and wispy with pain.

'Scrap heap?' she said. 'What are you talking about?'

136

Ten

'I meant to tell you, I'll be away for a while ... I don't really know how long.'

'Oh?'

'A rest.'

'But where are you going?'

'Somewhere I can get some peace,' she said.

Lawson trembled. It was bitterly cold, standing in the open doorway. Why had she left this till now? Because she was lying. He knew it. Mystery cults and Roman politics, gospel writers and inconsistencies – she had listened to it all; for once, he'd had her undivided attention, and this was his achievement. He had pushed her even further from him. To a hopeless distance. And now, this false statement.

'What do you need a rest for?'

'Because I do.'

Miserably he tugged at her sleeve.

'But you'll come back, won't you?' he begged. 'And what about the Poetry Society? ... That's next week, isn't it?'

'Oh, I'll miss it.' She moved away. His touch was obviously undesirable. 'I'll drop you a line,' she said.

'Or phone me. Phone me. I don't mind it that much.'

From the bottom of the steps, she turned and waved with a bright, escaper's smile. His eyes filled with tears. He stood watching as she drove to the gate, and every tree that sprang out into the glare of the headlights seemed to be shouting, 'Last time! Last time!' He knew for certain that it was. He had done her a disservice. He had shown her what a patched, fragile shell she had faith in, and she didn't love him for it. He had miscalculated, thinking her stronger ... Rubbish. He had neither thought nor cared. What he had done had been solely for his own comfort. He had only himself to blame.

I meant to tell you, I'll be away for a while ...

As he stood in the porch looking after her, a queasy, fluttery sensation rose in the pit of his stomach. Disaster. An evil-minded old fool. Upsetting people.

Not that he had meant any harm. Wouldn't Moira see that?

Returning to the library, he stared with dismay at the books that lay scattered about over his desk and the chairs. He could only just find the energy to put them back on the shelves. It took a long time, and when he had finished, he sat, faint and appalled, wishing the evening over again. He would drink large tumblers of whisky – and to hell with the doctor. He would ask her to play the piano, sing 'Greensleeves', 'Camptown Races' ... But wishing never solved anything. Then he longed to forget the evening, to fall asleep, or at least to get away from the subtle reproach of her perfume and the presence of her half-full gin glass that stood on the little table, glinting at him. In the end, he broke a rule, and went upstairs early.

Not yet half past two. He wasted all the time he could, standing in front of the bathroom mirror, noting how ridiculous he looked, with his pink cheeks and clamorous toupee, his blood-shot eyes.

Ugly. He passed judgment.

He hurried down the passage to his bedroom; but once he had his clothes off, instead of promptly pulling on his pyjamas, wearing nothing but his dressing gown he went back to the bathroom and the mirror. Naked, he confronted his reflection again. Another rule broken.

Suddenly he tried to imagine Moira Gelling naked. That was difficult. He hadn't seen a naked woman for more than twenty years. Come to think of it, he wasn't sure he had ever seen a women past her forties without clothes on. He thought there must be similarities, the same flabbiness of the belly, and soft folds near the armpits, the same creasing of the thighs, nests of dark blue veins, and brown flecks on the skin.

Lawson's breath came and went, whistling. Faintly he heard it. Just below his left hip, he could see a mole – a new one. Instability, corruption, that was what a mirror told him, and, really, he apologised. It was true, he was disgusting.

He went back to his bedroom, and as he pulled on his pyjamas, he tried to keep his hands from touching any part of his unclothed body.

Then he lay flat on his back with his eyes wide open.

I'm not upset, he told himself.

Of course not. But he found his bed had maliciously swollen. It had always been substantial, but tonight – it was huge. He probably looked like a dwarf in it ... Laughable. If he ever had to have visitors up ... but he wouldn't. Slowly, he stretched his legs apart, and felt for the bed's edges, the comforting walls made by the tucked-in blankets. Nothing. Stranded. In a cold desert. After a while, he carefully closed his legs again, and laid his hands over his genitals, like a napkin.

Throughout the week, the weather grew colder. Every night, a hard frost. He had the central heating turned up, until movement through the rooms felt like burrowing through flock or duck-down – not just warm and cosy, but suffocating. He needed all this heat. He shivered at the very thought of losing it, even though it gave him trouble with his breathing, and sometimes, when she came in with her tin of polish or a meal tray, the housekeeper found him red-faced, in a sweat. Then she would say cheerily, 'You must be ill again. It isn't natural, heat like this!' – a hint which he understood too well, and once, in an unlucky moment, he told her, 'You'll call that doctor again over my dead body!'

'I dare say I will. Very likely, the way you're going!'

Oh, she had loved it.

He refused to encourage her. Every other day, he forced himself to go out: grim promenades along the road, the air sinking teeth into his cheeks with all the vigour of a mad dog. Mostly on these walks he thought of nothing, but when he did contrive to keep alert, for much of the time he looked at trees. Every year, it was the same. Once their leaves were off, he rediscovered skeletons, breaking out of the ground, sky-aspiring. A doomsday image. It generally took a month or more to push down in his mind again, deep enough not to think about.

Nor were the trees the only things that worried him. Occasionally he would stop by the meadow wall and peer over at the unscrupulous-looking birds that liked to perch in the gorse bushes. They were large and black. He wondered what they were waiting for.

And in the garden, he sometimes encountered Briggs, or Biggs: too late now to ask the fellow which, and as for asking the housekeeper – never. At the start, Lawson had done his best to solve this mystery by poring over the gardener's references, but those had all been scrawled so impatiently or dismissively that the name had looked like Briggs on some and Biggs on others. He worried about it. He found that he couldn't ignore the man – not without knowing what his name was – and it made him break with precedent. Whenever he saw the gardener, he felt obliged to stop.

'Getting colder ...' He would stamp his feet on the gravel, or rub his gloved hands together. 'Not too bright today, is it?'

Briggs, or Biggs, would go on working, his own hands – brown and strong – gripping the throat of a weed, or his foot on a spade, pushing it into the earth.

'You're right there,' he would say. Or, 'True enough! We're getting into winter now ...' and his comments sounded rich with satisfaction. He was still working in his shirt-sleeves, despite the white vapour that his breath made, and as he spoke, he would glance up at the bare trees and overcast sky appreciatively.

Then Lawson would grunt and walk away. The man was rude, stupid too. Not much hope of communicating. Quite apart from the question of his name, there were other matters that Lawson still hadn't raised with him and knew he should – the trespassers, for one: something ought to be done to keep those boys out – but when he actually faced the gardener, he always kept to commonplaces. He sensed that this Briggs–Biggs wouldn't understand, that he would be totally out of sympathy with any talk of an owner's right to exclusive use of his garden, and, without knowing why exactly, he didn't want the man against him. Particularly not now, not after his last, disastrous evening with Moira. If anything, he felt a need to be extra cautious. It was as though, if Briggs–Biggs turned against him, he could be sure that whatever tolerance there had been of him in

140

the universe – it had all been withdrawn, lost along with Moira's.

On the eighth day after her visit, it snowed. Not much: only the kind of powder that might fall from a stone splitting open; and on that day, the Poetry Society met at the Hydro. Lawson didn't go. He couldn't, in case he found Moira there – proof beyond the last merciful doubt that she had lied to him. And in any case, what earthly reason had he for going, if not in the hope of seeing her? They could keep their poetry. The whole afternoon he sat huddled at his desk, weighed down by his decision.

In the evening, the housekeeper brought him a slice of delicious egg and tomato flan, the best he had tasted for years, followed by a large apple dumpling, piping hot and topped with fresh cream.

'Why the treats?' he asked suspiciously.

'What treats?'

But somehow, obviously, she knew. It was that Sibylline part of her. He had breathed not a word about Societies or meetings, but that there was a Society and a meeting and he chose not to go – these were facts she had plucked from the wind or the pattern of leaves on the back doorstep. And she approved.

She made that clear. For the next few days, she was – in her way – cheerful and industrious. While he watched by the window for Moira Gelling's car, or sat dozing with a book, distantly aware of whalesongs in his stomach, she 'did a spot of cleaning' – a brisk shampooing of carpets and washing out of cupboards that reminded Lawson of something he had read about the territorial instinct. Setting her mark on things. He suffered it. He couldn't do anything else.

He moved through the days numb and well-fed, dimly hoping for surprises – a letter or a phone call. But every night his thoughts sharpened. Complex yet distinct thoughts – contradictions, their edges scratching against each other; they were like a heap of pendants from a dismantled chandelier, and he would sit in his armchair by the fireplace, trying to sort them into order.

Moira was a shallow, callous women, he would tell himself, who enjoyed inflicting pain, and she knew that it was best done by seeming easily injured. She calculated everything.

No, she was a true coward. She never allowed herself to see

141

how she behaved. She just snatched what she wanted – what she thought she wanted – insisting people tell their secrets, then shrinking back, as much as to say, 'What are you trying to do? I don't want awkward truths and feelings . . .'

But she did. Feelings, at least. Those were a kind of drug to her. And what did *she* care if the price he paid for giving them was sky-high?

Not that she was heartless . . . That night, when he had splashed her with the gin and grabbed her hand – how quickly she had forgiven him. The way she had smiled and said, 'It's all right, Arnold.'

So much friendship.

Or pity. Was that it? Bothering to visit, only because she saw in him an old bore who had no one else to harangue? Dear God, no . . . Yes, possibly. And now she was angry.

He tortured himself. He gave her eleven days, by a super-human effort made it twelve. Then he acted.

Halfway through the afternoon, Lawson stood in the hall and sniffed, testing the air that came from the passage. Nothing yet. Hurrying to the telephone table, he clawed up the fat, heavy directory, and fled with it back to the library.

For the next part, he took special care, placing a ruler across the page to prevent a mistake, and then he checked and double-checked the figures, copying them out in slow, trembling curves on to a page from a note pad. Back to the hall. He sniffed again, and this time, from the direction of the kitchen came the aroma of buttered toast. Good. The house-keeper's tea. He approached the telephone.

3581   9 . . . His hand slipped; he started again.

3581 . . . 9585 . . .

He stood breathing into the mouthpiece; and now the process was under way, and a faint 'burr-burr' inside the phone – desperately faint – warned him his actions were taken seriously, Lawson hoped that no one would answer. And that he would hear.

What if he missed the first 'hello' and whoever it was hung up? What then?

Inevitably, he began to wheeze.

'– 9585 . . . Hello?'

'Hello!' He volleyed the word back.

'Yes?'

A woman's voice, but not hers. Probably some domestic. Lawson's cheeks went hot. Couldn't she say who she was, the fool?

'Who's that?' he hissed. 'Isn't that the Gellings? ... Mrs Moira Gelling?'

Hunched low over the table, terrified of any sound escaping down the passage, as far as the teapot and the buttered toast.

'Yes?'

'That's not you, Moira, is it?'

Then the woman gabbled something – and he made out not a syllable. Lawson felt the first waves of panic.

'What? Speak more clearly, can't you?'

'... not back yet. Another three days.' The woman sounded suddenly peeved, but that was the way of domestics. Lawson squeezed the receiver hard, as if trying to force the last fugitive whisper out of it, to boost the volume. Nothing helped. He lost a number of words. '... says the rest has done some good,' the woman said. 'She seems a little better ...'

'Ah.'

Not back yet. A rest. So what she had told him was true. He calmed down. His shoulders relaxed, and looking up, he saw that the hall had turned bright and spacious round him, full of serene pools of daylight, and that both the skirting board and the picture rail stood out clean and helpful, setting him in a decent framework. A blur had lifted from the afternoon.

'What?' he said. 'What was that?'

'Did you want to leave a message?'

'Wait a minute ...'

Tell her I phoned to apologise ... No, not that. Not to a stranger. *Just tell her I phoned.* Would she know that expressed contrition?

Lawson decided.

'Yes,' he said. 'You might tell her ... Kindly give her ...'

'Yes?'

But he was lost. Prompted by some obscure instinct, he had glanced round over his shoulder, and there, in the shadows of the passage stood the housekeeper, watching him.

143

'No! No message!' he croaked, and banged down the receiver.

On cue, she came forward. 'I'd have done that, if you'd asked!' she said. 'I could see you were having trouble!'

Witch. Sneak. Ruining everything. Horrible and everywhere! He edged away. He gasped, 'I'm not entirely helpless, you know!'

Her bitter face looked at him. He scuttled into the library.

And his day was just beginning.

The trouble was, of course, Moira Gelling could still be lying. He was woefully quick to realise that.

'If anyone phones who sounds like a deaf old man, for heaven's sake tell him ...'

Oh yes, that was plausible, and he thought about it for hours – a tedious, nagging suspicion that seemed an extremely poor reward for his heroics on the telephone. He should have earned some peace of mind, and here he was, depriving himself of the benefits.

He struggled not to be cheated. His own worst enemy, he scolded. And what more could he do? Damn it, there was call for a bit of optimism.

After supper, he was resolute. A good read. Take his mind off things ... He chose his book at random. *The History of Henry Esmond*. Thackeray again, he noted – but what about it? Nothing but coincidence.

Preface ...

His watch said half past one. Four and a half more hours to get through. Simple enough.

The estate of Castlewood, in Virginia, which was given to our ancestors by King Charles the First, as some return for the sacrifices made in His Majesty's cause by the Esmond family ...

Lawson read gratefully: he crept down into the printed words and hid, a runaway in the long grass. Not much chance of it happening, but if he ever met up with God, whatever he might jibe about, he would give thanks for this – the mercy of print, the escape it offered. A bounty far superior to those toxic gifts of alcohol or tranquillisers, or, so far as he remembered it, the teasing relief of sex.

If they say she's away, she's away ...

Emerging briefly to shift his legs and ease a cramp, he found his mood was already lightening. The fact of escape – that it was possible – soothed him, and now his mind seemed more disposed to trust a little. As to what he should do once Moira Gelling was home again – he would have to think, but not tonight. Tonight, he meant to forget his troubles and all the evening's batch of irritations – a smear of something on his sleeve, oddly acquired from his lunch tray, the wing-flapping motions in his chest, and the animal life in his left hand: warm and restless, some time since the afternoon, this hand had developed a mischievous habit of slipping down over his stomach to lie with a faint, nuzzling pressure below the zip of his trousers. It offended him, but ... well, he would ignore it.

There was a German officer of Webb's with whom we used to joke, and of whom a story (whereof I myself was the author) was got to be believed in the army ...

Creeping through the book to bed; what else?

Something –

Lawson held his breath. Chapter 6, page 44. Doing well. His eyes had been on the print. Excellent concentration – so what was that? It had flashed across the room in front of him, an indeterminate something, a ripple of astonishing speed coming from the fireplace. Heading, he sensed, for the door.

Slowly he turned and looked.

Nothing. Naturally. And the door was firmly shut. Now what? Another bout of indigestion? His heart was thumping ... But tonight there was no pain, there were none of his usual heartburn symptoms; what he felt was new, and made him ice-cold: a thing the lamps were supposed to keep at bay. A watcher in the room.

A presence.

Rubbish.

He took a deep breath, still looking at the door. Shut. Then – back towards the fireplace. Black, empty. Just a draught. He should have had the chimney blocked, and a firescreen would be useful. Bad nerves. Too much reading ... his own fault, since he never wore his spectacles. Tiredness, making his eyes jump ...

He raised the Thackeray again, and found his place. Back, back to the print ...

Incredibly, his eyes defied him. They swivelled to the door; they were straining in their sockets.

Was he being watched? Who by? And how? Through the keyhole?

His eyes ached.

Paranoia, he diagnosed. *I've been like this all day, but I'm not giving in to it!*

He clutched the book. His eyes continued to scan the door, and when they found what they were looking for, he gave a little grunt of fright. Peering out of the wood from beneath the gloss of the varnish, he could see a face – undeniably, a face – watching him. Narrow slits for eyes, and a long wispy beard that flowed down to the doorknob.

A living shape come from nowhere, without warning.

Lawson stared, and as he did so, gradually his strange intruder worked free, detaching itself from the wood, emerging through the varnish, until it floated clear of the door altogether; and then it began to drift towards him.

Pranks of the old fool ... Most ingenious. He wheezed gently. Nothing to get in a state about. This was a time to be rational ...

He got to his feet. The face watched. Its uneven lips smiled, and its eyes, although they remained fixed, promised that whichever way he moved, they could watch him.

He took a step forwards. And another. Cautiously, he put his hand in his pocket, and felt for his inhaler.

Another step.

The face hovered. Through it, he could see the door ... and he knew what must be done. He must call this ghoul's bluff. He must walk right through it if he had to ...

But what if it swooped at him like a bat? Lawson shook. These things had no rules. They came from outside rules, from the hiccup moments of the universe, when logic stopped, and there was no telling ...

146

Be rational!

One more step. He took it with a short, heavy thrust of his body, as if the air were pushing against him, and, to his joy, the face drifted back a fraction.

There! You see!

Another step: back it went ahead of him. He bullied it to the door, and all the time it smiled, as though it were beckoning.

Damned illusion . . .

A trick of cracks and polish. He forced it into the wood. Every step helped to disperse it, until finally, up against the actual varnish of the door, he saw that there was no face, although the lines and wrinkles that had made it – those were there: he could trace them one by one in the wood.

You see?

Sweating with relief, he ran his hands across the smooth mahogany. A triumph for the powers of reason! A door was just a door, nothing but a slab of wood on hinges, by means of which he could come and go exactly as he wanted – a fact he demonstrated by walking out into the hall; and there he stood, enjoying the vulgar brightness of the hall lights, and consolidating his victory. That old fool in his skull would have to think again: Arnold Lawson didn't scare so easily! How on guard he was! Finely tuned! For instance, he could tell that if it wasn't already raining, it soon would be. His hearing might be less than wonderful, but he could sense the dampness, and standing there in the hall, he could sense, too, the sanity of his house, how solid it was, and prosaic. Absolutely trustworthy.

With a smile, he turned to go back to the library – and just then, something shot past.

It brushed against his cheek, so that he flinched. He lost a breath. Transparent, shapeless, he almost saw it, vanishing into the sitting-room, and he gaped after it.

So we haven't finished yet! he told himself. *And now my asthma's playing up . . .*

The sitting-room door was open, and inside, the darkness had a shallow, tenuous quality, as if the slightest movement would be likely to disturb it, any moth or fly, and it seemed to Lawson as he watched that this darkness very delicately rippled.

Have to see this through . . .

The old fool had to be taught that he couldn't be intimidated. Lawson frowned. His heartbeat seemed to have doubled, and he discovered that he was shaking again.

What had touched him?

Imagination ... He gave the word his full scorn.

Natural explanations ... A small fly, perhaps, or one of his own eyelashes ...

Quick march to the sitting-room. He struck out boldly, and when he got there, he thrust his arm round the door-frame, reaching for the light switch. Then he peered in.

Piano ... vases ... cabinets ...

Suddenly he gripped the doorknob.

Across the room, near the piano, the largest of his cabinets ... in the central strip of wood between its glass panels: another face. And this time, it was unequivocally evil. What he had seen in the library was amateur stuff compared to this, a trial run. Here – here was the real face.

The old fool in his skull, this time he had surpassed himself.

A long, scalpless head, thinning into nothing. Downward slanting eyes that were formed, he knew, by wax-yellow knots in the wood – weak eyes, strangely opaque, but watchful. Taut cheeks, showing cracks round a mouth that was much too thin, much too wide, and smiling, Lawson might have thought, pathetically – but for the teeth. These were hardly visible, and they were all the more conspicuous because of it. They were long and narrow, some of them darker than others, and – those he could see – all tapered to sharp points. They effectively quelled any suggestion of innocence, before it was made. The whole face looked ravenous.

And imminent – almost in the room – as though it concealed an extraordinary store of energy that might break loose, at any moment.

'Imagination,' muttered Lawson.

Tentatively, he began to move.

It had seemed a healthy thing to do, speaking out his thought like that, a way to prompt his common sense, but immediately he wished he hadn't risked it. The word slithered through the room with unnatural weight, like oil.

Got to get this over with ...

The face watched. It watched, but it stayed where it was.

148

Well and good ...

He worked towards it like a hunter. One step and he paused, studying its eyes, trying to read some hint of its intentions: did it mean to come bursting out towards him, or to fade back, into the wood?

It chose to do neither; until at last his paunch was a bare six inches from the cabinet. The face held. It leered at his belly.

Varnish stains, said Lawson, but he put no voice in the words.

The face held. Varnish stains or anything else – he knew it now: this was the kind of illusion that couldn't be broken down. Once seen, it wouldn't be un-seen. A twist in the wood, a peculiar slant of the shadows, a flaw in the mind – just one more freak combination, but add bad luck, and what did you have? Not the passing scare that it should have been, but a chilling, permanent outlet for the secret malice in things. Oh yes. Lawson peeped down fearfully. The face was only a trick, of course, but it didn't help to know that. In fact, it made it worse. Why? he wondered.

He had no idea, he didn't want ideas. He hurried back to the library and succumbed to an overwhelming impulse. He rang the bell.

Being alone was terrible.

When the housekeeper came, wrapped in a monastic camel dressing gown, her feet in slippers with blue fluff round the tops, he asked for paracetamol.

She made a great show of yawning.

'Haven't you any of your own?' she asked.

'No.'

She didn't believe him, obviously. Despite her squinting eyes and deep yawns, all at once she looked incredibly wide awake. She would go and check in his bathroom cupboard, and there she would find a full bottle. Well, it couldn't be helped. Lawson sat back weakly, offering smiles. For once, he was glad to see her. Her blockish lack of sympathy, and that hard, inquisitive look which she couldn't quite keep out of her eyes – they were more than welcome; and he wished she didn't have to leave the room again to fetch the paracetamol.

Mercifully, she was quick. Only a couple of minutes passed

before she was back with two white pills on the palm of one hand, and a glass of water in the other.

'Been reading too much, haven't you?'

'Yes ... yes ... eye strain ...'

He gulped the pills down.

'I'm not surprised. Why don't you wear your glasses more?'

Arms folded, she stood in front of him, banal, resentful, marvellously devoid of any imagination, and at the thought of her going upstairs again and sinking back into sleep, Lawson felt desperate. Too much night left. There might be other tricks in store for him. He had to stop her somehow ... He smiled, swallowing the water, nodding gratefully.

'You don't look very good to me,' she said. 'Would you like a cup of cocoa?'

'Oh ...' He blinked, and his voice wavered. 'That would ... Now that you're up ...'

Her mouth twisted. 'A nice hot drink,' she said. 'And if you don't mind – after all, you've got me out of bed, haven't you? – I think I'll have one with you, in here ... I'm not going to freeze in the kitchen, and I don't suppose you've ever thought about it, but that back room takes a long time heating ... So you can't say no, can you?'

Lawson shook his head.

Eleven

Moira's Christmas card – a plump, Technicolor robin – took him by surprise. It arrived in the week following his fright about the faces.

Delivery rounds were taking longer as the Christmas mail built up, and so he was already downstairs, breaking the shell on a boiled egg, when the postman went past the library windows to shove his various offerings through the slit in the front door.

Lawson immediately abandoned his breakfast and went to retrieve them. It was a novelty, picking up these slightly damp envelopes in the knowledge that the housekeeper hadn't touched them. There was one small envelope for her, written in a hand which he had come to associate with church-going spinsters – ornate, but stiff and cramped – and there were two large envelopes for himself. One of these had been forwarded from the other place, and one had been posted locally.

He recognised Moira's writing with a twinge of fear. The dead-white, expensive envelope felt strangely impersonal, and it was sealed. Dropping the card for the housekeeper back on the mat, he carried his own two into the library, and opened the other one first.

A solemn little Renaissance madonna, with an obese infant on her knees.

The signature was illegible – all too plainly a painstaking effort by someone barely strong enough to hold a pen – but printed in the lower left hand corner was a name, and a Manchester address.

Old Arkwright. Lawson moaned in protest. Shrewdest business rival back in the 'thirties, Arkwright. A man who had put one over on him almost as often – maybe just as often – as he had put one over on Arkwright. Almost an equal. After a day spent zealously trying to sabotage one another's schemes, it had been nothing to sit down together at some civil function, or to leer at each other across a dinner table. Arkwright had been almost a friend. But now Lawson seldom thought of him. Whenever he got out his photographs, he gave the man no more than a cursory glance. Only at Christmas they signalled to each other, '*I'm* still alive ... what about you?' Arkwright always came up with the bawdiest, most irreverent card on the market, and Lawson would send back one of his specially designed, atheistic Yuletide greetings. Fair exchange.

But this year ... A signature that looked like something from an ancient manuscript, and a pale-lipped prude of a madonna? Arkwright must be cracking up! Lawson turned the card over. He turned it upside down and right way up again. He examined every part of it, the Tuscan landscape of the painting, the scroll lettering of the season's compliments, the printer's name on the back. There had to be a hidden joke in it somewhere, a penned-in cartoon, or some obscenity ... but he couldn't find one.

Well, of course not. There was something else on his mind.

The second envelope. Slicing it with his paperknife, he snatched the card and laid it flat on his desk, wide open. Four sprawling lines of ink. He read them through twice.

I've been away, as you know, and now the usual Christmas rush. Noel, noel! Why don't you come to dinner with us on the 25th? About seven. We would love to have you.
Moira

Christmas at Williston ... He turned to the glossy robin on the front and studied the detail of its feet, its pin-sharp eyes. With her, but not with her. With her family.

And she won't be coming here, he thought. *Not before then. That's what she's saying.*

Still, an invitation ... Did that mean he was forgiven? Or was this some subtle form of revenge?

Lawson scowled at the robin. There was something downright nasty about it. The log on which it was standing wellnigh dwarfed the holly bush that was only a couple of footprints away through the snow, but the robin, swelling out a muscular chest of remarkable proportions, wellnigh dwarfed the log ... These Christmas card conventions ... Was a giant-sized robin fun? Join the festive spirit, or else!

It was tempting to see in Moira Gelling's invitation the same dubious qualities, and quickly he reminded himself that this was a hectic time for women: they always fussed about Christmas; no doubt she considered herself too busy to come to Woodbourn ... And then there was another factor: friends, her small-town friends, who might have been saying, *'Don't you think you go there rather often? People will talk, you know.'*

'What? He's a very old man.'

'Oh, they're never too old!'

Yes, and then, too, he reasoned, after the coldness with which she had left him last time, possibly she felt awkward about coming back. An invitation like this gave her a chance to show goodwill on her own ground ...

Really, he supposed he should be pleased. He *was* pleased – but that didn't stop him worrying.

We would love to have you ... He hated that, her use of the plural. Withdrawing into the security of the fold. But the invitation itself must have been her own idea ... Who was there to force her into it? Not the husband he had never met, and surely not Rowena!

Christmas. Somewhere to go for Christmas. And not just somewhere.

Arkwright's card he stood on the mantelpiece, but he locked Moira's in his desk together with the envelope. No traumas, he promised himself. Whether he was going to accept or not, this was one decision that would have to creep up on him. No more strain on the nerves. Since the faces, he had been working through his days carefully, thinking carefully. That episode had implications, and he felt ready to admit that one can only take so much.

Also, if he was honest, things were very pleasant at the moment, with the housekeeper being so affable, even if it was because she had won a rare victory. A hot drink in the middle of the night, sitting opposite him in one of his leather armchairs, talking about her life in the war, fire-fighting up in Hull and her brother in the Navy – such a triumph for her! She had broken into his stronghold, and since that night, she had been all unintrusive helpfulness. The milk was no longer tepid. His portions of ice-cream were as large as an open hand. It was as though her saints had suddenly conferred a blessing on her, and her heart had grown bountiful.

Of course, if he went to Moira's, he would lose all that. It would be gone as soon as she knew.

So he stalled. He thought about the invitation most of the time, but never confused thinking with deciding. He advised himself not to go. Moira had asked him out of charity. But Christmas Day on his own, like last year and the year before, with the housekeeper in and out, keeping vigils at the charnel house and offering him a mince pie? Not a thrilling prospect. On the other hand, that was just the point: knowing what to expect from it ... Then he would start to wonder if Moira meant to have other guests, and was she planning to impress them by showing him off as her curio, her 'grand old eccentric'?

And there'll be turkey, he thought gloomily. *Which I can't eat.*

But the most worrying thing of all was that if he left it too long before replying, Moira might assume he wasn't interested, and fill his place with someone else.

After three days of studiously not agonising, the whole business was settled for him – and in an abrupt fashion that Lawson couldn't have contrived even if he had wanted to.

About two o'clock in the afternoon, all unlooked for, Dr Hewitt breezed in.

Lawson had been pacing round the library by way of a constitutional. He was in the mood to go out, but the long, blackish streaks of rain that he could see, smashing into the lawn and the gravel, made that out of the question. So it was round the room in slow circles, and after he got thoroughly sick of that, up and down ... He hadn't seen the car – Hewitt must have driven round the side of the house as he had on the previous occasion – and so the first Lawson knew of the visit was when the library door opened. Without a word, the housekeeper stood aside to let the doctor pass.

Hewitt, smiling like a sickle. This time, he wore no coat; and yet his green corduroy jacket didn't look wet at all, despite the fact that his hair was obviously soaked and rain-water dripped from his case on to the carpet. He must have hung up a coat in the passage, or the cloakroom. Making himself at home.

And now he banged his case on the arm of a chair, and sitting down, he pulled it round towards him, flung the lid back –

Lawson stood numb with horror.

'Well now, Mr Lawson ... I was going past the house, so I thought I'd just look in, check up on a couple of things ...'

At the door, the housekeeper smiled.

'You ... Did you do this?' croaked Lawson.

'I did not.' Calmly she straightened her overall, as anyone might who had nothing to hide. *So there you are!* said her bearing. *It's not just me. Other people can see that you need looking after!* – and as if that gave her quite enough gratification just for the moment, she turned and left.

Stupefied, Lawson had to submit to a whole new bout of blood-pressure reading, stethoscopes and questions about his bowel movements. He didn't dare refuse, or let too much of his anger show. There could be new and stronger tranquillisers, and next time, she might be put in charge of them, bringing them by the clock, and round the clock, and watching to make sure he swallowed them ... Yes, if he hadn't a mind to end up permanently doped he would have to be careful ... so what could he do?

He could only comply; and he did, although as he fluttered out of his shirt he protested, 'This is quite unnecessary ... I didn't send for you ...'

'Just want to make ab-so-lutely certain,' chanted Hewitt, and his fingers drummed professionally on the patient's chest.

Lawson suffered it. But was this to become a habit? Was he to be dropped in on whenever this boy saw fit? As if old age was a kind of fever that needed constant supervision, until – sooner or later – it reached its unpleasant little climax, and went away for good?

Yes. That's exactly how they see it!

At the thought, he forgot himself, and he grinned fiercely.

From between the prongs of his stethoscope, Hewitt gave back a quick smile, politely raising his eyebrows to ask for a share in the joke. Lawson didn't oblige.

Questions. Questions. How was the asthma? Any more palpitations? Any discomfort?

'No, no, none,' said Lawson flatly. 'No palpitations, nothing. I'm quite well, thank you.'

'Your eyes are all right?'

'Eyes?'

The doctor looked solicitous. 'I've heard', he said, 'that you're having some trouble with your eyes. A little strain.'

'You have, have you?' Lawson reddened.

'Your housekeeper happened to say something, as she was showing me in . . .'

'Well, she shouldn't have! I get a headache now and then, that's all. Because I read too much.'

'Oh?' said Hewitt soothingly, and he nodded at the room, the shelves. 'You like to read, do you?' Then, as if this imbecile comment daunted even him, he changed the subject.

The word 'improvement' was mentioned. Or rather it was offered, thought Lawson, angrily buttoning up his shirt, like a sweet at the end of an ordeal; and a minute later, the examination was over. The black case had shut, and Hewitt, jabbing down his biro into his breast-pocket, glanced at the windows, the torrents of rain.

'Well,' he said cheerily, 'I suppose I'd better get out there . . . Now aren't you glad I called, Mr Lawson? Isn't it good to know you're in the pink?'

'Can't say I was worrying . . .'

The doctor wasn't listening. He had grabbed hold of his case, he was making for the door. Lawson held his breath. Only a few more seconds, and he would be rid of the fellow . . . But it was then, when Hewitt's hand was already on the doorknob, that things went wrong: suddenly he turned back and added, 'I must say, Mr Lawson, your housekeeper's done an excellent job! Quiet living and a sensible diet . . . that's the tonic. Now you'll keep up the good work won't you? Lots of rest, and peace and quiet, eh?'

An excellent job. Oh, undoubtedly. A perfect use for her talents! Lawson felt his face distorting. Peace and quiet. Rest.

Monitored and molly-coddled ... never going anywhere, never doing anything – except, perhaps, breathing now and then ... that was what he meant, this oaf. That was his prescription ...

Hewitt's smile got on his nerves. The young man hovered by the door, apparently expecting thanks.

Easy enough, going round telling other poor buggers, 'Empty your life ... Don't cause trouble ... Have a bit of common sense, and fade away ...'

Lawson couldn't stop himself. 'It's all right for you!' he cried. 'Coming in here, telling me, "Don't do this and don't do that! ... Just sit quiet ..." I'm not a bloody puppet, you know! Just you wait till you get to my age ... Then you'll see.'

He stopped. The outburst sounded hysterical, and something white flashed through his mind – a warning: the image of a prescription pad. As it was, the doctor's round face grew prim, and he said coldly, 'When I'm your age, Mr Lawson, I'll be quite happy to put my feet up! I'll feel I've earned the rest!' – which was easy to interpret.

What do you think you're griping about? You're lucky to be alive!

That was the message.

And that settled it. The same afternoon, Lawson scribbled on one of his Yuletide greetings cards: 'Delighted to come on the 25th. See you then.' And towards evening, when the rain let up, he splashed out through the puddles to post it. He also had the housekeeper order a car for the following day. This she did without comment. Every year, he went out just before Christmas to buy a present for her, so she couldn't very well say anything. All the same, he fancied he saw a glint in her eyes – suspicion, and a veto.

To hell with her! he encouraged himself. *It's my life ...*

Commendably punctual at 2.30 the next day, a cream-coloured Mercedes drew up round the back, and Lawson issued forth in all his winter regalia: heavy coat, best hat, gloves, a cashmere scarf. It was a dull day, bitingly cold but dry, which was something to be grateful for, and waiting for him by the car, Lawson found a second mercy: Ruddy-cheeks – the long-suffering individual of his first outing from Woodbourn. That was something. The afternoon was likely to be bad enough, he thought, without that dandy in tight trousers rushing him off his feet, or all the strain of a new man ... He had no idea what he ought to buy for the Gellings, but he had made up his mind that he should take a separate gift for each of them, which meant three difficult decisions, and he anticipated much traumatic toing and froing between the High Street and the shopping precinct. Ruddy-cheeks was just the man for that. There was a steadiness – a relative one, of course – about this older chauffeur, and because the man had seen his tetchy side already in that business with the umbrella, Lawson felt all the more comfortable with him.

In fact, considering the weather and the chauffeur, as they started down the drive he began to hope that he was wrong about this shopping trip. Maybe it would all go smoothly ...

But the town, once he got there, soon put him right on that score.

Crowds. Festoons of tinsel in the shop windows. Plastic reindeer strung like beads on wires across the High Street ... and the Salvation Army, blaring 'Once in Royal David's City' outside Marks & Spencer's. Irritations, clutter, they made the simplest thinking difficult, let alone the subtleties required to choose offerings for the Gellings.

At first, the possibilities seemed legion, especially for Moira. Brooches, writing paper, soap, books ... No. Not books. He wanted to show her he had taste in other things besides books ...

He very nearly bought her a wine-red headscarf. A delicate silk, and just the colour, he imagined, to highlight that pale skin of hers, and her dark eyebrows, but then he suddenly remembered her hair, with its strident purple rinse. Impossible. What about a different colour? No. His heart was set on the red, and if he couldn't take that, he wouldn't take any. Besides, a scarf was rather commonplace ... And then he decided that writing paper and soap were also commonplace, whilst to give a woman jewellery in front of her husband might be considered provocative. Perhaps the answer was perfume ...

But everywhere he went, serving behind the cosmetics counters stood young girls with perfect faces, looking treacherous and arrogant. He couldn't approach any of those. A man in his eighties buying perfume? He could almost hear their giggles ... the joke of the afternoon. And he had to admit that bending over the wrist of one of those girls to sniff the tester ... yes ... definitely ... he would look suspect. So what could he do? He wasn't going to buy just anything – grabbing whatever came to hand by some well-known manufacturer, neatly boxed and Cellophaned, and smelling, for all he knew, like high-brow turpentine.

Round the stores he struggled, gasping in his heavy overcoat, the worthy Ruddy-cheeks at his side, acting as a shield against the other shoppers – women mostly: to Lawson's eyes, as huge and swift as dinosaurs, prowling about, snatching at price tags.

'Maybe the lady would like a nice piece of china?' suggested Ruddy-cheeks, as they pushed their way out of the third and last department store in the High Street.

'No ... no ... Too old-fashioned. Very Victorian ...'

The chauffeur gave him a strange look, which Lawson saw, and although he didn't say anything, he was offended. He expected better of Ruddy-cheeks. It wasn't a chauffeur's job, observing ironies. Damn it all, the man was paid to drive a car and carry his parcels for him, not to smirk ... It was one annoyance too many, and emerging into the cold, Lawson took a couple of steps then stopped abruptly. Exasperated, indignant, he had to vent his feelings somehow; and raising his head clear of his collar, he blinked round, his chin trembling.

'P-pagans!' he sputtered, grimacing at the street lights. How he hated everything. Not that he cared a fig about its being pagan, but the mindlessness of everything ... this bric-à-brac ... all these stupid people ...

It was growing dark. The suspended reindeer had lit up in their entrails. Their red noses shone belligerently, and lines of hard white light showed along the join beneath their bellies. Down the street, the band was blasting 'We Three Kings' to the accompaniment of several moneyboxes, crashing up and down in unison – he could hear those all right, the moneyboxes, despite the other racket. And he could see, across the backs of the crawling cars, on the other side of the street, a man in a brown work-coat doing a brisk trade, thank you, with his Christmas trees – miserable, half-fledged specimens propped up outside a butcher's shop, their lower branches sticking out at dislocated angles, and their thin tops seeming almost to touch the feet of the naked turkeys that hung by their necks in the window.

'Pagans! Philistines!' Lawson raised a fist, and a pale, dumpy woman in one of the cars that was passing, opened her mouth at him.

'Perhaps we should go back to the precinct, sir?'

Ruddy-cheeks sounded anxious. Why? What did it matter to him whether the presents were bought or not? Lawson turned to glare at the man's attentive face, and it occurred to him: *He doesn't want another afternoon like this one. Not with me, he doesn't!*

His glare provoked another burst of helpfulness.

'Maybe we should try the smaller shops, sir. We've only got an hour before ...'

'*Will* you be quiet?'

Lawson broke away, and plunged back into the store they had just left.

Minutes before the shops closed, things were bought. A reasonably cheap fountain pen for the girl, a hideous onyx paperweight for the husband he had never met, and – in desperation – a lead crystal vase, for Moira. The vase, cold and multi-faceted, wasn't right for his purpose, but it was expensive, and he would give a book with it, one from his own library. Burns, perhaps. He had a quaint Edwardian edition, with illustrations.

He had also bought something for his housekeeper – a neat, leather-bound diary, which was what she would be expecting. Every year he bought her one, brown or black. 'Diaries should never be gaudy, not for plain, honest living,' she had told him once, fifteen or sixteen years ago, trying to impress him, doubtless, with her modesty. Brown or black. Well, now she was stuck with them, and for next year, it would be black.

For himself, he bought nothing. The price of the vase had been very sobering, and in any case, he didn't need a treat. It was enough to have the job done. With profound relief, he loaded his last parcel on to Ruddy-cheeks, and ordered a retreat to the car.

Too late. All the shops were disgorging people at the same

time; the pavement had become a battleground of jabbing elbows, shoes coming down on heels, and everyone pushing for head-room. Soon, Lawson found he was panting; winter coats bulged above him, boxes stabbed him in the neck, and down there in the thick of it where he was, the air seemed poorly distributed, coming in a wave, and then, suddenly, nothing ... It wasn't a place to faint in. Necessity got the better of his pride, and taking a grip of the chauffeur's arm, he held on for dear life. Ruddy-cheeks was magnificent: he pretended not to notice; and in this he was greatly helped by the fact that the arm which Lawson clung to was curved like a handle anyway, for a totally different reason – under it, he was carrying the vase. But as well as that, he had the sense not to keep glancing down like a male nurse with an invalid.

Old-fashioned tact! thought Lawson, greatly surprised, and with vast approval. Coats and multitudinous objects heaved around in front of him. He was panting hard and his steps were unsteady. His fingers dug brutally into the chauffeur's sleeve, but Ruddy-cheeks didn't flinch; staring dead ahead, he advanced slowly down the High Street, and Lawson forgave him all his transgressions.

When they reached the car, he withdrew his hand with a smile.

'Thank you ...' he gasped. 'Most kind ... ' Shaking with exhaustion.

The chauffeur handled that well, too, deftly opening the car door, guiding Lawson in, and piling the goods on to the seat all in the one smooth, reassuring sequence.

'Now you wouldn't think that, would you, sir? All them people in a town the size of this one!'

Yes, Ruddy-cheeks was all right, remarkably so ...

As the Mercedes groaned into the High Street, Lawson focused on the chauffeur's cap, and wondered how he planned to spend his Christmas. Could he be persuaded to ferry an old man up to Williston and back? It was very tempting to ask, but the man's recent display of sensitivity had cast an awkward light on several other moments in the afternoon when he himself had been quite short, quite rude, in fact, and it was difficult to know how to go about things. He wouldn't give a hired man the chance to snub him.

'And you ... ' he said. 'Enjoy Christmas, do you?' The question shot out like a stiletto, straight at the chauffeur's neck.

'Me, sir?' Eyes showed in the driver's mirror. 'I do and I don't, sir ... '

Lawson grunted. The fellow was obviously playing safe – not a good sign; he was going to take some winning over.

I suppose I'd better ask his name ...

He gloomed at the thought. He disliked doing that – showing too much interest. There was no telling when it might put you at a disadvantage.

Maybe it would be simpler just to ring the car-hire firm and insist that they gave him Ruddy-cheeks. He could say, 'The man you sent me last time ... ' and never mind about the name. Dignified, and easier ... except that he would have to make the call himself. Booking a car for Christmas was one chore he could hardly entrust to the housekeeper, so there was no way out of it, unless he spoke to Ruddy-cheeks. Well, phoning wouldn't kill him ... and having decided on that, he sat back to watch the crowds. He made a study of their weaponry. Well-stuffed carrier-bags, long rolls of Christmas wrapping paper, trees of spikey tinsel, prams and fold-up pushchairs ... excellent weapons, all of them, for bashing one's neighbour, one's pagan neighbour, and clearing a little space for one's self.

He indulged in a spell of amused loathing. Now that he was out of it, the struggle on the pavements had real entertainment value – which was just as well, because, bumper to bumper in a long queue of traffic, progress down the High Street meant nudging forwards a yard or two, then stopping, nudging and stopping, and there was every chance that it would go on like that at least as far as the traffic lights. Lawson didn't mind. Warm now, and safe, he was beginning to relax. His breathing had eased, his shaking was phasing out, when, suddenly, a man with a huge pile of shopping dashed out from the pavement, trying to squeeze between the Mercedes and the bright yellow Cortina that edged along in front – and as he squeezed, one of his parcels flew from his arms like an uncaged bird, landing with a thump on the Mercedes bonnet.

The man stared. From beneath his shopping came a hand,

reaching out, while with his other hand, he tried to clamp the rest of his load to his chest ... No use ... Something spilled from one of the bags ... gloves, or socks, brilliant red and sticky-taped together, flopping down between the windscreen wipers ... He came lunging after them.

Incredible. Lawson sat taut with shock.

Blue-grey and puffy, the man's face gaped in through the windscreen with an unmistakable look of injury, as if all these cars had no right to be blocking up the High Street in the first place ... and at the sight of that, Lawson's blood pressure soared.

'Mad man!' he shrieked. 'Lunatic!'

Ruddy-cheeks was calm. The yellow Cortina had spurted forwards, but the Mercedes stayed where it was until the man had retrieved his parcel and the woollen things, and was well clear, dodging about in the oncoming traffic.

'It's a wonder more people don't get hurt!' said the chauffeur mildly.

'It's preposterous. Something should be done about it!'

'How's that, sir?'

Wary eyes could be seen again in the driver's mirror. Lawson gesticulated fiercely. What he'd had in mind was staggered closing times for shops, more and better policing, with fines for any wild pedestrian who didn't cross at the lights, but the moment he was asked his meaning changed, and he shouted, 'Scrapped! The whole damned farce! Done away with!' – and to leave no doubt that he meant Christmas, he banged the largest parcel on the seat beside him, but not hard; that vase had cost good money.

Ruddy-cheeks kept quiet. A minute or so later, he nosed the car into a side street, and not long after that, they had turned into a road that was comparatively clear. Then the chauffeur spoke with cheerfulness, apparently believing that thoughts expressed in traffic jams weren't to be taken seriously.

'Yes, but you know, sir ... Christmas ... it has its good side. It's for the kids, really, isn't it?'

'Kids!'

This, the last and most ingenuous of the afternoon's insults, was somehow also the worst. All that staggering about, agonising over presents, and not because it mattered, oh no, nothing

to do with him, just one old robot going through the motions
- but for kids.

Lawson leaned towards the chauffeur's ear.

'And what did kids ever do for me?' he cried. 'Paid my taxes
for me, have they? Fought in the wars? Why should I give a
damn about kids? Tell me that!'

But Ruddy-cheeks had learned his lesson, and sinking deep
inside some invisible protective shell, he let his passenger rage;
and when it seemed to be called for, he would laugh politely,
or punctuate the tirade with a little soothing assent:

'Never thought of that, sir . . .

'See what you mean . . .

'Yes, sir . . . '

Twelve

Not until December 21st did he tell the housekeeper, and then, only because she asked straight out: 'Would you be planning to go somewhere this Christmas?'

The cream cracker he was biting crumbled into tiny fragments.

'What do you mean?'

Moira's card still lay locked in his desk.

The housekeeper shrugged. Nothing, said her manner, could be less important – which was fair warning that she had rehearsed this scene very carefully.

'All that shopping you did ... Those parcels. Either you're going out, or having people in. One or the other. I only ask, because if you want any food bought, anything special ... '

She stopped.

Lawson's hands on the edge of the tray, trembled. He bunched them up.

'As a matter of fact ... ' he said, 'I *will* be going out on Christmas Day ... for a meal in the evening.'

He waited for the storm.

'To her? That ... Gelling's?'

'Yes.'

Silence. The other crackers had turned to chalk on the plate; he sipped his milk, and when he looked up again, there she was, actually smiling, which frightened him all the more.

'Queer, how you've changed,' she said. 'You were always harping on about a quiet life. How you wanted seclusion. Mens sano. Now it's women and societies and supper parties.'

'I didn't go to the Society.' He gazed at her. 'And she's not been here for weeks!'

'No, but you've changed, you must admit.'

Lawson didn't answer. He forced himself to appear more interested in his food than her opinions; he bit into a second cracker, but she didn't go. She walked over to the fireplace, and pulling a duster out of her pocket, began to swish it along under Arkwright's card and the other things on the mantelpiece, which didn't augur well for him. She knew he hated her in the room while he was eating, and besides, she never dusted in the evening, so this sudden burst of industry could only mean trouble.

Any minute now, she'll say something ... We're going to have a row about Moira ...

He made a point of ignoring her. He tried to concentrate on spearing a pickled onion, but at the corner of his eye he could see her elbow going, and the yellow cloth. When she had finished with the mantelpiece, she began to flap the duster at the fire-grate, bending low, full of her mean secrets and her petty outrage.

Why the devil can't she say what she wants to say ... ?

Dry cracker and onion stuck in his throat. He swallowed hard, and they went down sullenly. If she didn't break the silence soon, he would have to.

I'll simply say, 'Couldn't you do that some other time?' ... and that should start her!

He began to rally his nerve – but in another moment, she had straightened up and was stuffing the duster into her pocket again.

'By the way,' she said, 'on Christmas Day, I'll be going to church in the morning, as usual, but after that, I've decided to spend the day with a friend.'

'Oh ... ?'

'Someone who goes to the same church. A lady.' She stressed 'lady'. It was clear that she could have named some who were no such thing. 'A widow. She lives on her own ... so she's invited me.'

He fiddled with his serviette, dabbing his lips. A friend. Coming from her, the word had a quaint, deadly sound to it, like 'arsenic' ... and this was new ... not just for her sessions at the charnel house, but abandoning him for the whole day ... the whole of Christmas? He was dazed. If she had come creeping up in the quiet of an afternoon and pulled his ears or tweaked his nose, she couldn't have surprised him more.

'So that all works out quite well,' he said. 'I'll be going to the Gellings, so you can do what you like for once ... '

'Oh, I'd have gone anyway.'

She came towards him, and her face was extraordinarily neutral, as though the words she had just spoken, she hadn't spoken.

'Got everything you want? Enough cheese?'

'Yes ... thank you.'

He nodded, smiling. So the bitch had made plans, had she? When? That day when he had come back with the parcels? Or earlier? He saw now that all her recent cheerfulness and treats didn't count for anything: she might have planned this weeks before. Revenge. Punishment. Christmas Day on his own. Well, what did he care?

Go on ... get out ... As she headed for the door, he threw his will-power after her, pushing her along – but even then, there was something else.

'Oh yes ... and seeing as you're going out ... which coat will you want for Christmas?'

'Pardon?'

'Coats. Which coat? You're wearing your heavy one now, aren't you? That's what you went shopping in ... so I've sent the grey one to the cleaner's. I hope you didn't want it for the Gellings, because it won't be back before Christmas.'

'Of course I'll wear the heavy one. I always do, don't I, in winter?'

'Fine,' she said. Then, at long last, she left him to himself.

Tactics. Nasty little refinements. '*Oh, I'd have gone anyway!*' – and then to pretend that she cared about which coat he wanted!

There was a neat, orange block of cheese on the plate beside the last cracker, and now, very slowly, he began to cut it into thin slices, laying them down with the flat of his knife, one by one, like playing cards. It was delicate work ...

Suddenly, he let the knife go. He stood up, and went hurrying after her, across the hall, down the passage to her tightly cluttered sitting-room with its red bells and ribbons stuck to the mirror, its sprigs of holly everywhere, and a tinsel fir tree decked in fairylights on top of the television . . .

He burst in without ceremony.

There she stood behind an ironing-board, one of her pink, floral-printed nighties spread across it, the iron raised in her hand, and she was so cool, so collected-looking that she had obviously been waiting for him.

'Where is it?' he cried. 'If you've read it, I'll sack you! How dare you interfere with my correspondence!'

He came to a shaky standstill; he wanted to make a run at her, his fingers twitched – but what could he do?

'Where is what?' Calmly, she set the iron down dead centre in the square of asbestos, and in her face there was a peculiar contradiction, she looked both satisfied and shocked. 'Bursting in here like that!' she said. ' . . . and I wouldn't shout about sacking me, if I were you . . . at this rate, one of these days I just might take you at your word!'

'Give it me! There was a letter in that coat! I meant to tear it up . . . How dare you keep it?'

Her mouth fell in a hard crescent. She picked up the iron again. 'Why can't you ask like other people?'

'I know the things you do . . . poking your nose in . . . Give it me!'

'Oh, yes? . . . And what if I can't give it you?' she said coldly.

'What? Where is it? If you've read it, you're a thief! That's illegal!'

'You're getting yourself into a state.'

'Bitch!'

'No Christmas parties for you, if you carry on like this! We'll have you back on the tranquillisers. And what would I want, reading your letters? All I did was read the address. I suppose I can do that, can't I? It was stamped. I thought you'd forgotten to post it.'

'You . . . you evil woman! You stupid, interfering bitch!'

'Now stop that!'

Banging down the iron again, she came stepping over the flex. Lawson didn't move quickly enough: her hand folded round his arm, her grip tightened. Then she marched him out of the room and back along the passage. He resisted weakly. Close up like this, she smelt of bleach and cheap scent – lilies of the valley – an indescribably vile combination, forcing him to turn his head away while all the time he made his small bid to escape, to pull clear, wincing for his bruised arm.

His letter to the *Herald* ... damned nuisance ... dangerous nonsense ... should have dealt with it months ago ... Gone. Posted. His loud squeal to be left alone. Every man is entitled to his privacy ... What if they decided to print it? Out of spite? That was perfectly possible, he hadn't been kind about journalists ... They might put it in the next day's paper! How could he face the Gellings, walking in with his parcels, an old man out to dinner, smiling at a room full of people – knowing that the paper must be hidden somewhere, tucked away behind the sofa, with his letter and a headline: *Woodbourn Recluse Begs to be Left Alone* ... ?

Into the library, marching him up to a chair: only then did she let go.

'Now sit down!'

He collapsed back, helpless.

The housekeeper stood over him, and he saw with dismay that her mood had changed. Somewhere between her ironing-board and the library, she had lost her satisfaction in proceedings; now she was all cold anger: ice-still with fury, and strangely taller than usual. A slight thrill of fear ran through him. Those big hands of hers, capable of anything ... He waited silently; and when she spoke, her voice had an extra sharpness to it, straight from the heart.

'I just want to say', she said, 'that I'm sick and tired of being called names! You've no right. I do my best for you, and it's never thanks. It's insult after insult ... I've had about as much as I can take ... '

He breathed painfully.

'You didn't really post it, did you?'

'Did I say I did?'

She brought it out of her overall, white and decently stuck down, the address in his boldest handwriting.

'I wasn't going to mention it. When the coat came back, I was going to put it back in the pocket. Here.'

Meekly he took it. The envelope steamed open over the kettle and glued together again? Never mind. Never mind.

'You had no right to talk to me like that!' she said.

On Christmas morning, when he came downstairs she had

already gone, and a breakfast tray had been left for him on the library desk: two buttered wholemeal rolls, a jar of honey, orange juice and a Thermos flask of coffee. Propped up against the honey jar was a small box, only slightly larger than a matchbox, wrapped in scarlet paper – he had expected something of the sort; but round his plate was something that he hadn't expected: ivy. A thin, spiky circlet of it. He stared at that. It was years since she had imposed her Christmas trimmings on him, so why now? And, ivy ... Well, it would be. No doubt that was her instinctive choice where he was concerned, so he wasn't going to look for hidden meanings in it. But after all these years, why bother? Now and then she would do these occult things, breaking out of her habits for reasons that were never entirely clear to him. It was disconcerting. He picked up the box and rattled it. Maybe she was in the mood to give him a couple of nail-clippings, or a dead beetle ...

But when he tore the paper off and lifted the lid, it was a tie pin. A silver-plated yacht, its sails filled in with yellow enamel, cruising along on a wavy line of blue. Grotesquely commonplace, like all her presents.

As for the ivy ... With great caution, he drew it out from under the rim of the plate and coiled it into the wastepaper basket. Then he threw the piece of wrapping paper in on top, and went to wash his hands.

When he came back, he sat in his chair and did nothing. The truth was that he didn't really feel like breakfast. For the past few days, he had been sleeping badly – more so than usual; he felt queasy; his nerves seemed to twitter like small birds, and it was all the housekeeper's fault. That fracas about the letter hadn't been forgiven easily – if it was forgiven. It had next to nothing to do, of course, with anything he might have said: whatever names he might have called her – and they weren't so very terrible – she had heard far worse in the past, but this time, she had gathered them up and hugged them to her, not because she cared about the names, presumably, but because of the Gellings.

It had made things very difficult. For two days, she had gone around tight-lipped, speaking to him only when she absolutely had to, and then, in hard, cold monosyllables. There had been stodgy food again, and all the lights turned out in the hall when she went to bed. She had done her best to make him jumpy, and play havoc with his digestion – but he hadn't complained. He had submitted. He had made a point of thanking her for everything. He had offered smiles in fair exchange for meal trays, he had cheerfully ignored her silences and made hopeful little comments on the weather and so on. It had been a dreadful strain, the whole business, bringing on palpitations, stomach pains – but in the end, his remarkable restraint had paid off. Late on the 23rd, for no apparent reason, she had changed. There had been egg and cress sandwiches for supper, and a slice of strawberry cheesecake; and the next day, Christmas Eve, apart from being a touch more martyred than she had been lately, which was understandable, she had seemed to be back to normal, her great displeasure about the Gellings wrapped round her like a dismal vapour which she stoically pretended wasn't there; and he had thought to himself:

Hostilities postponed. This is Goodwill at Christmas, as decreed by the charnel house!

Was that the meaning of the ivy? A seasonal truce?

Well, he would be a fool to worry about it ... she had upset him quite enough already. Thanks to the housekeeper, he was not the calm and well-ordered being that he had planned to be for Christmas. During those two days, she had made the house so oppressive that when he wasn't actually trying to placate her, he had done what he could to escape, focusing his thoughts on the very thing that had caused the trouble in the first place, a thing he was dreading – or had been: Christmas dinner at the Gellings. After he had given a smile for the cold toast or the solid bread-and-butter pudding that she slammed down in front of him, he had allowed himself to spend several hours imagining every detail of his evening up at Williston, practising things to say, and, in general, building the visit into a kind of grand rebellion against the housekeeper, which hadn't been wise. Gradually, he had diverted so much of his time into wondering how to behave and what to expect, that when at last, late on the 23rd, the tension with the housekeeper had eased up, he had immediately reacted by plunging into a spiral of anxiety centred on Moira.

Would she be glad to see him? Would she refer to that last time, here at Woodbourn? Should he somehow mention it? Was she going to make fun of him? And what about this husband of hers? Once he had met him, would it be impossible to invite Moira on her own ever again?

Throughout Christmas Eve, the questions had come crowding on each other, and he had suffered. They had taken full advantage of his weak stomach. Finding him already tense, they had nearly brought his asthma on, and before he had gone to bed, in desperation he had gulped down a large shot of whisky. Not that it had helped much; today, he felt no better, but tossing about for six hours, somewhere between sleeping and waking, had finally dulled his brain, and now he was less aware of all the things he had to worry about than of a vague sense of disaster, which, at the very thought of Williston, caused a spark of fright. It was incredible, what he would have to live through, before he could go to bed again.

No, he wouldn't eat.

Come to think of it, he shouldn't have touched the ivy; he shouldn't have touched anything. It would have been a way of saying to the bitch, 'Look! I can do without your damned breakfast!' A great pity that it would be childish to fish the ivy out of the basket again, and re-arrange it. He would have liked to, and to stop himself, he had to do something else. He pulled out his watch. Another six whole hours to fill . . .

Opening the flask, he began to drink the coffee, and then he ate both of the rolls.

Afterwards, he went out into the garden.

It was a Christmas Day for the card designers – bright and crisp. Frost had whiskered the shaded side of the lawn and the edges of the dead leaves, but the sky was stridently blue with not a cloud in it, a scrubbed, wholesome sky, and, it seemed to Lawson, evangelistic – all that sunlight for the big day. To get away from it, he ventured down the gentlest track into the spinney. He spat, and watched the blob of saliva seeping into the leafmould. He prodded the earth with his cane. Once, he stopped to look up through the branches, and he saw how the sun made every twig stand out sharply and separately, countless thousands of them. It was as though each one was silently clamouring to be noted. For some reason that depressed him, and he didn't stay out long.

For the next half-hour he explored the kitchen, gaping at the great rows of shining pans and at the grey deal table. Her realm. As spotless as an operating theatre. It smelt of disinfectant and detergent. He opened drawers and examined knives, spoons, peelers and scrapers – so much equipment just for the two of them! He opened cupboards and inspected ranks of tin cans – peaches, pears, soups – and he peered inside the huge, throbbing fridge, which was well stocked. Rather too well stocked, as a matter of fact: was it really necessary to horde such mounds of cheese and butter? It occurred to Lawson that he himself ate very little, and that most of these stores must be for her own consumption – the housekeeper's. What a farmhouse appetite! His money, down her gullet.

And what other secrets was she keeping from him? He might just take a look in her sitting-room . . .

But the door was locked. Impossible. He rattled the doorknob. Yes, the bitch had locked it. Did that mean she always locked it when she went out? He had never noticed before. He hadn't even known there was a key. Maybe there were keys to all the doors, somewhere . . . Maybe on her first day in the house, she had gone around pocketing them . . .

Wheezing heavily, he climbed the stairs and hurried along the landing to her bedroom. He tried the door. Locked. Well, so that proved it . . . She must have the key to *his* room! His heart gave a jolt. She could lock him in whenever she liked.

Bad . . . bad . . . paranoid . . . He put out a hand against the wall, steadying himself. It was one thing to keep his thoughts off the Gellings, but getting himself into a frenzy about these keys – that was another . . . and she was entitled to her privacy, wasn't she? Like anyone else?

True. But not to the keys.

I'll have to talk to her tomorrow, he decided. *I'll tell her, 'Look, it's my house . . .'* How could she argue with that? He calmed down. His house. An extremely soothing thing, proprietorship. Then he had a good idea. He would spend the afternoon looking at his jades and ivories. It would be a harmless way to pass the time, and they had been neglected lately. Excellent ... He set off down the stairs again.

The only snag was the sitting-room. He hadn't really liked it ever since the autumn and that strange fainting fit, or whatever it was, standing in there, watching the sunset; and although that particularly nasty episode had been cancelled out, more or less, by Moira, by jolly singing round the piano and gin and tonic and whisky – there had still been the face. The night of the face. He hadn't been back in the room since: not that he had avoided it, of course, but in the normal run of a day, he had no reason to go in.

There were only the times like now, when he needed his carvings. If he was thorough, it could take him hours to clean them.

He walked in quickly and boldly – and threw one glance at the cabinet near the piano: there it was, the face, just as he had known it would be, and yet, he told himself, it didn't matter. He could keep away from it. By a remarkable coincidence, all the figures that were overdue for cleaning were in the other cabinets, anyway.

He took them out one by one, and examined them.

Fine, cunning objects: tiny ladies laughing behind their fans; bullocks pulling miniature carts; a group of peasants, no taller than his little finger. Objects that were exclusively his, never handled by anyone else, unless he gave his permission.

Tenderly he brushed dust from folds of jade, wheel-spokes of ivory, and somehow the patience in these carvings, the humour and skill in them, helped to reinforce his contempt for the housekeeper. What did she know about anything? Come to that, what did Moira Gelling know?

A wrinkled Chinese sage, about the length of a hat pin, smiled up at him from the palm of his hand.

Have you done a lot of travelling, Mr Lawson?

He carefully rubbed the old man's beard.

At last it was evening, and things went wrong from the start. The cab, infamously expensive and booked well in advance because no chauffeurs were to be had from the car-hire firm, not Ruddy-cheeks or anyone else – came fifteen minutes early; and despite the fact that he had been bathed and dressed

174

almost an hour before, this severely flustered Lawson. He threw on his coat in a panic, and found, once he was under way, that he had forgotten his gloves. He had also had no time for a final check in the hall mirror, so that he worried about his rouge and the angle of his tie, which must have shifted when he pulled his coat on.

Not the most auspicious way of setting out ...

As he rode up the hill towards the bungalows, his heart was pumping hard, his face already felt damp with sweat, and the evening was going to be one long catastrophe, he knew it – or if he had the slightest doubt, it was very quickly taken from him. The cab had just pulled away from the first set of traffic lights, when he made a discovery: there was something wrong with the parcels that he had on his knees. Something to do with the wrapping paper ...

From all the Gellings' presents, the dye was coming off on his hands.

Worse and worse ...

He studied his hands anxiously. A street light or a passing car would throw a sudden gleam across his wrists.

No mistake ... red and green streaks down the inside of his fingers, and smears across the palms. It was one of those practical jokes, those small, mindless betrayals ...

Devil take this Christmas rubbish!

Lawson slumped back hopelessly. And now what? When Moira introduced him to her husband, was he going to stick out this multi-coloured paw at the man? Or the moment he arrived, before she could push him at anyone, should he ask her for the bathroom?

Nerves, she would think. They all would. An old man's bladder.

Getting out his handkerchief, he worked up a froth of spittle, and spat. Then he rubbed until his fingers hurt. Next, he began on the palms, and first – the right hand. He was still engrossed, rubbing away at that, when the cab slowed down. He went on rubbing. Soon the cab shuddered to a halt, and a gentle violet shine from one of the street lights fell in on the passenger seat. Lawson stared out, horrified. Williston. Already. And this ... presumably this was the 'Hillcrest' of the address on the Christmas card: a piece of mock-Tudor whimsy, with a privet hedge, a wrought-iron gate, and an uncomfortably short path to the front door. It was homely by the standards of the area, at the other end of the scale to the daunting Williston fortresses, but he didn't like the look of the place any better for that. As if to compensate for its obvious shortcomings so far as size and grandeur went, Hillcrest's windows were all ablaze, spelling out a clear message: *Lively people! Sociable goings on!*

Stuffing away his handkerchief, Lawson pulled out money, and when he had paid, for once he couldn't be bothered with the change; he dropped it into his pocket without so much as looking at it. Then he clambered out, hugging the vase close to his chest with his other two offerings balanced on top. The dye ... the red and green, rubbing off on his good coat ... Nothing he could do about it.

He pushed at the gate, and it swung open. Here he was. The garden path. And now that the door was only a couple of yards ahead, he realised how ill he felt – not just sick, as he nearly always felt when he was nervous, although he was that, too, but ill, with weak legs, a throbbing headache.

He stopped and looked back at the cab. Although he didn't know why he had done it, he had asked the driver to wait until he was safely in the house; but now, all things considered – feeling so ill, and his crooked tie, and the sweating parcels – the question was, should he let the cab go? He thought with longing of his library. His stupidity astonished him. Standing in a Williston garden, seconds away from the very worst kind of festivities – and for what? If he never set eyes on Moira Gelling again – what did *he* care? Of one thing he was certain. She wasn't worth *this*.

I'll just go home, he thought.

But he didn't move. The cab driver's bored white face was watching him, and apparently the fellow expected normal behaviour. From the rear of the cab, little puffs of blue-grey exhaust fumes rose in the road – signals to get on with it.

Lawson turned to the house again. He took a step forwards, and eyed the downstairs windows. In the room on his right, shadows moved behind the curtains. Giants at their rituals.

Was he going to feel as ill as this all evening?

I can manage, he countered, and because it was a healthy thing to do, he breathed in deeply. A tang of manure from the rose-beds reached him, but he didn't mind. The sharpness of the air helped.

Give it another minute ...

Late in the afternoon, the sky had clouded over, and now, when he put back his head, looking up in search of stars, he found there were none.

It was time. He arranged his face. He took the last few steps, and rang the bell.

The door opened, and it was Rowena; his smile slipped. It was not just that he had expected Moira: the girl had performed horrible wonders with make-up. Her round face shone a bright baby-pink in contrast to the pallor of her neck, as white and strong as a cabbage stalk; her lips were pearly orange, and she had left off her spectacles for the occasion, she had caked her eyes in several layers of oily mascara.

'Ah ...' He took a step back at the sight of her. All her cosmetic radiance beamed at him.

'Mr Lawson!'

She came bearing forwards, plump and sleek in bottle-green velvet, reaching for his elbow. 'Merry Christmas! We were really so glad you could come!' she enthused, drawing him over the threshold. And the door closed. He thought he heard the cab make off. He clutched his parcels. The sickness in his stomach billowed.

'Won't you let me take your coat?'

'I can hardly get out of it holding these,' he gasped, 'now can I?'

Rowena's smile grew brighter and brighter. Lawson stood where he was, panting. A fussy hall, with potted plants and pictures. There was also a chandelier, and over a half-moon table hung a brass plate, like a great egg yolk. The carpet was so thick that it seemed to suck at his feet.

Then she began to strip him of his largesse: 'How kind of you! What pretty paper!'

Grimly, he delivered up his burdens. To his right, a door was ajar, and through the crack, he could hear a churning of voices, while through another door to his left, he had already glimpsed a confirmation of everything bad: a long, glossy dining table set with a disobliging number of places, squadrons of tall wine glasses, glinting tumblers, and red serviettes – eight, or maybe ten of them. All the trimmings of a fair-sized banquet. Hardly a quiet bite with the family, this.

Well, there's no way out of it now!

He started to struggle with his coat buttons. As usual in a time of crisis, they had become unaccountably stiff, like a set of bolts, and he took so long pushing them out through the buttonholes, that the girl came creeping round behind, her hands hovering near his shoulders, ready to help with the disrobing – like a nurse.

'All right?'

'Yes! Yes!' he snapped, and he looked round wildly for a mirror – every hall had a mirror – but there wasn't one. There was only the brass plate.

Rowena said, 'I'll just put this ... ' and vanished with his coat through a door at the foot of the stairs.

A hall without a mirror! And what an inept, revolting creature Rowena Gelling was. She might have asked, 'Would you like to straighten your tie?' but no, not her. And he was damned if he was going to ask. Glaring after her, Lawson had a vision of mirrors, whole corridors of mirrors, just beyond the door, wherever his coat had gone. Then he took to squinting at himself in the brass plate. He fiddled with his tie. He felt the line of his toupee. He looked carefully at his hands. A little red, perhaps, but not green. They would have to do. Everything would have to do.

His presents lay in a sorry heap on the half-moon table, and thanks to the way in which they had been taken from him and plonked down, one of the smaller parcels had pushed against a gift tag – Moira's, of course – and bent it. He was busy trying to straighten it out when Rowena re-appeared.

'Would you like to bring those in with you?' she asked.

'No, I wouldn't.'

A geriatric Santa Claus, the other guests – and there were definitely others – watching the hand-out. Lawson drew back smartly from the table.

'Well then,' said Rowena, 'shall we ... ?'

Miserably he shuffled after her, into the lounge.

'Arnold!'

Now Moira saw him.

There were five, no, six people in the room, three of them seated, and she was sitting on the end of a sofa near the drinks cabinet. When he came in, she didn't get up, but she quickly stretched out her hand towards him, smiling, and his heart leapt. He saw the affection in her eyes. He could scarcely believe it. Oh, she was pleased, genuinely pleased to see him. Brimming with gratitude, he hurried forward, seized her hand, and daringly kissed her on the cheek.

'A happy Yuletide, my dear.'

'Oh, that sounds so romantic!'

Moira laughed. He stood stupidly, holding her hand, and after a second or two, the husband came – tall and solid, and speaking gustily in a voice which sounded accustomed to being listened to. His jolly manner said that here was a man who wanted things to go smoothly.

'Delighted you could come.' He gave a strong handshake. 'Any trouble finding the place?' – and he nodded at his wife: 'She's looking well, isn't she?'

'Yes,' said Lawson. 'Yes.'

'Come and meet ... '

A new disaster. He was shepherded away from Moira, away across the room. Names were recited. There was a surgeon and a lawyer. There were wives ... He was brought to a standstill, then made to sit by the surgeon's wife who was writing a novel, and she would be so pleased to know what he thought ...

The doorbell rang piercingly. Full of purpose, Rowena clumped from the room. David Gelling brought him a glass of whisky, and a jug of water.

'Say when ... '

New arrivals.

From her place on the sofa, Moira greeted a blonde young woman dressed in black, and a man in a leather jacket who wore his hair greasy and low on his collar – a kind of ageing teddy boy. An artist, perhaps? One of her protegés? A plaything, like himself?

' ... and so, you see,' went on the surgeon's wife, her head nodding and bobbing across his line of vision, 'what I need is a motive, Mr Lawson. A really strong reason why a girl would

do such a thing. Now you, with all your literary experience
... Moira tells me ... '

Moira. She could have been a thousand miles away. He
watched her laughing with the leather jacket, and he thought
that she was softer and more fragile-looking than he had ever
seen her. Even her laughter, usually on the loud side, was
gentle tonight, and her clothes were soft, too – she was wearing
a cloud-blue dress in some fine-spun woollen stuff – and the
purple rinse had gone from her hair. Now she was grey, a mild
smoke-grey. Also, she was very ladylike. She was sitting with
her knees together, whereas often down at Woodbourn, she
had disconcerted him by her masculine way of sprawling.
None of that tonight. There was a strange, languid elegance
about her. She was very much the hostess, but without the
servile or officious part – no racing around with the peanut
dish: chores like that were left to Rowena or the husband –
and Lawson felt a pang of love as it occurred to him how
much of Moira's style for this particular event was at the
expense of her family, the daughter hurrying to open doors,
the husband serving up the drinks and marshalling people into
groups – while she sat. Yes, she was exploiting them, and he
loved her for it.

If only he could get rid of everyone else ...

Oddly enough, although he had come in terror, and for days
he had been warning himself that there would probably be
other guests, he had still hoped for special treatment. He had
hoped she would feel the same need he felt, and would keep
him near her. Despite repeated cautions to himself, he had still
cherished a belief in moments when he would have her on her
own, and, by a look or a word, he could try to make her
understand that it was safe: she really could come back to
Woodbourn, because he would never again force her to think
anything she didn't want to think, God or no God; that it was
a new covenant between them ...

Dreams of the old fool!

There she was, chatting to the leather jacket and his girl-
friend, apparently just as happy to see them as she was to see
him.

From where he had kissed her, there was a trace of face powder
on his lips, and he moved his tongue discreetly, savouring it.

He needed her attention badly, so very badly that it seemed impossible for her not to look at him. She did look. She waved – but immediately turned away again.

' ... so what do you think, Mr Lawson?' inquired the surgeon's wife, earnest over her gin. 'Do I make her run away at that point? Or earlier, when the stepfather tries to seduce her?'

Lawson brought his eyes back to focus on this woman's goodnatured face, and spluttered, 'I'm afraid I wasn't ... I haven't heard a word you were saying!'

'You haven't?' The surgeon's wife turned red. 'How silly of me!' she cried. 'Moira did mention you're a little ... ' And she started the plot of her novel all over again, an octave higher.

Dinner promised no improvement. As everyone flocked out of the lounge, he broke away from the surgeon's wife, rushed up to Moira and hissed, 'I can sit next to you, can't I?'

'Of course!'

To his immense joy, she squeezed his arm.

But when they entered the dining-room, David Gelling had already placed the surgeon and the lawyer at the end of the table where Moira was to sit, and from the other end, he shouted out to Lawson, 'Up here, Arnold! Near me! Between Rowena and Elizabeth here!'

'Oh ... '

He turned to Moira pleadingly, but she deserted him. *Don't play up!* – he saw it, the danger light in her eyes – and letting go of his arm, she very gently pushed him from her. No scenes. He was not to disgrace her. He shambled to his appointed chair. Penned in between the daughter and the lawyer's wife ... Near the husband. A good sign, possibly? David Gelling wanted to get to know him?

Moira, out of reach.

I'll never get through this ...

Soup, mushroom. A kind of maid, not in uniform – black skirt and red jumper – but not a member of the family either, someone large and silent, padding about, setting down plates. A home help, working at Christmas.

They must pay a lot for this! he thought.

David Gelling, pouring out the wine.

'You'll take a little of this, Arnold?'

'Certainly. Certainly.' It could hardly make him feel worse than he did already.

Rowena, launching into clumsy flights of erudition. 'I've been reading *A Passage to India*, Mr Lawson ... I think it's Forster's best novel, don't you? I do think his Indians are wonderful ... Especially the Hindus.'

The soup was too rich, and he belched. On and on went the daughter's monologue, and when he turned from her, it was to find the Leather Jacket's thin-faced girlfriend staring across the table with undisguised revulsion at his toupee.

Moira's husband gulped down his soup greedily, and said nothing. The lawyer's wife ignored Lawson and talked incessantly about a strange noise in her washing machine and a missing teaspoon ... All the fun was down the other end of the table, where Moira was apparently also telling a story, her voice low and confidential, the lawyer and the surgeon leaning eagerly towards her, and soon, down there, everyone laughed.

After the soup – the turkey; it was borne in crisp-skinned and glistening, and the ritual of carving began. This was going to be the difficult part. David Gelling's knife sliced into the white of the breast; with a dessert spoon, he gouged out sage-and-onion stuffing from the space between the bird's ribs, and Lawson's stomach heaved. He should have mentioned this ... He had intended to, and it would have been easy if he had been sitting next to Moira ... As it was, what could he say? At this meal, of all meals, wouldn't the very word 'vegetarian' brand him as a kill-joy? He kept quiet and hoped for the best. Moira knew, of course – thanks to the *Herald*, everyone knew – but would she remember? If someone would just slip him an empty plate on which he could pile a few vegetables ...

The home help moved soundlessly round the room, distributing servings of turkey, and when she wasn't doing that, she stood by David Gelling's elbow, waiting for the next plate. Lawson tried to catch her eye. No good. The cutting up and scooping processes seemed to have a wonderful fascination for her. As for Moira, far away at the other end of the table, she was giving her undivided attention to something that the lawyer was saying; and even Rowena wasn't to be signalled at: the girl had pushed back her chair and got up, and now she was busy transferring vegetable dishes and pretty sauceboats on to the table from a trolley.

I suppose I'm going to have to say something!

But, no, he decided. He would look less graceless and altogether less conspicuous if he simply pushed the meat to one side of his plate and left it there. That was the answer. He must steel himself to having a piece of meat in front of him ... He waited. Soon, all the women had been served except Rowena, and all the men except himself and David Gelling. Then Rowena came and sat down, clutching her own plate, and a moment later, the home help came stealing round to his side with a plate for him. On it lay something wet and yellow.

Finnan haddock.

He shrank at the sight of it.

'What's this?' he gasped.

The home help muttered something.

Dead, reeking fish. A white and yellow liquid seeped out from its sides.

'What's this?' he cried over the clutter of dishes at Moira. She went pale. The conversation stopped. Rowena said quickly, 'Well, as you're a vegetarian, we thought ... '

'No.' He turned to her bitterly. She was so crass, he couldn't bear it, and he guessed. Oh yes, this was her idea, this obscenity they had given him. Whose but Rowena's? 'You didn't think at all!'

The girl's mouth sagged.

Lawson trembled.

Terrible. Terrible. Now look what you've done ...

Silence. The unavoidable odour of turkey meat. And fish. He twisted his serviette in his fingers.

I've embarrassed them, he thought. *All this fuss. So rude.*

Tears sprang to his eyes. An exhibition of himself. Every face at the table watching him ... He glared defiantly. Stupid, over-fed, disapproving fools ...

'Fish ... turkeys ... ' he croaked, 'they're all dead bodies, aren't they? What's the difference? They're all corpses!'

On the seat next to his, Rowena's fleshy body winced.

'If you'd prefer cheese,' said David Gelling, and Moira rose softly, coming to his side to remove his plate herself, as if in penance.

'Just vegetables ... I'll be quite happy ... Please don't trouble.'

He couldn't bring himself to look at her.

The Gellings heaped his plate with potatoes, sprouts and carrots, so that after David Gelling had taken a third of a spoon of each for himself, there was nothing left. Nothing for seconds for anyone.

Disaster on disaster. How could she forgive him? When everyone began to eat, Lawson ate humbly, his hand quivering on his fork, and between bites, he swallowed down David Gelling's excellent wine. It was a long time before he spoke again.

Still, by the pudding stage, he felt better. Rowena had finally got caught up in a discussion with the Leather Jacket's girl-friend about exams and universitites, which was a great mercy; and now that he had taken care of his appetite, David Gelling seemed prepared to talk more, and to extend his sense of obligation beyond the women who sat next to him:

'Maybe Arnold can help. You're the scholar, Arnold ... Moira says you've got a book about everything. This kissing under the mistletoe, it's to do with the shape of the leaves, isn't it? The waxing moon, and all that?'

The lawyer's wife smiled round. 'I wish you could have heard her,' she said. 'Going on like that in this day and age! The vicar looked absolutely stunned, poor man. But you know, she had a point. I don't remember any mistletoe in churches when I was a girl. Is it really forbidden, Mr Lawson?'

He perked up. Oh, he knew all about mistletoe, and holly, too, if they wanted it. He could tell about the Yule log and the Christmas rose, and – yes, he knew the Celtic traditions, animals kneeling in the farmyards on Old Christmas Night, and – no, he didn't believe such things ... On the other hand, the sensitivity of animals shouldn't be dismissed lightly. He could name a couple of very persuasive writers on the sub-ject. And as for this business in the States, these intelligence tests, teaching chimps to speak in sign language – well, he had looked into that; he had read a good deal about the mysteries of syntax and the structure of the human brain, and he was willing to say this much ... Pioneer days yet, of course, but the findings had their implications. The chimps, for a start ... and then, these studies – the serious ones – of whale songs. In fact, there was an excellent book he could recommend ... No, he didn't have a television, but he read. He read ...

Alcohol enlarged his brain. David Gelling and the ladies made comments or asked questions, and he flourished his knowledge like a magnificent set of peacock feathers; and as he talked, his voice acquired a fine bold ring to it, so that after a while, the entire table – Moira as well – fell silent and listened. He knew so much that they had skimped on, these people, that they had half read, or only glanced at. A suspicion at first, this soon became a certainty, and his confidences soared. He risked a joke, and heard the slightly startled respect in everyone's laughter. Then he told another – a cruder one – and this time, the laughter round the table came more easily, the lawyer putting back his head to give a loud guffaw. Better still, he saw the surgeon nod at Moira, as much as to say, 'You're right. This old boy's got something ... '

He glowed.

I'm doing well ... I'm doing well ...

Coffee was served, and brandy. The Leather Jacket came up with a witticism about Finnan haddock, and the whole question of whether to eat meat or not to eat meat was, declared the surgeon's wife, very interesting. A debate began, frivolous but lively, on the subject of vivisection, with both sides referring to him along the table for facts, or some statistic.

The room bulged with his happiness. Moira, walking round with a box of chocolate mints, laid her hand on his shoulder as she offered him one. Success. Success. In her smile, he thought he saw something more than friendliness; it seemed that she was proud of him, and that there was a conspiracy between them: We'll show them!

Eventually – an adjournment to the lounge, and more brandy. Rowena mentioned 'Mr Lawson's parcels in the hall', and wasn't it time to open them?

'Not now! Not in front of me!' he protested, but he didn't really mind, so they were brought in, his undistinguished offerings, and pulled out of their wrappings in a general surge of enthusiasm. 'What a beautiful vase!' 'What a thundering big paperweight! That'll keep your bills down, David!'

185

'I meant to bring you something else as well,' he confided to Moira, 'something special, but I forgot ... '

She laughed. They all did. He was so roguish, so charming. 'What kind of thing?' she asked. She was holding the vase extremely carefully on her lap, as though its sides were sharp enough to slice a finger off.

'Oh, a book ... '

One of his rare, wonderful books ... To his delight, Moira looked a trifle piqued. That was as it should be, he thought. She deserved some small punishment for his discomforts earlier in the evening; and perhaps if she knew there was a present waiting for her, she would come back all the more quickly to Woodbourn.

'Yes,' he said. 'I'm sorry ... I don't know how it slipped my mind ... '

It hadn't. He had wrapped up the Burns lovingly, and laid it ready with the other parcels, but at the last minute, the thought of making such a sacrifice with strangers looking on, with turkey, and the wine flowing – with paper hats and whistles, for all he knew – it had seemed too hazardous. Moira might just glance at the Burns, then fling it down somewhere, or let her other guests look at it – maul it – and what if someone spilled their drink on it? He hadn't forgotten how she had tossed his Thackeray into the back of her car – so very revealing, so different to the reverence that she showed for his books in his library, and it had suddenly been obvious to him that if he was going to give her the Burns, he would have to do it there, at Woodbourn. Anywhere else, it might hurt too much.

The right decision, surely. He had brought enough without it. Moira set the vase in pride of place on the mantelpiece. Rowena suffered raptures over her cheap fountain pen, and David Gelling, examining his paperweight, looked amazingly pleased with it.

At last, the whole ceremony was over; the torn paper was gathered up; and Lawson pinkened. The Gellings, it appeared, hadn't thought to buy *him* anything ... Quickly he squirmed round in his chair to listen in on an argument that had just begun between the surgeon and the Leather Jacket. Old movies ... Dietrich versus Garbo ... not so much these women's acting talents, apparently, as their anatomies ... Elaborately, he displayed interest. What, after all, did a present matter? He hadn't made a fool of himself. It was right for guests to come with presents. No one need feel awkward ... They had given him his dinner, and he hadn't expected more than that ... Lawson grinned, nodding away eagerly at the finer points of Dietrich, and when the surgeon cried, 'As for Garbo's legs, good God, there's no comparison! Stumps! Awful little stumps!' he heard himself giving a shout, 'Hear, hear!'

Then Moira stood in front of him, holding out a slim parcel wrapped in silver paper, and he almost fainted with relief.

'Happy Yule, Arnold.' She smiled.

He shoved the gift into his pocket.

'Is it from *you* ... or all of you?'

'You can decide.'

'I'll open it', he whispered, 'when I'm alone!' – and, again, everyone laughed. A theatrical, mischievous old chap – that was how they saw him, and what was wrong with that? he thought happily. They didn't mean any harm.

As a matter of fact, they had all become remarkably easy to like. He leered at the Leather Jacket's girlfriend, and the young woman threw him back a coquettish smile. Then David Gelling offered a cigar with gratifying deference: 'I don't know what you'll think of these, Arnold ... ' And when he bantered with the lawyer, who had thoughts of his own on Garbo and the properties of a beautiful leg, drunk as both of them were, he could have sworn that he made the legal man blush. Everything was all right. He relaxed. He listened with enormous goodwill and credulity to a panegyric on the Japanese delivered by the Leather Jacket, who turned out not to be an artist but a businessman, and, no doubt, a very good one. He was secure. Among friends. These fine, intelligent people.

Even Rowena could be tolerated.

There was a piano in the room – an apologetic-looking upright that stood against the wall by the door, and at some point near the end of his second brandy, Rowena took it on herself to persuade Moira to play.

'Oh do, Mummy. Just a few carols. I'm sure Mr Lawson would like that. Wouldn't you, Mr Lawson?'

Carols were hardly to his taste, but it didn't occur to him to say so.

'It would give me the greatest pleasure,' he said gravely.

The lawyer's wife also insisted, and so, after adjustments to the piano stool, and prolonged rummaging around for music, a carol began – 'Si-iLENT NIGHT, Ho-oLEE NIGHT' ... Moira pounding it out like a rugby song, and the brash, careless notes filled him with an aching happiness. He let the others sing; he sat quietly. Moira, playing at Woodbourn – such fun, such good times! He should have let her play more often. From now on, he promised himself, there would be fewer sober talks, and more of this. Life, in the end, was very simple. It was wrong notes and odd rhythms, it was bad singing. Yes ... yes ... His emotions rose in a great wave. Everything was glorious, magnificent ... or almost everything. There was still Rowena. For obscure reasons of her own, in the middle of the second carol, she abruptly left her post near the piano and came to sit beside him on the sofa; then, as soon as Moira stopped playing, while the others shouted out suggestions for the carol they should have next, the girl leaned towards him, and she spoke slowly and deliberately into his ear.

'What?' He jerked away from her.

She pushed her face close to his again.

'Mother,' she repeated. 'Looking dreadful. That's why ... '

The piano started up, and whatever she had to say, he lost it.

Moira, looking dreadful? He stared at her, then back at the girl. Rowena's round, watchful face had taken on a sanctimonious expression, and in a trice he understood: *She's jealous!* he thought.

What else could Rowena be? Moira's lipstick might be smudged, and it was true that her hair was not quite right for once, so that there was a bald patch showing, and if he bothered to think about it, he could see the powder-line across her jaw, but – looking dreadful? Hands crashing on the keyboard, the gold charms on her bracelet trembling, tossing back her head as she sang so much worse than everyone ... Moira was superb, stupendous, and this, this poor mooncalf, plainest of plain teenagers, how could she be anything but jealous? Lawson felt suddenly moved to pity. He smiled. Forgivingly, he patted Rowena's arm, and the girl drew away from him, surprised. He sat back with a sigh of contentment. *Why can't I always be kind?* he wondered. Thoughts came and went like goldfish in a still pond. *I get ruffled much too easily,* he observed, *which is nonsense.* The knowledge didn't worry him much.

'While SHEPherds watched their FLOCKS by night ... ' thumped the piano. Moira had begun to use the foot pedals. As she hammered at the keys and pressed down with her feet, she swayed, she played with her whole body, but after the third verse, she brought the music to an end with a harsh chord, and she stood up, laughing, 'That's enough!' Pale and a little breathless, she came to sit beside Rowena on the sofa.

'I'm puffed!' she said, smiling at him across her daughter.

'Oh, I know the feeling ... '

They sat in a row, the three of them, while the surgeon's wife sang 'Hark the Herald Angels' – an operatic rendering that somehow led David Gelling into ribald jokes. Then Lawson opened up his own store, coming out with jokes far closer to the bone than any Gelling had to offer – damn funny stories, some of them, that he could only marvel at. Where had he heard such stuff?

Am I offending them? – a flash of doubt in the final line of a limerick on a certain old spinster of Worcester, but really, he was too quick, too clever, and in their flushed, attentive faces, Rowena's as well as the others, all he saw was approval.

I'm in charge ... I always was in charge, he remembered with astonishment. *That's how I made my money ...* and, remembering, he doubled his efforts. He held them spellbound ... until, inexplicably, a bell rang.

A tight, sharp-edged sound, it cut across his voice and the haze of cigar and cigarette smoke like a fine wire. He wavered. He had just embarked on a long, extremely rude account of a parson's wife and a turkey ... one to show he knew rather more than a thing or two ... He carried on. But Rowena rose stolidly, and left the room. Seconds later, she was back to announce that Mr Lawson's cab had arrived.

Mr Lawson's cab. No one spoke.

So soon? Inquiring faces turned towards him, but even as they turned, he could see them rapidly adjusting. Of course. An old man. Eleven thirty. Such a very old chap ... Into their smiles crept an unpleasant softness, and Lawson's heart plummeted.

So soon.

He hadn't dared leave this cab to chance, and when he had booked it, the truth was, he had quailed at the thought of outstaying his welcome, of being trapped for hours neglected in a corner, so he had played safe, and 11.30 had seemed a very suitable time, considering.

But now, confound it, when he was game for hours yet ...

Could he send the cab away? If he did, would any of these new friends take him home? Would Moira get her car out? Or the husband?

Everyone waited; and it felt to Lawson like a purist kind of waiting that makes one's obligations plain.

An old man, about to leave.

Moira was already heading for the door: 'I'll get your coat, Arnold.'

Mechanically, he got to his feet, and David Gelling shook his hand, and slapped him on the back, saying with lavish heartiness, 'Now you know where we are, you must come again. Really you must!' But, 'Why don't you stay and we'll run you home?' - that he didn't say. No one did. Rowena held the door open.

'Good-night!'

Blearily he smiled round, and the Gellings' guests chorused back, 'Good-night! Goodbye ... ' Kind eyes, kind, kind ... Adults to the child, on his way upstairs.

Out, then, into the hall.

Beneath the chandelier, Moira stood clutching a coat. The front door was open, and a draught caused the chandelier's pendants to shiver, unsettling the light - an effect he had always hated, and yet it seemed to suit Moira. It made her look so gentle. Despite his misery - being hustled out - he noticed that, and he was struck, too, by the way in which she held his coat. She might be anxious to be rid of him - certainly it felt as though she was - but this one token of him, she was holding pressed against her, as though she didn't mean to give it up too easily. At the idea, his breath faltered.

No sign of the cab driver. Presumably he had gone back to wait in the car - the usual hint to be quick.

'Here you are.' Suddenly she held the coat out to him, but he didn't take it. He had come to a standstill. It was quiet in the hall. Private. And there was so much that he needed to explain. Why he was leaving early ... She mustn't think that he wanted to ... What he wanted was absolution – for leaving, and for the Finnan haddock, for the forgotten Burns. He wanted signs and promises, and he wanted them so badly that, for the moment, he was speechless.

Pulling out of his pocket the silver-wrapped Christmas present, he waved it at her, meaning, 'This I'll treasure, whatever it is ... ' but Moira didn't help. She gave him such a strange smile. Not necessarily a warm one.

I'm alone with her ...

Untrue. Dutifully Rowena had followed him from the lounge, and now her bulky form passed between him and Moira, grabbing the coat.

'Shall I help you on with this, Mr Lawson?'

With great reluctance he stepped forward, and he was just beginning to pull the coat on, when Moira said, 'Thank you for coming, Arnold. I wanted to have a *special* Christmas ... and you've really helped to make this one.'

The alcohol on her breath lapping over his face.

Words, just words – or did she mean it? Full of hope, he grinned at her. He tried to think of something gallant to say, devastatingly gallant, but his arm had stuck in the coat shoulder, and it took all his concentration to punch his way into the sleeve.

'All right?' asked Rowena.

'Yes ... except, this isn't my coat.'

'Oh.'

'Oh God, no it isn't,' said Moira, and she broke into a fit of giggles.

Rowena smiled slyly.

It reached down to his ankles. His hands were lost deep inside the sleeves. The belt hung low round his backside. The weight of the coat, like a sheet of lead, was crushing, stifling ...

He struggled to get out of it.

'Oh dear,' tittered Rowena, 'can I help?'

'No. Don't touch me!'

She recoiled. On his cheeks, he felt twin spots of heat beneath the rouge. Moira's giggles he could take – just – but not this, not the girl.

Out of the sleeves at last ... He bundled the coat back at Moira, and she gathered it into her arms, saying quietly, 'Ro, why don't you go and organise some more coffee, while I find Mr Lawson's coat?'

The daughter's plump face considered: 'If you like ... ' but she seemed uncertain how to leave, and first she stared, and then she thrust her hand out: 'Good-night, Mr Lawson. And thank you again for the pen.'

'Yes ... ' He forced himself to touch her fingers. 'Goodnight.'

'And happy new year!' said Rowena with a prim, upward curve of her mouth, making allowances.

Lawson nodded. She clumped away.

'Back in a moment ... ' Moira vanished too.

Then the cab horn sounded, and he moved to the open door. The night had become icily cold, but he felt obliged to stand there, so that the driver would see him. Ironic, if the fellow chose to lose his patience now, and make off ... The confusion over the coats had somehow changed everything, and although Lawson didn't want to go, he didn't want to stay, either – not as the result of a muddle, with explanations in the lounge and laughter, and everybody wondering how to get him home, who should volunteer ...

He peered out.

The street lamps of Williston were shining on to cloud – a thick, even blanket of it – and the sky had a grey, luminous quality. Not a single star, of course. He contemplated the poplars in the garden opposite. They were quite different to other trees. He almost liked poplars. Flame shaped. Then he spotted the man in the cab watching him, and he turned away. Maybe Moira couldn't find his coat ... but as he turned, she was already coming back with it across her arm.

'Here it is!' She was panting a little, and laughing. 'I don't know how I missed it ... Now off you go ... ' Her arms opened, and she draped it round his shoulders. Her haste was terrifying.

'Go on ... ' She nudged him.

Lawson didn't move; and and what happened next wasn't planned, and neither could he prevent it.

'Oh, Moira!' he wailed, a terrible noise, even to his own ears, and as he reached out, he saw her flinch: in the next moment he had pressed her to him, his cheek buried in her hair. And now what? He had sprung a trap on both of them. He had no idea. His voice was out of control. He could hear it saying over and over, 'Moira ... '

He breathed in her hair lacquer. It was sticky, like a fine mesh of sugar droplets scented with jasmine; and he could feel how fragile she was, and warm ... If he let go, there might never be another time, so he hugged hard.

She didn't seem to mind. In fact she seemed to like it. She stood there so passive, allowing him to rub his lips over her hair, and a vague, beautiful sadness welled up in Lawson, which was only slightly marred by his awareness of the risk, the absurd risk, of someone coming from the lounge ... David Gelling ... Or Rowena and the home help coming from the kitchen with the coffee pots. And in all probability, the driver was watching ...

He knew they couldn't stand like that for ever.

Now I'm going to kiss her, he thought, and he began to release his hold, just enough to let her raise her head.

'Moira ... '

She pushed him. Her face flashed up, red and contorted. At once his arms dropped from her. One of her fingers jabbed against his waistcoat.

'You ... you old goat!'

'No ... '

She laughed, the loud, vulgar laugh that she had been avoiding all evening.

'Yes you are. An old goat!' and she began to shove him through the doorway.

Lawson was too stunned to resist. Obedient to her proddings, he retreated across the threshold, twisting back to her: 'Moira, I ... '

'Ye-es?'

What? That he loved her? She went on laughing. He stumbled backwards down the step, out into the cold.

'Good-night ... Don't ... It wasn't ... '

193

'Oh, sleep it off, Arnold.'

Still laughing, she closed the door, and as he set off down the path, he had no doubt at all that behind the brightly lit curtains, everyone in the lounge was laughing at him, too.

Thirteen

It wasn't the driver who had brought him. It was some other fellow, smirking as he helped his customer into the back of the cab, and there Lawson sprawled, misery rising in his throat like a huge bubble that couldn't be swallowed and couldn't be forced up either. He had great difficulty breathing.

'Had a good time, have you?' said the driver. 'Well, and why not? I'd have had a few meself, only I'm working ... '

His words came lunging in at Lawson on a wave of stale beer. Then the passenger door slammed shut. The man struggled in behind the steering wheel. The driver's door shut, and they drove away, leaving Williston.

At first, Lawson didn't attempt to collect himself. He allowed his body to spread across the seat, and gave himself up to his helplessness. He felt as unco-ordinated as an infant, and found it very comforting. What was he, after all, but an overgrown infant? He couldn't be held responsible ...

You old goat.

Oh, but that was unjust. She couldn't really have meant it, not in the way he understood her: senile, lecherous, pawing at her. He told himself that Moira must have drunk at least as much as he had, probably more. One too many. So why should he take her seriously? That couldn't possibly be how she saw him. And yet – how had she seen him? His red-rimmed eyes, askew toupee, the yellow skin, and his mouth, slackening for the kiss ... revolting her.

At the thought, he let out a croak. It was quite loud, and it startled him, but apparently used to all sorts in the back of his cab, the driver didn't turn round. Even so, Lawson made visible corrections. He sat up straighter. He put his hand to his mouth and felt his lips. His hand seemed to have the consis-

tency of a rubber mitten, and his lips were little rolls of rubber
... So he was not only losing co-ordination, his senses were
going, as well. Maybe he was dying.

Just this once, the notion soothed him.

'Well', would you believe it,' sang out the cabman suddenly.
'A bleedin' white Christmas. That's snow, that is.'

The windscreen wipers began to move, ponk-ponk, pushing
flakes aside as they fell against the glass. Large, soft flakes: a
few, then quite a few, and within seconds, legions of them,
they came hurtling out of the dark, and whenever the cab
passed beneath a street lamp, the latest flakes to have spattered
on to the windscreen shone like brilliant goosedown, while in
the centre of the screen and low down on either side, a wedge
appeared – compressed sludge, gathering under the wipers.
Black wedges, fringed with white.

Ponk-ponk ... A gentle but insistent sound, Lawson could
just hear it, directing him to watch the wipers. This way, that
way, pushing sludge, they mesmerised him. Spatter of flakes,
white, soft – sweep of wipers – black sludge. Spatter of flakes
... ponk-ponk ...

After a time, his vision blurred, and he looked away through
a side window. Viewed like this, the flakes weren't rushing
straight at the cab at all: they were swirling round in grey
currents, so that Lawson had a peculiar impression of the car
as a covered boat, falling through a cataract.

'Not much out and about tonight!' shouted the driver,
although there was no need to shout. 'Less than I expected!'

'It's early yet,' said Lawson.

Away across the eddies of snow, he could see a row of
houses, and in them lights were shining. The downstairs lights
caused him pain, but he stared for as long as possible at any
upstairs lights. He needed to know that for other people, too,
whatever hope the day had held, it was over.

Past the bungalows, falling down the hill, a slow, endless
fall in whiteness.

I don't believe we'll ever arrive, he told himself, and like the
thought of infancy or dying, this seemed to offer something
most desirable.

Never to be alone again. Never to have to examine the
evening, picking it over ...

Not much hope of that. They turned into the drive at Wood-bourn. The trees came arcing over them; and then the house rose out of the gravel, with all its windows blind – all except for those of the library, which were giving out an orange glow through the curtains.

'Round the back is it, guv?'

Lawson didn't answer. The sight of the house shocked him. No light in the porch ... He should have thought of that, a light to welcome him ... and what had happened to the hall lights? He had left in such a flurry, he must have switched them off ... extraordinary. Or was this a trick of the house-keeper's, switching them off as she went to bed? Whatever had happened, seeing the place from the outside, his library snugly lit as if he was already in there, and the rest of the house so quiet, so dark – it was unnerving. He could have done without it ...

Round the back, and one small mercy: the naked bulb above the door was burning. So at least he'd had the presence of mind to leave that on! But nothing else. Every window dark. The house felt massive with darkness, and all at once, squint-ing at it from the cab, Lawson knew that he couldn't face unlocking it himself – the door swinging in on to the black emptiness of the passage.

'This is it, then.'

The cab drew up, and the driver let the engine run as he twisted in his seat to look his passenger right in the eye.

'That's five pounds. Special rates for Christmas.'

Lawson stared.

'I didn't pay that going ... '

'Christmas rates. You should have.'

Robbery ... of course. Why not? No justice. Why expect it? And even if he had wanted to, he couldn't have complained. He needed the man. He fumbled with his wallet, and as he was pulling out a note, several more came fluttering down on to his knees.

'Careful there!' said the cabman, watching eagerly.

Lawson rammed them into his pocket. Five pounds ... He thrust it out, a single note that he saw between his fingers, although he couldn't feel it, and then another note – a grand, placatory one pound tip – and his keys.

'If you'd just see me in ... The door sticks ... '

'Thanks very much.' The pound note disappeared along with the five pounds. 'Right ... ' said the driver, and switching off the engine, he jumped out, flung open the passenger door, then ran for the house. The back door was unlocked and the passage lit by the time that Lawson, gasping in the bitter air, took his first step on the gravel. The snow, he discovered, was not snow – it was wet, stinging sleet – but despite that, he moved slowly. He crept. He wanted to keep this stranger with him, just for a little longer ...

When he arrived in the entrance, at the prospect of the stern passage stretching past the kitchen, he made one last attempt to stave off being alone.

'Would you ... ' he turned back shivering, 'care for a quick ... '

'Got to go, guv,' said the driver with appalling promptness, backing off. 'Another call.'

'But just ... '

'Can't do it.'

Lawson managed a smile.

'Merry Christmas,' he said.

'Same to you.'

The man hurried, his shoulders rounded, becoming a bearish shape in the sleet, and just before he burrowed into the car, he raised his arm and waved.

Lawson felt himself obliged to wave back.

'Merry Christmas,' he called again, although, at midnight it was a little late for that.

He hadn't used the words for years.

There was no sign of the housekeeper. He reeled down the passage into the hall, switching on lights and coughing to announce himself. He banged the cloakroom door. Nothing. Then he went upstairs and banged his bathroom door. Still nothing – but he decided not to ring a bell: it wasn't as though he wanted her for anything, and it would be unpleasant if she didn't answer, the emptiness of the house rushing at him. He felt quite sure that it *was* empty ... He had tried the door to her sitting-room and found it locked; and now he stood beside her bedroom, listening, but he hadn't the courage to turn the doorknob: what if she was in there? Only, he knew she wasn't.

The house to himself, just when he least wanted it. He went downstairs to the library.

His breakfast tray was where he had left it, on the desk.

Gone midnight and not back yet. Gossiping with her Christian widow. Mugs of cocoa and sentimental nonsense on the television.

Lawson slumped into an armchair. Hours of night ahead of him ... shaky ... nauseous ... and one thing that he mustn't do: think about Moira. Anything else but that – what she had said ... Soon, he began to talk to himself in random snatches.

'Turkeys and fish,' he muttered, 'what's the difference?' Quite right. Eggs, now. One could argue the case for eggs ...

And concerning those criteria for a lovely thigh, the main point, which he hadn't mentioned, because of the ladies ...

'Drunk again,' he whispered.

He huddled in his overcoat. The energy required to take it off was too much and too complicated. He raised a foot and very carefully brought it down on the carpet. Neither his foot nor the floor felt right. Then suddenly he noticed that his well-ordered bookshelves had begun to move; they were gliding inwards from the walls, then back again ... in–out, contracting and expanding like a ribcage, with himself at the centre. His fingers tightened on the armchair.

Better try to calm down ... breath steadily, he warned himself, and so he concentrated. He worked at keeping every breath he took a perfect match with all the others, gauging his success by the movement of his coat buttons. Gradually, this relaxed him, until he forgot to guard his thoughts.

Up there in Williston, Moira and the Leather Jacket and the rest of them – were they still telling jokes and drinking brandies? Light years away. It was as though his evening with the Gellings had happened on a bright planet that he had somehow visited and then been pushed off ... Now here he was, drifting, drifting ...

What was Moira doing? Sitting by the drinks cabinet, with the Leather Jacket and the lawyer or the surgeon. Moira, entertaining:

' ... *and I was just handing him his coat, when he made a kind of lurch* ... '

Laughter. Universal laughter. The old goat.

'Ooooh ... ' moaned Lawson, coming to with a start, and wrapping his arms around himself, he rocked gently. In his suit pocket, Moira's thin Christmas present bent stiffly as he bent.

'Oh ... oooh ... '

In the end, he fell asleep.

Incredible. When he woke up, according to his watch, it was 11.40 and this had every chance of being true, because, on his drawing back the library curtains, a mature day confronted him. There was no trace of the night's sleet, and none of the previous day's brilliance, either. The trees looked like frozen smoke, and the grass was like a mat of smoke. Everything was colourless.

Standing by the windows, Lawson rubbed the cramp from his neck. Downstairs at twenty to twelve ... not that it mattered. Against all probability, he had just enjoyed the longest, soundest sleep that he could remember having in years. All the same, looking out from the library in this last hour of morning, he was breaking a taboo; and maybe it was that, or an after-effect of the alcohol – he didn't know – but there was a nervousness in his heart-beat, and his whole body was keyed up, tuned and ready for something he should worry about ... Last night, of course. Making such a fool of himself. But Moira had been drunk, too ... On the other hand, *in vino veritas?* Well, if he had to agonise about that – and he had, no doubt – it would have to keep till later ... Astonishingly, the sense of panic growing in him now seemed to have nothing at all to do with Moira. It was ... whatever it was ...

The housekeeper –

She must have seen me.

Oh God, yes. Lawson stiffened at the thought. That was it. First thing every morning, she came in to the library for his supper tray, and to check that he hadn't left the lights on. So she must have seen him, collapsed in the chair with his chin bulging on his overcoat, his mouth wide open, smudged rouge, toupee slipping –

He stared round, dismayed, as if her cold smile, which he

could see so clearly in his own mind, must be imprinted on the room somewhere, and there, on the desk, he saw yesterday's breakfast tray, with the honey jar and the Thermos flask.

At the same moment, it occurred to him that all the library lights were still blazing. She hadn't switched them off . . .

What was that supposed to mean?

Tact. The bitch's version of tact, sneaking out again: *'When I saw you were asleep in there, I thought I'd better leave things. Come back later.'* Her scornful toleration. And then there would be questions, her spiky offerings of interest, like a bunch of thistles.

'You must have been very tired to fall asleep like that. Did you have a nice time at the Gellings?'

'Yes. Thank you.'

'You didn't eat too much, did you?'

'No.'

'Well, it's plain fare today, anyway – remember what the doctor said. You did drink, I suppose?'

Damn it, get it over with . . . Lawson set about taking his coat off. The cramp in his neck hurt, and he moved so awkwardly that as he was finally pulling free of the second sleeve, the coat caught on something that was sticking out of his suit pocket. Moira's Christmas present. It fell and lay at his feet, a silent invitation.

Later . . . Scooping it up, he hid it in his desk drawer, flattening it down on top of a wad of papers – his unfinished poem: there were nine lines of it in all, but in how many forms and combinations, he had long since lost count. Just as well he had never sent it. If Moira Gelling couldn't take a little drunken tenderness, what would she have made of this – this most vulnerable of tributes? Poetry wasn't his forte.

She'll be in the kitchen . . .

He went as far as the head of the passage, and stood there, ears straining.

Not a sound – none that he could hear, at any rate, like her radio, or the grinding of the washing machine.

'Hello?'

No answer. Half-way down the passage, he stopped again.

'Hello?'

Her sitting-room door was shut.

'Edith?'

He ran: he tried to turn the doorknob.

Locked. Still locked.

Into the kitchen ... No one. Bleach-clean. For a second, he was stupefied; and then the explanation, which was obvious and also very convenient, came to him. He grinned with relief. She simply wasn't used to late nights. She must have come back in the small hours, and so, of course, she had slept in. Why not? She would hardly expect him to find out. He wasn't due downstairs for another fifteen minutes yet. Any moment now, he would see her coming along the passage, rolling up her sleeves to start his breakfast. Or better still, if he was quick, he could get upstairs before that happened; he could shave and smarten up, rumple his bed ...

He set off.

But in the hall he stopped, and stared at his face in the mirror.

I don't really need a shave, he thought; and now that it actually came to it, he didn't feel much like racing about un-making beds, either. It wasn't that he felt weak exactly, just incapable of doing things, so he wandered into the sitting-room, and perched on the edge of the sofa.

From there, through the open doorway, he had a good view of the staircase.

A long, shivery time passed. His stomach rumbled. A draught stole over the back of the grand piano and pressed against his neck.

At last, he knew it must be twelve, and he looked at his watch.

Long gone. Almost half past.

He climbed the stairs, calling to her. She didn't appear. And when he tried her bedroom door, he found it locked.

She hadn't come back. It was scandalous, and it was true. Lawson retreated into the library. He was furious, he told himself, disgusted ... To abandon someone his age without a word of warning ... It was immoral, very nearly criminal ... His heart thudded. He could see all sorts of havoc heading for him. When she came back – as she would, of course – he was going to have to sack her. No choice – unless she had some highly plausible excuse. 'Pack up and get out,' he would have to say. And advertise, and interview, and find someone . . .

After so many years, to do this to him.

He lit a cigar, one of his great treasures which he kept for mellow evenings; he puffed at it once or twice, and then forgot he was holding it.

Uncanny malice. At any other time, he could have coped with this. What was she after all? Only today, because of the Gellings and his catastrophic fumbling with Moira, he badly needed normality, the reassurance of order in his life, his rituals . . .

As usual when it came to an attack, the housekeeper had shown perfect timing.

Minutes crawled past.

What now?

He craved company. What he needed was advice. Should he phone Moira? Who else could he talk to?

She'd only laugh, he decided. *Calling me a thing like that, even if she was drunk . . . She's not to be trusted . . .*

In search of comfort, he went over to the desk, took out the neatly wrapped Christmas present, and tore it open. Inside, packed in Cellophane, a tie. Paisley-patterned silk. He spread it out and fingered it in dismay. Moira's choice? More commonplace than soap, more of a cliché than gloves or writing-paper – and this one, stunningly ugly. The sort of thing Rowena might have bought.

'*Ro, we'll have to get the old goat something.*'

'*Leave it to me, Mummy.*'

The afternoon grew black. He didn't eat. If he went out into the kitchen and made himself a sandwich, he would be surrendering. The housekeeper's delinquency would then have become a force which altered his behaviour . . . Far wiser to keep still. His one concession to the situation was a guilty minute in the bathroom, where he gulped down a large tumbler of water.

This restraint lasted well into the evening, until long after dark and his lunchtime, but in the end he broke it with a frenzied burst of activity that centred, for a start, on the waste-paper basket. He plucked out from the wilting ivy the piece of scarlet paper that had wrapped the housekeeper's gift to him, and examined it meticulously. Had he missed something? A note, spitefully under-sized, hidden somewhere?

No.

Next, he inspected the box, especially its base, and inside its lid. Nothing. He took out the yacht and scrutinised the flimsy square of card behind it. Blank. After that, he hunted round the library – his desk, the mantelpiece – in case a message had been left propped up somewhere, very discreetly.

There wasn't one.

He went out into the hall, and flicked through the pad by the telephone; and all the time his hunger was ballooning in him. *I can't go on and on like this* . . . he thought.

He stood undecided by the telephone, trying to resist the thought of food and the well-stocked fridge in the kitchen, the temptation to go foraging, and he was just about to give in, when a door bell rang: the harsh, almost guttural bell of the back door. A huge weight dropped from his shoulders. Here she was.

She hasn't got her keys with her . . .

Then he thought of the bolt; and he thought of the snig on the Yale lock. She couldn't get in because of those. He must have pushed the bolt home last night, out of habit, pressed the snig . . . whether she was in or not.

He hurried down the passage. So long as the bell had actually rung, not one of those noises that his head made . . .

His hands trembled as he pulled the bolt back.

'About time!' he snarled. 'You might have let me know . . . ' and there he left it. In the raw glare of the outside light, he saw a man, oddly dressed in old trousers and a smart tweed jacket, with a cap pulled forward over his eyes.

The gardener nodded civilly.

'Evening, Mr Lawson. Compliments of the season.'

For one long moment, Lawson stood paralysed; then he ducked in behind the edge of the door.

'What do you want?' he whined. 'It's Biggs, isn't it? Go away.'

The gardener's face didn't change; it was smiling neutrally and courteously. Because of his cap, the man's eyes were only just visible.

204

'Oh,' he said, 'I'm not stopping. I've got a surprise for you, Mr Lawson.'

'Pardon?'

'She said to drop it in any time on Boxing Night.'

An envelope was held out.

Lawson snatched it.

'What's this?'

'Some sort of present,' said the gardener. 'From your house-keeper. She gave it me a couple of days ago. An extra little surprise for you – that's what she said it was.'

Lawson was scratching at the sealed back.

'I must say, B-Briggs,' he panted, 'you might have brought it sooner ... '

The man's shoulders lifted slightly.

'Just doing what she said. A favour, like ... '

But Lawson wasn't listening. He had ripped open the envelope, and he was following with horror the crabbed words on the sheet of paper.

You seem to think you can do without me. So you won't mind if I stay away a few days.

Edith

Fourteen

After Briggs-Biggs had gone, Lawson's first reaction was to rush into the kitchen, seize a pint of milk from the fridge, and pour himself a full glass: ice-cold, far too cold, but he drank it anyway. Then he took a packet of biscuits from a cupboard, spilt them out on to the table, and wolfed down about half of them.

This convinced him that he wouldn't starve. In fact, contemplating the crumbs, and the rings he had made on the table with his glass, and the puddles of milk, he understood: all this must be exactly as she had planned it. She had left the place packed to bursting point with food for him, and – if he were honest – he was grateful.

Yes, grateful.

He went back to the fridge, took out a great slab of cheese, and sliced off a chunk. He nibbled it furtively. Here he was ... She had withdrawn from him, a kind of act of terrorism ... and here he was, mentally thanking her for providing for him.

Bitterly and humbly he ate, an unavoidable demonstration of his dependence on her. And now that he understood, he could feel the entire kitchen – the pans, and the clinically white cupboard doors and all the rest of it – watching him. They were her spies, her allies.

Clutching a replenished glass of milk, he escaped to the library.

Away a few days ...

The truth might be very different. She might have cleared out altogether. Behind the locked door of her sitting-room, there might be nothing left but the hired television and some bits of furniture. No cuckoo-clock, no swan from Caernarvon, no calendars. And in her locked bedroom, there might be empty drawers, and an empty wardrobe.

Fiercely, he tried to reject these speculations.

Rubbish ... She'll be back. She knows when she's well off ...

But was she so well off? He realised with a shock that he didn't know. Maybe it wasn't much of a life for her – alone all day at his beck and call, long hours with nothing much to do, and a somewhat modest wage. Of course, he paid her fairly, but how could he tell whether she knew she was 'well off'? He had always thought the life suited her – martyrdom: the power and satisfaction of it. Then there was the bonus: he had provided her with a passion in life – someone to hate. Wasn't that better than nothing?

But if this Christian widow had come out with an invitation: *'Why don't you leave him, Edith? There's enough room here for the two of us, and I could do with the company ...'*

What then?

Oh, what then? A pale, leech of a widow, stealing other people's help.

No. She would be back. He remembered that night she had brought him the paracetamol – the night of the face – how, afterwards, she had carried in mugs of cocoa, and sitting down, she had crossed her legs and she hadn't jutted her foot at him but pointed it at the carpet; then how carefully she had re-arranged the overlap in her dressing gown – extraordinary, womanly behaviour; and as she had talked about the war, he had watched, fascinated, a semi-animation in her; he had seen the ghost of a person struggling up to the surface, trying to break out of the stone. And for what? Because she was sitting in his library?

She was bound to him by twenty years. To him, or to his money.

And now he would have to sack her. Stupid, selfish bitch ... She had suddenly made things impossible. Her note was an ultimatum. If he gave in, she would have him, to his last gasp.

Devil take all women ... Treacherous, deceiving bitches. When had they brought him anything but misery, right from the start with his cringing mother: 'Ah've got nowt t'give yer,

Arnie ... but if yer say yer prayers ...'

Shortly before midnight, he settled in an armchair with a book of memoirs – *My Life and Loves* by Frank Harris – and in defiance of women, he began to read all the prurient passages. No supper tray; and if he rang the bell, there wouldn't be anyone to answer – but none of that mattered. He wasn't hungry in any case. He had no needs. He read the book.

If things start scuttling round tonight, faces playing up ... I'm on my own ...

He kept his eyes on the print. Harris trotted out his beauties. Bold or coy, simpering or protesting, once they were stripped of their skirts, these Victorian females all became indistinguishable from one another, or so it seemed to Lawson. He sat like a statue, holding the book unnaturally high in front of him to reduce the chance that he might catch sight of anything either round it or over it; and he read desperately, forcing himself to pay attention even to the most absurd details. But for all that, his mind brought him a visitor: it created a monster for him – a hybrid woman with the small face and brown eyes of Moira Gelling, and the thin lips and square jaw of the housekeeper, a hybrid that talked incessantly – gibberish which he couldn't hear exactly, and yet he was aware of it going on behind the print; and the creature smiled in a way that was neither Moira's nor the housekeeper's. As for its body – he had only the vaguest idea of that, but he knew that it was strong: this visitor had a hand that could have squeezed his to jelly.

It stayed with him all night; but at least it stayed in his skull. Then, in the last hour, somewhere between five and six, it disintegrated; he could feel it fading piecemeal as he read less and less and dozed more. Secretly he watched it going; he was very careful not to make any attempt to hurry it.

Meanwhile, he had taken out his watch and laid it on the arm of his chair, and every now and then he glanced at it, wishing for six. As soon as the minute finger closed the circle and reached twelve, he banged shut Frank Harris. He was for bed. Despite his marathon sleep of the night before, he was exhausted. The only problem was, with the house empty – now that he *knew* it was empty – it seemed extremely doubtful he could sleep in it ... Well, he was going to have to. From now on, until he found someone, there would be nothing much but emptiness - except for the great sacking, and what a vile, sickening scene that would be ...

Another thing - he would have to find a replacement fast. The house meant work. Nothing stayed clean by magic.

Bad luck, thinking of that, just as he was going to bed. At once his head began to throb: he was full of alarm.

He was going to have to wash up dishes. There would be shirts and pants and socks - could he work the washing machine? Where did she keep the iron? Maybe she would take it with her. He imagined himself, tussling with the ironing board ...

And the house - the hyooooge house, as someone had said ... Carpets to hoover; and dirty bathrooms - he had a horror of those: stains in toilet bowls and grime in the sinks. And he hated unmade beds, and most of all, dust.

A place like this needs constant attention. You've no idea ...

Edith's words, following him up the stairs. His tiredness thinned out and sharpened ...

It was true. On the bathroom mirror and the one in his bedroom - dust: the enemy of man and books ... and a thin layer of it powdered the top of the chest of drawers. Already. After only two days of neglect. When he got up, he would have a thorough go at it, he really would ... With this promise to himself, he started to undress, but a minute later, he was standing by the bed in his shirt tails, rubbing a finger along the headboard. No, he couldn't sleep in this. He had his asthma to think of.

On with the trousers, and downstairs for a duster.

It was hard work, but he rather enjoyed slapping on polish and rubbing up a shine. This would show her, he thought. He began on the banister, working his way not down from the top but up from the bottom, and sometimes stopping to sit on the stairs and catch his breath. Sweat trickled down his cheeks.

Slowly ... much more slowly ...

Gradually he learned to pace himself, and he got round all the important places - the staircase and his bedroom, the library - the parts he would notice, anyway - but the bathroom and the sitting-room would have to wait. It was not bad going, for a first effort. Encouraged, he thought he might go out into

the kitchen and experiment with the gas stove, poach himself
an egg ...
Instead, he fell asleep.
Only for a few minutes. He knew it couldn't have been for
long, because when he woke up, the day light was no brighter.
It was probably around nine.
Something slid across his knees ... The tin of polish. He
wiped a patch of wet from his chin – he had been dribbling –
and then realised where he was: slumped in a chair in the
library, with a yellow duster on his chest. And the time ... He
groped for his watch, but he wasn't wearing his waistcoat. He
was sitting in his shirt sleeves.
I suppose I'd better get to bed ...
Giving in to a whim like that – cleaning in his sleeping time
– it was wrong, wrong. He went upstairs quickly, guiltily, but
the smell of polish that rose from the banister and greeted him
all over again in his bedroom was extremely gratifying.
Really, he felt much better.
On the bed, he found his jacket, tossed down; so he picked
it up and hung it in the wardrobe. His waistcoat he had left
draped, after a fashion, over the chair, and now, because he
always did when he went to bed, he took out his watch, meaning to put it on the chest of drawers; he enjoyed that moment
of contact – silver case on polished wood ...
1.55.
He had to stare hard, before he could make any sense of the
figures.
His watch said 1.55.
He twisted round to the bedside table and his clock.
1.55.
What's happening to me?
Hours gone. Vanished, like pins dropped on floorboards. Like
water from a cracked glass ...
He sat down weakly on the bed.
I mustn't panic.
This was what happened when you chucked routine away;
things merged together, or they disappeared through one an-
other, and – time? There was no controlling it.
I must get things back to normal ...
Too late for bed. Pulling on his waistcoat, and pushing his

watch down in the pocket, he hurried from the room; but half-way along the landing, he remembered that he always wore his jacket or a cardigan when downstairs, so he went back and dressed carefully, taking a fresh handkerchief from the little stack in his top drawer; and he changed his toupee from his best to his second best.

Then he made for the library again. It was very nearly two days, he realised, since he had washed or had a shave, but to mess about in the bathroom now, at this time of day – that would be another transgression; and, in any case, what he wanted – what he really needed – was to be surrounded by his books ... He almost ran into the library and snapped on all the lights to bring up a glow in the place, calling up from every book its full colour: the maroons and ruby reds, the warm black and sapphire ... shelf after shelf of books, comfort and civilisation. Flopping into the nearest chair, he breathed deeply, drawing calm from the wonder of his library, its systematised, catalogued richness.

Normal behaviour, sitting in there in the afternoon ... The lights were on a fraction early, it was true ... Still, it was a dark day: nothing wrong with that.

But he soon discovered a new problem. He had missed his breakfast time. He felt giddy, he was so hungry, and his lunch-time wasn't for hours yet.

Stick it out ...

It couldn't be done.

A quick raid on the kitchen.

Sultanas. A lump of fruit cake. A soup bowl of ice-cream. A bar of chocolate. Nothing but the sweetest things, and why not? For the next day, he told himself, he would plan some sensible menus, but today, when his hands had begun to shake the moment he set eyes on food, all that mattered was plenty of sugar ... the treats that Edith loved to ration: as he piled them on to a tray, he could feel the kitchen watching him, and disapproving; so he piled on more.

If I take enough into the library with me, I can eat half of it now, and half for supper ... I won't have to come out here again, not today.

December 28th dawned uncomfortably. It brought a sharp,

silver light to the sky above the spinney, and a restlessness to the trees: they looked as if they were creeping – not as whole trees, so far as he could tell, but in parts: a creeping of twigs and branches, making off to an unknown destination somewhere beyond the window – only, they never reached it. Propped up on his pillows, Lawson watched through the gap in the curtains. He couldn't sleep. He had hardly expected to. Here he was, he had come to bed at six, as usual, fitting into the pattern again, but from the start, it hadn't felt 'as usual'; he had found himself behaving strangely.

For one thing, as he had pulled on his pyjamas, a very unpleasant thought had struck him, and he had felt compelled to drag the chair, which was heavy, right across the room and wedge the door open with it. Apparently, the old fool in his skull had a fixed idea that if he did fall asleep, someone would come sneaking up the stairs with a key, and lock him in. Lawson had deemed it best not to argue.

And that hadn't been the end of it. When he had finally climbed in between the sheets, there had come another odd prompting, and he had tugged out the bolster from beneath the undersheet – quite a strenuous job – and stuffed it down alongside him in the bed.

All this had magically soothed the old fool, but Lawson had been left wide awake and breathless, so he watched the trees, creeping, creeping, getting nowhere.

A couple of hours went by before he thought it worthwhile to lie down, and close his eyes.

Empty your brain . . . Relax . . .

Nothing could be more exhausting than this struggle for sleep, but in the end it paid off, and he slipped into a shallow blackness, which didn't last for very long, and when he suddenly came out of it, he was muddle-headed; nevertheless, it was an achievement, and to celebrate, he decided to allow himself an early escape – not to go downstairs, oh no, not at 11.15, but he could go to the bathroom, he could pass the time with a long wash and a leisurely sit on the toilet . . .

He got up gratefully. Soon, he was out on the landing in his dressing gown – or he wouldn't have heard it: a faint, hypothetical sound that seemed to come from somewhere beneath him. He stopped to listen. In his head, or out of it? When

212

standing still didn't tell him, he made off down the stairs ...
A burr ... now he was certain ... and by the time he reached
the hall, it had taken on a higher pitch ... Soft and discreet to
his ears, maybe, it was the telephone ringing ...

He ran.

Too late. Silence.

All the same, he snatched up the receiver, and gasped,
'Hello?'

Nothing.

'Hello?'

He hung up, and shuffled out to the kitchen. Bad start ...
Edith? He didn't really think so, not before twelve; not even
as a tease. She knew he couldn't hear the phone up in his
bedroom. Who, then? Moira – his one friend? If she was. Who
else could it have been?

The car-hire people, about his account.

Thieves, casing the joint.

A wrong number ...

The stove, at least, co-operated. When he lit the gas, a docile
ring of blue flames came up at once, and he scrambled eggs.
They stuck to the bottom of the pan, but there wasn't anything
wrong with them, so he scraped them out on to a side plate,
and ate them with a spoon, sitting at the deal table – which
didn't exactly tally with his resolutions: his intention had been
to carry every meal into the library, but as he hadn't cleared
the tray from in there yet, with last night's things, he thought
he might as well eat where he was. Besides, the phone call had
upset him, and so he excused himself from the washing up,
too.

Why would Moira Gelling ring?

To apologise, or – far more likely, to embarrass him?

'*Are you all right, Arnold? You were so drunk the other
night ...*'

Maybe something worse than that: '*Listen ... Arnold, can
you hear me? I've been thinking it over, and I just want to say,
after that little scene the other night ... I can't come down to
Woodbourn again. Not unless you promise me ...*'

I haven't thanked her, he thought. *Thank you for Christmas
... I suppose I could phone ...*

But wasn't he in disgrace? How could he tell? And what

213

would *she* care, anyway, that his housekeeper had gone?

Groaning to himself, Lawson moved round the library, taking books from the shelves, opening them, and staring at a glazed page, then banging them shut and shoving them back in their slots. After four or five times through this ritual, his eyes lit on the collected works of Samuel Johnson, and he pulled out a volume eagerly – the letters – opening it at random. There was always something wise to read in Johnson.

Sure enough. Immediately, a sentence cracked through the glaze.

'Solitude excludes pleasure, and does not always secure peace ...'

Ha. He rammed the book back; and then, for no good reason, hurried into the hall, and stood, breathing anxiously.

He felt in his pocket for his inhaler. Yes, he had it.

Up the stairs ... all the way to the second floor.

It was a harder climb than it should have been. Once, he had to stop and actually use the inhaler, but perseverance got him there, to the bleak passage with the doors that had so excited Moira in the autumn, that carnival night; and at once he found that he hadn't come to the same place.

Damp, and dust. Bitter smells, well established – and yet he had never noticed damp up here before. As for the dust, he had known there would be that, of course, but up here in the dark with Moira, he hadn't been able to see it; he hadn't understood how much there was. Now, he discovered a thick layer on the skirting board, and a skin of it on the lino; and everywhere, in corners, and the cracks of the lino, there were little growths of fluff.

Then he saw the mould.

It was high up on the wall at the end of the passage, facing him. A white stain speckled with black. Somehow, when he had come to view the place, he must have missed it. Fungicide ... He would have to get the experts in ...

In fact, now that he took a good look in the daylight, it seemed to Lawson that he had missed the most obvious things – the wall-paper, for instance, a faded apple green with brown flowers, darkening and narrowing the passage: in several places it was peeling back at the joins. Then there was the picture, a cheap print in a plastic frame that hung by the first door on the left, unmissable, but he couldn't remember ever having seen it before: Christ, with His face the pink and white of sugar mice, displaying in His chest a vast plum of a heart. That had to go.

Lawson shivered in his dressing gown. It was cold up here. Arctic. Standing at the top of the stairs, he could feel a draught – a small gale, rather – being funnelled down the passage. Surely none of the windows were open? It was probably the window frames, the glass working loose ...

I'll have to get them seen to. My heating bills ...

But he really couldn't bring himself to worry about his heating bills. He had just caught sight of a ghostly shape on the floor, a thin and frightening phantom lying only inches from his feet, and then he spotted another one. Bleached - no, dust-coated – leaves. Leaves. In the house.

How could he have let this happen? Good God ... He was going to have to change things. He couldn't have this ... Sitting snug in his library ... Splashing about like an idiot in his bath ... All tucked up in his bed – and this going on.

Library, bathroom, bedroom – they were three bright tents in a wilderness (he felt he couldn't count the sitting-room). Three bright tents. That was what 'home' came to, and he didn't mind, it was enough; but he had always thought that the rest of the house served as a screen, that at least it kept the weather out, while all the time – dust, damp, leaves ... There had been this anarchy overhead, edging towards the stairs.

And what had *she* done about it? She could have cleaned up, put some effort into the place ... What did she think he paid her for? Well, now he wouldn't. Not a penny when he sacked her, unless she came up here first, and put things right.

Oh yes, there would be changes. He felt ill at the thought of how many.

Turning up his dressing gown collar, he held it tight across his throat, to keep the draught out.

Better get down, into the warm ...

What on earth was he doing up here?

Incredible, that this was the place; this was where they had come that night, he and Moira.

215

He began to potter from room to room. Boxes ... broken
furniture ...

*This is where they spread the apples ... This must be the
butler's bedroom* - Moira's preposterous make-believe.

And this room's mine.

He floundered in. The least impressive room of all, with its
sloping ceiling and its window - not much more than a cupboard really, opening to the sky and a tall, smoke-blackened
chimney stack.

What had the woman seen in it?

Nothing, he suspected. She had run out of ideas, and that
was why she had claimed this room. It had been something for
her to say. Either that, or because it had been the last room,
she had felt that urge which people have with last things, to
put her mark on it. A room with no particular charm - except
for the moonlight: it had been awash with that, he remembered,
and he thought of Moira's hand, deadly pale in front of the
window.

Isn't this beautiful?

Moira ...

The air was icy, and the walls seemed to quake with shadows. The window was rattling.

This is where I come when I want to hide, she had said -
but the room was empty. She was so emphatically not in it,
that her absence was as strong as a presence. Yes, he could
almost feel her there, and he crossed to the window to stand
as close to her as possible, where she had stood.

Trying to focus on her ...

When he failed, he turned to look out; and now he saw that
what had begun as a sly breeze in the spinney had developed
into a blusterer. Corpulent clouds rushed past the chimney,
and it was their shadows, pooling in the room then vanishing
again, that made the walls seem so unstable, as if the house
were about to shatter.

Lawson watched, horrified. The frenzy of the sky astonished
him. He wasn't used to attics. He felt he'd had no conception
of this energy, this speed skimming over the tiles ... The sky
whirled. He resisted it. He threw against it all his loathing of
open spaces and shifting seasons; he brought his defiance from
some angry point inside himself that meant to stay fixed and

hidden, never mind what force challenged it ... 'Damn you! Damn you!' he whispered. Then his rebellion went wrong: he began to spiral up and out. He became elongated, tenuous ... The sky was drawing him through the glass, over the roof ...

He closed his eyes. The floor was spinning under him. He pressed his hands against the window and waited for the dizziness to pass.

Coroner: And what did the old goat die of, Dr Hewitt?

Hewitt: A fractured skull. When he fell, he struck his head on the window ledge.

Coroner: But what caused the fall? Did he have a heart attack?

Hewitt: Oh no. He was in excellent shape for his age. He just keeled over.

Quickly Lawson opened his eyes again. If he was going to fall ... but he knew he wouldn't. The floor was already levelling out. Soon, he would be able to move. Patience. So he stood, numbed by the air that squeezed in round the window frame, and gaped straight ahead at the chimney. It steadied him. Rigid, sharp-lined, black against the sky. Lawson gave it his full attention, until its blackness was complicated by patches of grey and details of brick and cement; and suddenly, down at its base, in a spot he could probably have reached from the window, he noticed a cobweb. There was a fly trapped in it, and with each gust of wind, as the web came billowing out like a sail, the insect twitched, putting up a frantic struggle; but as soon as the web fell back against the chimney, the fly lay still.

Alive?

He couldn't tell, although he watched for a long time, his forehead hard against the glass. A fly with a shiny patch on its body, shiny blue, that glowed or darkened as the clouds passed over ... There. That was a movement, wasn't it?

He couldn't tell

Fifteen

'Hello?'

'Yes?'

'Who's that? Who's speaking?'

'This is Rowena Gelling speaking.' Silence. 'Is that you, Mr Lawson?'

'I want to speak to your mother ...'

'Yes ... Look, I'm very sorry. I'm afraid you can't.'

'I beg your pardon?'

'She simply isn't well enough ...'

'What?'

'I tried to phone you, Mr Lawson. This morning. And yesterday ... She wanted you to know ...'

'Why won't she speak to me?'

'She can't. Honestly.'

'She can.'

But the girl was adamant. Curses didn't budge her, and when he called her a liar, all she said was, 'Can't you understand? Christmas was just too much for her. I'm sorry, Mr Lawson.' Then she hung up on him.

Never mind. Never mind. He should have known.

'If you ever answer the phone, Ro, and it's Arnold Lawson – tell him I'm ill. Tell him anything.'

All that again.

Numbly, he went back to the library. He shouldn't have gambled. Thinking that he *could* phone and he might, that had been infinitely more comforting, but trivial things – flies in cobwebs – could force one's hand occasionally, and there was no point regretting it. Why fuss? Hadn't he said, over and over, that women always let him down? He was relieved. If he had been proved wrong at this time of life – what good would that have done him?

Better to know for certain that Moira Gelling was no different to the others. Playing games. Bright lips and quick smiles – but make one move towards her, one mistake, and no forgiveness. *Christmas was just too much for her.*

Damn it all. It wasn't as though he had shoved his hand up her skirt.

Just one more teasing bitch. Well, what did he care?

After several minutes spent moving objects round on his desk, he lowered himself into an armchair – gingerly, as if his body had sustained blows and was covered with bruises.

So here he was. Alone, with his books. These, at least, couldn't be taken from him. He blinked round; and as he began to recover from the shock of his phone call, he realised this was right: an old man, sitting in his library, packed in with the essence of brains, dry words. He and they, brought together over the years, at great cost.

All that schoolboy eagerness for women, dreams of affairs at his age, if there had been dreams – what lunatic stuff!

Books were his only appropriate company ... and yet, today, if he were honest, he could find no pleasure in them. Quite the reverse ... His neck sank low between his shoulders.

Shelf after shelf, sealing him in ...

Of course, in a room like this, which had three walls covered with books, it was natural to lose one's sense of perspective sometimes. The other night, hadn't that happened, after the wine and the brandy? And very often, when he was tired, deep in the small hours, the walls would shift in or out a little, especially while he wasn't watching. But this sensation gaining on him now wasn't like that. It was claustrophobia.

Hundreds of them ... What were they, these judiciously selected volumes, but so many bricks? They were first-class bricks, and their prime function was – not to be read, but to thicken the walls.

He forced himself to regulate his breathing, unclench his fists ...

Then, something else he had never thought of ... Turning his eyes to a huge Greek lexicon, he began to consider all the weight in his library, so many tons of books; and if he was to pull a book from one of the shelves, and by some freakish chance, it dislodged all the books on all the other shelves, and they came with it, crashing down ...?

Books were this, too. A dead weight.

Nonsense. He could take one out and see for himself that the others stayed put. He could open it at any page and read the clever, communicating print. Any time.

He sat still. The trouble was, he knew he could go through these motions without changing his feelings in the least. They were certainly bricks, these things lined up along the walls, and the fact that there were words in them – what made that so special? Words were only marks, patterns pressed on the brick in the mould.

How could his most loved treasures have become so horrible? He couldn't bear to look at them. He got up, hurried to the door ... but there he checked himself. This was his library, his sanctuary. He couldn't give it up.

Your head's not right ... Sit down.

Back he went to his armchair: and now he did his best not to see the books. He sat staring down the room and through the French windows. The sky had turned a lead grey. The wind raked the spinney. Full winter had come.

I suppose I ought to get dressed ...

What for? Who cared? Better not risk making things worse. Keep still. Ask for nothing. Think of nothing.

Lawson curled up. He put away his hands between his legs, and drew his knees up on to one of the arms of the chair, and there he stayed, curled inside his dressing gown.

Now he was learning. This was where they wanted him, everything. This was it. Give up thinking altogether.

And eventually, the music started: piano music, reaching into him long before he realised it, but when at last he did – he felt no surprise.

Something had been bound to come.

Yes. He raised his head, and saw, with fear – no lights, just a glow of night above the spinney, and black trees tossing. Then, shapes: old familiar chairs and lamps made strange and watchful by the darkness; and through the library came the music.

Lawson wheezed softly. The piano in the sitting-room ... it was giving out those irritating spurts, those flourishes and wrong stresses ... Si-iLENT NIGHT, Ho-oLEE NIGHT ... just the way Moira played.

He could see her, gold bracelet, shoulders swaying, and his heart-beat quickened.

So here we are, he thought, *the old fool, he thinks he's got me now.*

The piano in the sitting-room, in his skull. Ingenious. And if he went creeping out, if he stole across the hall, hoping to find Moira, what was it that was waiting for him?

Not her. Oh no. It wouldn't be Moira Gelling seated at the piano. The old fool could arrange a joke very much better than that. It would be the face ...

Of course. Bunched up in the dark and trembling, Lawson had the most perfect insight. Piano music just like Moira's – that was to entice him, lure him out ... and if he had a mind to ask himself how a face could play the piano – oh, there were possibilities.

Teeth. Long rows of flexible teeth, like fingers.

The music clanged and shuddered. It filled out with eccentric phrases – Moira's own. It was a faultless imitation; and now it broke out of the carol, into songs ...

Smoke Gets in Your Eyes ...

So like her.

Could it be? Had he checked the bolts last night? Rowena might have told her that he'd phoned ... and Moira might have come down, wanting to make peace, and when she had found no lights on ...

Don't be tricked. The back door's locked.

Tears welled in his eyes.

She had let him hold her, hadn't she? She was not all bad. She wouldn't want this, tormenting him like this ... She was kind, kind ... Weak and cruel as well, maybe, but not this wicked.

It's got to stop.

He struggled to his feet. The dark had a granular quality, as though there were flecks inside his eyes.

I've been asleep, he told himself, groping his way to the door.

A moment's panic – but he found it, and it opened.

Then a wide space confronted him, totally black.

Old MAN river ... jangled the piano. Just KEEP rolling ...

Lawson scuttled back into the library, and switched on every light. The music surged after him. Out into the dark again ... But now he could see the switches to the hall and landing lights. Stealthily he moved towards them, stretched his hand ... and the place lit up, the red stairs stridently red, the white telephone dazzling.

And there was silence.

'Moira?' he said quietly.

Not a sound. He could see, across the hall, that the sitting-room door was ajar, and inside – nothing but blackness. Not a single lamp was lit.

'Moira?'

TIPTOE THROUGH THE TULIPS ... shrilled the piano suddenly, and he started forward, his breath scratching in his throat as he headed for the sitting-room.

How else could he stop it?

I'm not mad yet ... I'm not ...

Whatever was in there, it was nothing.

He reached the door; and here, the music was no louder, he discovered, than it had been in the library – but for that, he supposed he could blame his ears. Wasn't he deaf? Everyone said so.

Yes, but don't deceive yourself.

Leaning against the wall, he sweated; he looked back at the library, and the staircase. No help there.

Change of tempo ...

And now the modern song broke off, and softly, tenderly, like a heart-felt plea for understanding, the opening bars of 'Greensleeves' came drifting out to him.

All he had to do ...

He held his breath, and reached in for the lights. He thrust his head round the door

He thrust his head round the door, and saw the sofa and the vases; and he heard the tune of 'Greensleeves' cracking into ironies – loud, discordant notes rising from the piano. And he saw the lid down over the keyboard, and the sheets of music lying on the piano stool. Then the playing stopped, mid-note. No one, nothing: he just had time to register that, before he felt an intimate touch on his elbow – a purposeful touch – and he focused clearly: in the cabinet near the piano, in its central panel – a gaping hole . . .

He let out a squeal.

'What *are* you doing?'

He could only squeal.

It was behind him. A trick. A trick.

He wrenched himself round, and, as he'd feared, the face had become embodied. There it stood in a pale grey raincoat, with its terrible smile.

Now it had him.

Lawson swayed gently forwards into the housekeeper's arms.

Sixteen

He recovered.

To bed at eleven, and up at eight, when Edith led him down-stairs to the library. She would settle him at his desk, then she would sit by the fireplace and watch while he ate his breakfast. Afterwards, she would guide him through a cautious transfer from the desk chair to an armchair, and some days he would ask: 'Any post?'

'Now if there was, I'd have given it to you. Wouldn't I?'

'Yes. Of course.'

'Well ... what books do you want?'

'Oh, the same as yesterday ... That big blue one.'

'This? *Origin of the Species?*'

'Yes ...'

'Here you are, then ... Now don't start moving about, and ring the bell if you want anything.'

Dark drawings of shellfish, lizards, birds – he would turn the pages, marvelling at these creatures and at details in the backgrounds: a rocky stretch of coast, a bare branch. The blocks of words he ignored, but the pictures were a source of endless fascination.

And every day, the book grew heavy. Then he would let it rest on his knees, and folding his hands across it, he would wait. What for, he didn't know – he didn't ask himself – but he knew that he was waiting.

Sometimes, he saw boys running in the spinney, or scooping up snow on the lawn, and once or twice, they came right up to the French windows, and gaped in. White, oval faces that suddenly grimaced at him.

But, for the most part, things were quiet. When the curtains had been drawn and the library lamps were shining, after his supper, if there was nothing she wanted on the television, Edith would come with her knitting, and sit opposite him. Neither of them would say much, but he could watch her needles flicking, flicking . . . watch them for hours.

And twice a week, on Edith's arm he ventured down to the gate, peering across the meadow at the bungalows. He noticed things on these excursions: the silvery look of the river, the coal-blue of the gorse bushes, and, when there was snow, how creamy yellow the bungalows were. In the drive, he noticed blackbirds in the undergrowth, pads of snow in the forks of twigs, and the dark gloss of the ivy and rhododendron leaves. All this beauty puzzled him, so he didn't like to mention it. Underfoot, the going was difficult. He leaned hard on Edith's arm.

Then there were baths. Excursions in their own right. Up with Edith to the bathroom – shuttered tight and smelling of soap, misty with steam: she always ran the water before collecting him – and when they had arrived up there together, she would test the temperature again, her red arm splashing like a lobster.

Only once she was satisfied that it was as it should be, did he start to undress, holding on to the side of the bath with one hand, while with the other he pushed his trousers down.

Edith would help him to step out of them. She would help ease off his underpants, and pull his vest up over his head. Then she would tightly hold his arms, both of them, while he clambered in.

She was a veritable godsend.

She soaped him, rinsed him, and hauled him out for a towelling. She wrapped him in his dressing gown and helped him into bed. She would bring him a book. It would spend the night on top of the covers, over his knees. And so he would lie, waiting.

This was how a whole month passed. He didn't know it was a month, only that there was snow on some days, and rain or wind – or both – on others. Some days, there would be boys in the spinney, and on others, they kept out of sight.

On rare occasions, he thought he heard the telephone ringing, but he must have been mistaken, because Edith always denied it.

And who would phone?

On the whole, he was content. The big, blue book was his favourite, but once she understood that what he liked was pictures, Edith chose some others for him: a book about the Himalayas, with colour plates of mountains, temples; and a comprehensive history of the aircraft industry, with plenty of sketches and glossy photographs.

And there were visits. Short, cheerful visits. Then Edith helped him with his buttons. She would open up his shirt for him, and the young man, who smiled a lot, would take a tube from a case, and listen to his heart.

Before he left, this visitor would never fail to make some pleasant comment, and in the second week of February, he declared Lawson was 'as good as new'.

The next day, Edith dressed him in his winter coat, hat, gloves, and she herself put on her Sunday coat.

'Where are we going? Down to the gate?'

'Not this time,' she said.

She led him along the passage past the kitchen, and held the back door open for him. Outside stood a black Mercedes.

'A little drive,' said Edith. 'It's time we got you out again.'

Side by side in the back of the car they sat, in the plush warmth, and Lawson tried to make up his mind as to whether he knew the driver – a man with a rosy face, who had more than once smiled at him as Edith tucked a rug round his waist. He felt that perhaps he did, and out like this, driving along, he would have talked – he wanted to – but the atmosphere in the back of the car discouraged it, so he only said, 'It's cold, isn't it?'

'Certainly is,' said the driver.

They stopped in front of a florist's shop, and Edith looked at it through the window. Then she got out.

'Well, sir,' said the driver. 'How was Christmas?'

'Very nice, thank you.'

The driver's face beamed at him in the mirror, and then he knew where he must have seen it: years ago, in Manchester – in one of those big department stores that sell everything from

226

a handkerchief to peppermints, from bubble bath to tableware . . . Perhaps he had been a lift attendant.

'Have you ever lived in Manchester?' he asked, but before the man could tell him, Edith re-appeared, and the driver hurried out to help, handing after her into the car a large bunch of yellow chrysanthemums.

They drove on in silence. Through the town, down the High Street, out past the General Hospital. Lawson felt alert and anxious when he saw the hospital: glistening corridors, green partitions, tinsel round the windows, cotton-wool snow and red blankets . . . Images came so vividly, that he knew he must have been there . . . Was Edith taking him back? He looked at her. She smiled, and patted his hand.

Past the General Hospital . . . along the road to the cemetery. The car stopped. Wrought-iron gates barred the way, so the red-faced man sprang out, and pushed them back to open on to an avenue, broad and gently rising, with little trees on either side between the crowds of gravestones –

Black, grey or white gravestones, strictly placed in lines to make the most of the space; but from the road, the impression they gave wasn't one of order. It was chaos. There were too many shapes. There were crosses squat and tall, square-shaped crosses and circular Celtic crosses; there were obelisks and angels, pyramids and urns, all stiffly jostling together, pushing to be noted.

From the crest of the rise, a shell-pink chapel smiled down on anyone who came.

Lawson turned icy – despite the heat in the car, his coat, and the rug on his knees. He watched the red-faced man come back, and he felt the Mercedes purr forward, into the avenue.

'Edith . . .' He stared round at her.

She smiled, and patted his hand again.

'Now that you're well,' she said, 'I thought I should bring you. Just once. I thought you'd want it.'

Just once to the cemetery. Climbing down to lie on his back in the earth . . . or would they push him? Looking up at the red-faced man on the sky-line, setting his foot to the spade, and Edith ·. . . So this was what he had waited for.

Everything done with propriety – the driver in his uniform, Edith in her Sunday coat.

Fright silenced him.

They turned off from the avenue down one of the wider paths, nosing among the graves, and when they reached a junction with a narrower path, the Mercedes stopped again. Then Edith got out first, coming round to the door on his side with the driver, and when he didn't move, her sharp eyes came in at him:

'What's the matter? Don't you want to?'

'Let me give a hand, sir,' said the driver.

They helped him out, and, one to each arm, they supported him along the path. The air made movements on his face. He let them take him, gravestone after gravestone ... His knees buckled.

'Maybe you'd better leave it,' said the driver – not to him, but to Edith, and Edith said, 'Is that what you want? We can always come another day ... But we're here now ...'

And they stood him still before the grave.

All the funeral flowers had gone. A single vase of red carnations stood in the soil; there didn't seem to be any other vase, but in the grass at the head of the grave were jamjars, so the driver picked up one of those and went off with it to the tap, which was back near the junction and the Mercedes.

Lawson leaned on Edith heavily.

It wasn't for him, it wasn't for him, it was occupied ... A wave of sweet blankness came, and replaced the terror.

'I thought I ought to bring you once,' she said again.

Then the driver had come back, and she unwrapped the chrysanthemums. She snapped their stems, ripped off some of their leaves, and pushed the flowers into the jamjar.

'Where do you want it? At her feet?'

Lawson nodded.

The driver obliged, screwing the jar well down in the soil – so well down, that only the neck was left above it, choked with the chrysanthemums, which didn't look right, not to Lawson. There ought to be another vase ... He had an idea that there was one somewhere, lying in the grass, and a second's irritation crinkled through him.

Silence followed.

There they stood, the three of them, the driver at a

little distance, and very slowly, a question formed: whose grave? But Lawson sensed that he shouldn't ask. They presumed he knew, this man and Edith, so he must have been told.

And now that he wasn't frightened, he began to mind how cold he was. The air on his cheeks was making him shiver. It bewildered him that he could be out on a day like this, in the bleakest, rawest kind of weather – and that on a day like this, there could be flowers, red and yellow: the deep glow of carnations, the flash of these chrysanthemums. As he looked at the colours, they seemed to kindle something in him, and, moments later, he was angry.

He didn't want this. He didn't want graveyards. Standing out here, catching a chill – what would that prove, anyway? What right did she have, bringing him here? He wasn't dead yet ...

He shuffled his feet and glanced at her. He sniffed.

Edith gazed solemnly at the grave.

'I want to go,' he told her.

'Just a minute ... I'm saying a prayer ...'

But Lawson broke away. Shakily, he started off on his own, back towards the Mercedes. Edith turned and looked at that, but she stayed by the grave, finishing her prayer, and only the red-faced man came after him.

By the time she caught them up, they were almost back at the car, and her mouth had stiffened into a line.

She gripped his arm.

'For goodness sake ... We're not in the Derby, are we?'

He shook his head. The cold had become intolerable. He felt chilled to the marrow. His legs ached, and he longed to go home. He wanted warmth and boiled milk. He wanted pictures ...

'Rushing ahead like that!' she scolded.

Then the red-faced man let go of him, to push the paper and the pieces of chrysanthemum into a rubbish container. Lawson wouldn't wait. He opened the Mercedes door himself – and he would have bundled in by himself, but Edith chose to help; and as she was trying to steady him, she squeezed his arm so hard, that despite the layers of his cardigan and winter coat, she achieved a pinch.

He hated that. He twisted round, and he saw her face and the gravestones. She was always either pinching him or pushing him.

'Don't! Just ... stop it!' he panted, tugging to get free.

R. M. LAMMING was born on the Isle of Man in 1949. She was educated at a boarding school in North Wales and at St. Anne's College, Oxford, where she read English language and literature. She has worked as a teacher and in libraries and bookshops. Her first novel, *The Notebook of Gismondo Cavalletti,* received the coveted David Higham Prize for Fiction. She lives in a shaky north London flat that overlooks several railway lines and is working on a new novel.